ELIZABETH FENTON

THE EDGE OF THE WATER

A NOVEL

Cover Art by: Paul F. Fenton, III

The Characters and events in this book are fictitious. Any
similarity to real persons, living or dead, is coincidental and
not intended by the author.

Copyright © 2008 by Elizabeth Fenton

First Edition

ISBN # 978-0-6152-1689-8

Library of Congress Control Number: 008907020

Published by Elizabeth Fenton

DEDICATED TO MY FATHER

PAUL F. FENTON, JR.

CHAPTER ONE – From Coast to Coast

The request was simple but the distance was long—from one coast to the other, and Molly was still unsure if she would follow through with it. One step at a time, she reminded herself. Unable to afford both her rent and the trip, Molly had placed her belongings, including a stack of unsold paintings, in a small storage unit, packed up her truck and started the drive from Seattle to Maine. It took longer than anticipated and so when Molly arrived in Maine a week later, she was almost out of money. Why had she made this trip in the first place?

When Molly saw the sign to Hopeville, where she would catch a ferry to her final destination— Ridgeport Island, a feeling of dread came over her. *I'm really losing it*, she thought to herself. Thinking back to the day a few days before her fortieth birthday when she decided to just pack up and go, Molly knew she had acted irrationally. During the drive across the country, it had been easy to ignore her impulsive actions as she had spent the entire time thinking about her ex-boyfriend Joel who had very suddenly broken up with her. The Midwest states had been the most pathetic as the only stations that came in on the radio played country music that only served to fuel the fire of her rejected heart.

With much trepidation, Molly arrived in Hopeville and followed the signs for the ferryboat. Getting in line for the 11:00 am boat, she immediately noticed that the ferry line looped around the corner. Molly pulled up and parked her old truck behind the last car. As she shut off her engine which always gave a few sputters before stopping, Molly gave a sigh herself. 'You've been a good scout,' Molly said aloud to her old truck realizing it was fairly amazing that the 1963 vehicle had made the journey without breaking down. *I must have some luck on my side*, Molly thought as she jumped out of the truck to buy her ferry ticket.

There was a small shack toward the front that she assumed must be the place to buy tickets. Molly took a big whiff of ocean air before going in to get a ticket. The salty air was invigorating and lifted her mood.

When Molly stepped into the shack, there were a couple of people already in line. An older man got in behind her. It was close to the departure time, and Molly was a little worried about getting on the ferry. The man in back of her pulled on his suspenders and the snapping sound startled her. She quickly turned around to face him, then felt embarrassed about how obviously on edge she was.

"How many vehicles can they get on this ferry?" Molly asked the man quickly.

"Depends on the size and how many trucks are in line," he said.

"Ain't many trucks going on this time a day so I suppose right about where that yellow truck is parked is the cut off for the 11:00 o'clock."

Molly noticed that the man was pointing at her truck. "That's my truck," Molly said, "I sure hope I make it on. It's been a long trip."

"Where you coming from?" The man asked. Her reply was cut short by a loud shout from the other side of the ticket window.

"Car and passenger? What do you need?" a woman behind the window asked Molly, who was next in line.

Molly turned away from the man towards the window. "Just the car," she said. "I don't have a passenger."

"Car and passenger then," the woman said matter-of-factly.

"You're the passenger," the man behind her explained. "I sure hope you get on. And I hope you leave a little room because I'm right behind you."

Molly stepped out of the way of the counter. As she walked back to her truck with her ticket, she wondered if the protocol for ferryboats is the same as with buses. Maybe she should have given up her space for the older man. She didn't have much time to ponder this possibility, however. When she got to the truck, the line had already started moving and she quickly got ready to board the boat.

Molly pulled forward after a ferry attendant waved her onboard. He motioned several times for her to drive up a little further forward until she was practically touching the bumper of the car in front of her truck. He held his hand up for her to stop and wedged a block under her tire. She had made it, but not by much. The man who had been behind her in the ticket line was the last one on board. Molly smiled as she saw him being waved on. Then she turned her own vehicle off and sat for a moment, looking around. She saw that other people were getting out of their vehicles, weaving through the parked cars to a stairway and re-emerging on a passenger deck above. Molly decided to follow them. The other cars had parked just as closely as she so she had to turn sideways and squeeze herself between them to get to the entry of the stairs.

Once on deck, she leaned against the rail and took in yet another generous breath of the ocean air. As she inhaled, she closed her eyes, and as she exhaled she opened them again. Molly dropped her elbows down and leaned her chin against the white painted iron railing. She suddenly remembered being on a larger, but similar boat with her uncle. When she was a child, he would take her every summer to Martha's Vineyard. She used to love to rest her chin on the side of the ferry and look down to watch the white froth dance off the side of the boat. Molly kept looking across the water. In the far distance she could see the mast of a sailboat. She thought some more about her uncle, who had been from a seaport town in Ireland. He had always dreamed of having a boat of his own. It had been a while since Molly had thought about him. She remembered on one of their trips, they had stopped in a souvenir shop for some salt water taffy, and in that store they were selling cans with sailboats painted on them that advertised they were full of Cape Cod Sea Salt Air. Molly remembered how disappointed she had been when, after pleading with her uncle to buy her one, and opening it, there was no sudden ocean breeze gusting out of the can. Her uncle had tried to explain that it was just a gimmick, but she had been a child. She hadn't understood the empty promise of that kind of joke.

Molly missed her uncle. The last trip she took back East was to his funeral. It was hard to believe she had no family left.

The ferry ride to Ridgeport was not long. Molly was surprised to see the lighthouse and the Ridgeport dock appear so quickly in the horizon. As the Captain steered the boat into the dock, he bumped its edges lightly until it fit neatly up to a ramp that was lowered and ready to let cars off. Molly quickly returned to the truck. As she waited to disembark, her thoughts turned to her destination that she was now approaching and how she got there in the first place. She thought back to the day she received Electra's letter and how intrigued she was by the address on the return envelope. 'Electra Richards, 3 Misty Cove, Ridgeport, Maine.' *What kind of place is named Misty Cove?* Molly looked behind her at the deep blue of the Atlantic and realized that the mysterious letter and all that it contained had become, if not the motivator, the purpose for her trip. Suddenly, she was terrified to be faced with the reality that may soon be upon her.

The note had been short. It was as if whoever wrote it did not expect it to reach the person for whom it was intended.

"*Dear Molly,* the letter began. "*My name is Electra. I was adopted and I am now trying to locate my biological parents. I have reason to believe that you might be my biological mother. I was hoping that if you are, in fact, the mother of a daughter who was born on July 6, 1981, at Brigham Women's Hospital in Boston Massachusetts, that you would be willing to meet me. I have already been in touch with my biological father, Jimmy O'Conner. Enclosed is my address- Respectively, Electra Richards.*

Molly had tried to write a response until her wastebasket was full of discarded wads of paper. She didn't know what to say. *What if I say the wrong thing and Electra decides that she does not want to meet me?* She had thought over and over. In the end, Molly decided to drive to Maine and see Electra in person. Her life up to that point had come to a grinding halt and she just didn't think things could be going any worse for her. Some of Molly's paintings were on display in a tavern back in Bell Town in downtown Seattle. After being on display for two months, only one had sold, and the owners had asked her to collect them. She couldn't bear to bring the unsold paintings back into her apartment. In fact, she could hardly bare to go back to her apartment herself. She had lived there with her boyfriend, Joel, until just a few months earlier when he packed his bags and left her after three years. The letter from Electra had arrived a week before Molly's fortieth birthday and the same week she was asked to retrieve her paintings. The trip to see her estranged daughter had become the sole purpose of her life.

Molly had thought that by the time she was thirty, she would be married and have kids. When thirty came and went and she was alone, she had justified it by the fact that she was young and she had her career as an artist ahead of her. But when she found herself carrying the unsold paintings to her truck, still alone, and a few days away from forty, she felt she had come to the end of a path. She knew it was a cliché—but she needed to find herself. The letter that had arrived with an address to her past suddenly opened up that path for her. She would take the trip and find her daughter. Maybe along the way, she would figure out her life.

Molly was now only miles away from her destination, and she hadn't figured anything out about her life. She put the truck into gear and drove up the ramp onto the island. Still following the directions she had printed out from the Internet, Molly arrived in front of the house whose number matched the address on the return envelope from Electra. She had assumed back in Seattle that this would be some kind of small cottage in Maine, and so she was a bit taken aback when at the end of a neatly-combed, pebble driveway, there was before her a mansion similar to what Molly had only seen in movies. Unsure if she wanted her presence to be known, she parked off to the side of the road and slowly walked up the U-shaped, gravel driveway that led to the entrance of the house.

Finally, Molly stood in front of the door that symbolized the end of her path. She raised her hand to knock on the door. Then she paused. The lion's face on the large brass knocker stared back at her, challenging her to take it in hand. Molly knew this action wouldn't simply be about knocking on a door. It would be about the door that would be opened after many, many years. She thought of all the miles she had traveled and the money she didn't have that she spent. She thought of her apartment all crammed into a tiny storage unit, and not wanting to have done all that for nothing, she scolded herself, and raised her hand once more.

Like a statue, she stood with her hand almost touching the knocker until a bird flying past broke her thought. She tried several more times to knock on the door, but it seemed to her to be just out of reach. Finally, she gave up. Molly lowered both her hand and her head as she slowly retreated to the truck. The harsh sound of the vehicle's door slamming unnerved her and she sat in silence for a while before starting the truck up. She wanted to cry. Each day of the trip, she planned out the drive and decided where to stop for food or sleep. Now that she had arrived, she had no plan left. It seemed to her that she suddenly had no purpose at all.

Molly felt an immediate need to drive away from Electra's house and rethink what she was doing. She started up the truck and drove on, though she had no idea where she was going. She continued down the narrow road that had been paved, but had many potholes. Either side of the road was lined with different sized pine trees. Every so often there was a break in the trees and another small gravel driveway. In most cases she couldn't see the houses that lie at the end of those neatly combed driveways. They were tucked away. When Molly got back on to the main road, she wondered which end of the island was closer. She took a right. *Maybe I should drive straight off this island*, she thought—and pictured herself slowly sinking to the bottom of the ocean, a crooked smile on her face.

Someone passing her on the road going the other direction waved to her and Molly thought for a moment that they were mocking her imagined departure. Whatever sense of purpose or will had brought her to this point had ceased to guide her and she was again at a point in her life where she absolutely did not know what to do. Giving up her baby was a decision she had made so many years ago and it didn't seem right at the time to reverse it. *Anyhow, it looked as though things must have turned out well for Electra.*

The island was only 13 miles long and eventually the road ended at a small, ocean park. *This is a dead end in more ways than one*, Molly mused. At the park's entrance, there was a round driveway and a sign that read, "Ridgeport Town Beach." She parked and walked down a footpath, pinecones crunching under her feet. Molly was happy to see some white birch trees amongst the many pine trees. It wasn't often she saw those. She loved how they each had bits and pieces of their white bark peeling off as if to offer a passerby a piece of notepaper. Molly recalled when she was younger how she had written a poem on such on a piece of birch. She smiled at the memory.

Not far down the path there was an opening to the beach. Looking ahead she saw that there were several similar paths for beach access. She wandered down the first one which led to a small rocky beach. It didn't quite look like an inviting place to stop. The second path led to another rocky beach, however this time Molly spotted a picnic table where she decided to take a seat and gather her thoughts. Molly stared out at the ocean, mesmerized by the water's rhythm as it slowly crept up to the shore. It appeared as though the tide was coming in. The warm sun made her sleepy and so she stretched out across the length of the bench. When the sun started to feel as though it was burning her cheeks, she rolled to the side with her face away from the sun and she fell asleep.

Molly wasn't sure how long she had been napping when a black fly bit her ankle. The sting of the bug bite caused her to wake suddenly and bang her head on the top of the table. Molly shifted from the bench to sit on top of the table. Rubbing first her sore head and then her eyes, Molly focused again on the gentle waves breaking against the shore. She hadn't been sitting like that for long before she felt the presence of someone else nearby. Instead of being afraid or alarmed, however, she felt a warmth envelope her, as if the sun had come out from behind a cloud. She closed her eyes and turned her head up to the sky to bath her face in the warm glow. Then she heard a voice directed at her,

"Is that your truck up there?"

Molly saw that the voice came from a man who looked to be around her age. The man was a local named Nathan. He had jumped down from a large rock that separated the first beach. He was walking towards her with his arms out as he balanced himself stepping across the different sized rocks. Nathan was wearing jeans and a blue sweatshirt that had a sailboat and a logo which as he got closer she could see said, "Ridgeport Boat Yard." His sandy hair was disheveled as though he had recently taken off a hat.

"Yes it is. Is it in your way?" she responded when Nathan had come even closer.

"Naw I'm on foot," he said in a thick Maine accent. "I was just noticing the Washington State plates. Did you drive that thing clear across the country?" While he waited for her to answer Nathan looked around to see if she was with anyone.

As Nathan reached the picnic table, Molly at once noticed his eyes. They reminded her of her uncle's. He had sparkly blue eyes too. The familiarity made her feel instantly at ease and she continued speaking to him as though they were old friends.

"Yeah, I'm amazed it made it," she said.

"What year is it?"

"It's a 1963,"

"Phew! Cars rust before they get that old out here."

"Yeah, that was the first thing I noticed when I moved out West. Lots of old cars

"So how long did it take you?" Nathan said and then fishing for information added, "You didn't drive that thing yourself did you?"

"I did drive myself," Molly answered thinking to herself she probably shouldn't be telling a strange man that she was alone.

"That's a long drive," Nathan said. He hadn't meant to pry any further, but before he could stop himself he had already asked, "Are you here to see family?"

"I just have some stuff to do," Molly said.

"Well, there's not much stuff to do here," Nathan said with a chuckle. Molly noticed that he had the stereotypical Maine accent that she had been hearing a lot of in the last couple days. She thought however, that this man's voice had a very rich tone and many intonations in-between.

"I suppose not," Molly answered. She looked up at his tall frame. He was standing slightly in front of her in the direction of the sun, which had indeed emerged from behind a cloud. As she squinted with her eyes, the sun's rays shadowed his body and he appeared to glow.

Realizing that he had not properly introduced himself, Nathan put out his hand. "My name is Nathan Potter," he said.

Molly jumped down from the table to shake it.

"Nice to meet you, Nathan," she said with a smile, "My name is Molly Callahan."

From the moment he saw Molly, Nathan thought she was the most beautiful woman he had ever seen. Her dark hair was thick and wavy and it dramatically framed her delicate porcelain white face that was currently slightly pink from too much sun. Her smile intoxicated him and he had to steady himself with his back foot, as if he were drunk, to keep his balance. He was pleased to hear that she was on her own.

A brief moment of silence followed their introductions. Nathan, who had a tendency towards shyness with women, was embarrassed by how flustered he had become. He quickly turned to go. "Well, you have a nice visit," he said, waving his hand over his head as went.

Molly was disappointed by how quickly Nathan retreated. There was something peaceful about him and she wouldn't have minded if he had sat on the beach with her a little while longer. As he disappeared, she felt lonelier than she could ever remember feeling in her whole life. Her eyes filled with tears. Soon, she was sobbing uncontrollably. When the tears finally passed, Molly rubbed her eyes and looked back out at the ocean.

The tide continued to come in and the rocks nearby had mostly disappeared under the water. She could only see a few brown tips of the seaweed that clung to them. They swayed gently as the waves slowly pulled them toward the shore. Molly wondered if the crabs that lived under the seaweed counted their days by each time the tide covered them.

Molly remained at the beach as the afternoon wore on and it started to cool down. She thought about Electra writing that she had been in touch with her father, Jimmy. *Had she written him a letter, like she did with her, or had she already met him*? Molly wondered. It seemed impossible to imagine that the daughter she gave up so many years ago had been in contact with Jimmy. It had been years after their break up when Molly finally put him out of her mind. Then, one night not long after that, she heard what she thought was his voice bellowing out of the loudspeaker at the *Triangle Bar* back in Seattle. She remembered asking someone on the stool next to her who was playing. They had told her it was a band named Quarter Moon. She was at first relieved to hear it wasn't Jimmy's band. Then the young girl who was filling her in said, "Yeah, they really took off after Jimmy O'Conner joined the band. Aren't they great?"

Molly had gotten very drunk that night. She knew she should be happy that Jimmy had gotten what he wanted, but somehow his success only seemed to accent her own failure. To add insult to injury, he may have already met their daughter before she did.

Molly did not feel anywhere near ready to meet Electra. What would she tell her—that she had to give her up to pursue an art career? She was sure Electra must have been very impressed to discover her biological father was a big rock star. What a failure her mother would seem like. Yet she couldn't simply have come to collect her after she realized she was failing as an artist, could she? *Life doesn't give you those kinds of choices*, she thought. *I had to make a decision that would be best for everyone*. She nearly said the words aloud.

Molly had hoped during the first few months of her pregnancy that Jimmy would change his mind and want to raise the baby with her. When that didn't happen she believed she could take care of the baby on her own. It was her uncle who had finally convinced her that she needed to give the baby up for adoption. He had urged her to take the scholarship to art school that she had been given before she was pregnant. He comforted her by telling her that there were plenty of loving families who would love to adopt a 'wee little thing in perfect health. It would be much better for the child and for her own future,' he had said. At the time, she had thought that, in his own way, her uncle was trying to tell her how hard it was to raise a child on one's own. She wondered if he resented raising her after her parents had died and she had been sent from the coast of Ireland to Boston to be in his care. She felt as though she had spent a great deal of her life up until then wondering 'what if.'

Molly started to get cold and the sensation brought her out of her thoughts. She was reminded of the immediate decisions that needed to be made. Molly still hadn't met Electra, yet she was nearly out of cash, and returning to Seattle was not a possibility. She was familiar with living month to month, so she decided that she would stay on the island for a while and get a summer job. There must be some sort of general store that would have a community bulletin board where jobs may be listed.

Molly drove down the main road until she came to the Island Store. She was searching for a bulletin board inside when she heard someone approach.

"So I see shopping is on that list of 'stuff to do' for you?" It was Nathan. Molly felt her cheeks flush a bit.

"Actually, I'm afraid finding work is before shopping on my list. I'm looking to see if there is a place that might list jobs. You know, like as a waitress or something."

"Finding a job 'round here is a word of mouth sort of thing," Nathan chuckled.

"Oh," Molly replied, disappointed. She paused for a moment and then continued.

"Then do you know of any jobs?" Her tone was slightly joking.

"Well, Molly—you did say your name is Molly right?" Nathan asked. However, he had not only remembered her name, but also not stopped thinking about Molly since he so hastily retreated from the beach.

"Yes, and yours is Nathan."

"At least that's what I answer to on most days," Nathan said, and then added, "Molly, today might just be your lucky day." *And a lucky day for me as well*, Nathan thought. "I happen to be the Captain for a family whose housekeeper Benilde had to leave suddenly and go back to Portugal to take care of her family," Nathan continued. "The family I work for is desperately looking for a replacement."

"Really," Molly asked. "But what does a Captain do?"

"I take care of the family's boats, pick up their houseguests over on the mainland, take them out on picnics," he explained. "Most importantly, I skipper their boat for the summer sailing races."

"Oh," Molly replied. "I never met anyone who had that kind of job before."

"Well, if you're interested in the housekeeping job, I'd be happy to take you on over to meet Mrs. Geld."

"Just like that?" Molly said surprised. "But you don't know a thing about me."

"Call it Yankee intuition. You look like a good sort," Nathan said matter-of-factly, he was afraid he might have been a bit too forward and hoped that made him seem more indifferent.

"Well, that's very generous of you," Molly replied. She didn't really have any other options, and she didn't see how it could hurt to at least check the possibility out. "I would really appreciate the job opportunity for a couple of months or so, long enough to help me get enough money for the trip back home." *Or until I work up the nerve to do what I came here for*, she thought.

Nathan realized that he had flinched when she mentioned her trip home. He hoped it wasn't obvious to Molly. He quickly looked away from her, and put the rest of his items on the checkout counter and without looking at her said, "If you're ready, I could take you over after I get these things rung up."

Molly waited with him as though they had been shopping together. She noticed the bachelor simplicity of the items he was purchasing, a six pack of beer, carton of eggs, bacon, orange juice, and a bag of chips. After his groceries were packed up, she followed him out of the store.

"Let's go introduce Mrs. Geld to her new housekeeper," Nathan said, as he put his groceries in the back seat and then got into his vehicle. He suggested that she could either ride with him or follow. She decided to ride with him. As they passed by cars going in the other direction, Molly noticed that Nathan waved to all of them.

"People sure are friendly here," Molly said.

"It's one way you can tell whether someone's an islander or not," Nathan said. Then he added, "Of course, you've also got your summer folks who've been here a while and who have adopted the ritual. They always add a little smirk with the wave, like they're real proud to be in on the local tradition. I suppose it's quaint to them." Nathan was glad for the conversation Molly started. It put him more at ease.

"I suppose so," replied Molly. When Molly recognized that they were turning on to the same road she had gone on to get to Electra's house, she panicked. Her voice was shaky as she asked Nathan, "What did you say this family's name was?"

"Geld," Nathan answered, pulling into an estate just past the familiar U-Shaped driveway. Molly felt a wave of relief sweep over her.

"They actually refer to these places as 'summer cottages,' " Nathan said as he led her into a large foyer. A spiral staircase was to the right and, directly in front of them, a pair of French doors lined with long silk white curtains. The doors opened to a back lawn that spilled down to the shore. Nathan shouted for Mrs. Geld as they both waited in the entrance.

"Some cottage," Molly said under her breath as Mrs. Geld appeared from a side door, wearing light linen pants neatly pleated and a soft yellow cashmere sweater. Her fine blonde hair fell neatly on her shoulder in a bob. She was what most people would describe as very attractive for her age—striking, but by no means beautiful. She looked as though she took great care in her appearance.

"Nathan, I thought that was you pulling into the drive," Mrs. Geld began, "I can always tell the sound of a SAAB. I wasn't expecting you to come round this evening."

"Hello, Mrs. Geld. Sorry to disturb you, but I have a surprise. Just last night I got a call from Molly," Nathan said, stopping to introduce the two women. "Mrs. Geld, this is Molly. Molly, Mrs. Geld," Molly shook Mrs. Geld's hand, noticing how cold it was. Nathan continued with the introductions.

"Molly worked with my sister Sarah over on the mainland at the Lighthouse Inn as a housekeeper. She lives in Seattle now, but she is out East for a couple months. I told her about Benilde and how you could use some help."

"This is a remarkable home," Molly quickly interjected. She was uneasy with Nathan's lies. Mrs. Geld turned to Molly and looked her up and down.

"I am in a terrible bind," she said with a slightly exasperated voice. "Poor Benilde, I don't know when or even if she'll be rejoining us."

"I can stay and help until she does," Molly offered. "I'm a very hard worker and I'm never late."

"This is a live-in position, so you won't need to worry about being late." Mrs. Geld said. The woman made the remark in such a way that Molly was uncertain of her intent. She suddenly pictured herself slipping off to sleep in the attic after working all day and night.

"Exactly what are the hours?" Molly asked.

"It's six days a week. You get one day off, but if you're efficient, you should have plenty of time to yourself during the day. I might require that you help out during cocktail parties, but that wouldn't be more than once or twice a week. Do you know how to mix a drink?"

"Yes, I do," Molly answered. "I've been a housekeeper, a cook, a waitress and a bartender so I can help out in any way you need me."

"Well, Nathan, you are right. You did bring me a surprise." Mrs. Geld stared at Molly a while longer.

"You're quite an attractive woman," she said to Molly. "You're not going to get my husband's friends in any trouble, now are you?" Molly was alarmed by the question. She didn't quite know how to answer.

"Nathan, I'm holding you completely responsible for this one," Mrs. Geld stated, turning to him. "Show Molly down to Benilde's room in the guest cottage and then send her back up so we can talk about the pay."

"What was that all about?" Molly asked as Nathan escorted her down to the guest cottage. "She's not one of those jealous wives is she?"

"Mrs. Geld?" asked Nathan. "Not the kind of jealous you have in mind. She prides herself in being the matriarch of her home and running it with the same efficiency I would imagine her husband runs his brokerage firm in New York. Every year she tells me how the other wives marvel at her parties. 'They are simply the best,' she always tells me proudly. She is obsessed with entertaining." Nathan paused as he opened the door to the guest cottage with a spare key he kept on him.

As they entered, Molly said, "Now this is a cottage. It's lovely."

"I thought you'd like it. I think you'll find it very peaceful." After showing her around, Nathan and Molly turned to go. "Let's get you back up to the house to talk about the pay," Nathan said.

Mrs. Geld had decided almost as quickly as Nathan that Molly was the perfect person to take on Benilde's job. She had an offer letter ready and when Nathan and Molly returned from the guest cottage, she extended it out to her. Molly had never been offered a formal letter. She was more familiar with the one-page application form and a quick nod. Molly's eyes lingered on the last paragraph. It read, "Should you complete your 60 days with utmost satisfaction on the part of the Geld family, you shall also receive a bonus of $3,000." Molly was beside herself with this good fortune. She half expected to wake up back at the town beach having never met Nathan or Mrs. Geld. The $3,000 dollars would be most helpful in getting her back to Seattle.

"You can take the night to think it over, but I do need an answer soon." Mrs. Geld said.

"Oh, no. I don't need time to think it over," Molly answered, rushing to sign the bottom. "This will be perfect and I am most grateful. If it's okay, I will go and get my things. That way I can get started tomorrow morning."

"Glad to hear it." Mrs. Geld said. She knew her offer would be accepted when she thought to offer the bonus. Mrs. Geld held her hand out to get the signed offer back.

"I will make you a copy and get you a key to the guest cottage," she said, with a self-satisfied smile.

"That worked out well," Nathan said as they drove back to the store to get Molly's truck.

"I really don't know how I can thank you enough," Molly said as she got out of Nathan's car back at the Islander General Store. "This is too amazing, finding a job and a place to stay all in one day."

"I believe that sometimes things just work out, and I'm never one to question good fate. Chances were high you'd meet me down at the town beach. I live just down the road and love to walk along the beach path. On the other hand, that I would know about a good summer job—that was fate."

At the store, Molly got back in her truck and drove back down to the Geld's. As she pulled her truck into the driveway, Mrs. Geld came out and took a good look at Molly's vehicle. "My goodness what is that thing?" she asked.

"It's an International Scout, 1963." Molly said brightly. "Do you like it?"

"It's a rather unusual vehicle for a woman," Mrs. Geld answered with obvious disapproval.

"I hope it doesn't bother you," Molly said.

"Of course not," said Mrs. Geld, brushing the question away with her hand as if it were a tick she had for when she told little white lies. Mrs. Geld noticed an unwelcome weed had popped up in the driveway and she bent down and pulled it out. "The yard people aren't as thorough as they used to be," she said looking back up at

Molly who was still standing in front of her. "And about that truck, you will need to park that in the side lot. Just go back out and take the next driveway." Molly's eyes followed Mrs. Geld's arm which was pointing to the right. She could see another driveway through the bushes. "Ok. No problem," Molly said as she got in her truck and started it up.

Mrs. Geld took a few quick steps back as though she expected the truck to blow up, and then shouted out, "Come back up when you're done and we can go over the agenda for tomorrow." Molly rolled down the window, and stuck her head out to hear Mrs. Geld more clearly. "Anything else I need to know," Molly asked before putting the truck into gear.

"Oh, yes," Mrs. Geld added, "My husband William won't be up until Friday. He's only here on the weekends until the last two weeks in August and then he is here for the remainder of the season. My son comes up on the weekends a lot. He will bring some of his friends from time to time. Don't worry. They're always very polite. He's a very good boy. He just started working in my husband's firm in New York. We're so terribly proud of him. You'll meet him this weekend. He's coming up with a couple of friends for our annual Fourth of July lobster bake. Oh, my goodness! That reminds me! There is so much work to be done. This is such a relief you are able to start so suddenly. Well, I'll leave you to settle in."

As Molly pulled her truck into the side driveway, she thought, this is going to be an interesting two months. For a moment, she completely forgot the real reason she was on the island.

Molly unpacked her duffel bag full of dirty clothes and then made her way back up the side driveway so that she could rejoin Mrs. Geld at the front hall. Mrs. Geld was waiting there with a notepad in hand.

"Take notes," she said, handing the notebook and a pen to Molly. "I get up at eight every morning. Gina, who you will meet, is our cook. She has breakfast ready for me at nine thirty after I do my yoga. I would like for you to have my bed made and the room tidied up by nine. I expect the linens on my bed to be changed every three days. The linens for each room match the color of the room. Make yourself familiar with which linens go with which rooms because I don't want to see yellow linens going on the blue room's bed. When we have guests, I expect you to clean their rooms while they are at breakfast. I also expect you to change the guests' linens every day. Please use a different set each day. We don't want them thinking I only have one set for each room. You will need to go through every room before lunch to make sure everything is in order. I don't want you vacuuming until we are out of the house—so you'll need to plan your chores accordingly. We often have lunch down at the yacht club or out on our boat, so lunch clean up will vary. Like I said, if you are efficient, you could have quite some time to yourself in the afternoons. I need you back up at the house by five for cocktail hour when the men or guests are here. Then you need to return again to clean up after dinner. I'm afraid that can get quite late, depending on the guests. Gina will help you with the serving and the kitchen cleanup. She runs a very orderly kitchen." Mrs. Geld paused for a moment to make sure she was taking notes. When she was sure she had Molly's attention Mrs. Geld continued, "You will also be asked to help with the shopping. "Is this clear so far?" she asked.

"Sounds straightforward to me," Molly replied, "If you could show me where you keep the linens, your laundry room, and the closet where you keep your brooms, vacuum and such, that would help."

"Of course," Mrs. Geld led her down a hallway. "This is the pantry," she said, pointing to a room along the hall. Then she swung open a door that exposed a long beautiful dining room table, "and this is our dining room." Mrs. Geld went back through the pantry into a large kitchen that was equipped with a restaurant-style stove and an island with pots and pans hanging overhead. "This is Gina's territory so be sure to check with her on everything that goes on in the kitchen." There was a small, less formal looking eating room that was also equipped with a refrigerator. "That is the refrigerator that Gina has designated for my son and any of the employees. You are free to help yourself to anything in that refrigerator or the cabinets in this room. Gina found that this was the best way to avoid missing important ingredients to her scheduled meals."

They continued through the second kitchen. On the backside of the kitchen was a laundry room. Mrs. Geld pointed to a laundry basket that was placed underneath a very low cabinet. She opened the cabinet door and a pile of towels tumbled into the basket.

"There is a laundry shoot upstairs in the maids' quarters. You can throw the linens down there. That is also where the linen closet is, and on the other side is a dumb waiter that you can use to pull the clean laundry up as well."

"Maid's quarters?" Molly asked, wondering what she meant by that.

"Back when my grandfather owned this place, the help lived in the side rooms. Benilde used to stay in one of those rooms, but I had the boathouse converted to a guest cottage a few years back when our last cook from France quit and we got Gina. Gina lives down-island with her boyfriend so she didn't need a room. She has been to the California Culinary Institute and is every bit the cook Pierre was, and ever so much less trouble. Pierre was always grumpy. Gina, on the other hand—you'll see, she is truly a vivacious gal. Nathan, of course, has lived on this island his whole life. So with only needing one room for live-in help, we thought it would be nicer to use the guest cottage instead of those small rooms." Mrs. Geld remembered the day that Benilde handed her back the key to the guest cottage and told her she had to leave. She shuttered and continued, "Molly, I can't tell you how relieved I am that you are here. I'm going to take a bath so you can help yourself to something to eat. Since it's only me here, Gina took the night off. You won't meet her until the morning. I've already had a nice salad that she left for me."

Molly realized that she hadn't eaten all day so she took Mrs. Geld up on the offer for food. *Gina certainly is efficient*, Molly thought, as she noted everything in neat storage containers, properly labeled and dated. There was a container that said "lobster salad." It was only a couple days old. Molly felt a bit guilty taking something so extravagant. On the other hand, she hadn't had any lobster since she had been in Maine. As she helped herself to the salad, Molly wondered if her cleaning skills could match up to the apparent efficiency of this cook. It was interesting how Mrs. Geld had referred to Gina as vivacious. Molly wondered what the lady of the house thought of her.

Molly wanted to look decent for her first day's work. She was collecting her dirty clothes to take up to the laundry room when she heard a knock at the door of the cottage.

"Molly?" It was Nathan's voice.

"Come on in," she shouted from the bedroom. *What was Nathan doing coming round the cottage at this hour*? She was slightly worried. Molly came out and saw Nathan with an attractive couple in their thirties.

"Sorry to bother you, Molly. I just thought you might like to meet Gina." Nathan said as he stepped in the cottage.

"Nice to meet you," Gina waved at Molly and proceeded to enter the cottage as well. "I hope we're not coming by too late. Nathan came to our house for a barbecue and told us about you. He was against the idea of bothering you like this. It's totally my fault. To be honest, I was burning with curiosity." Gina gave the place a quick look over. "I hope you don't mind. This is my boyfriend, Stew." Stew, who was used to following Gina's lead, smiled at her with a slight apologetic look in his eyes.

Molly did mind, but her quick answer covered up her feelings.

"It's nice to meet you," she said, throwing a towel over the pile of laundry that she had collected. "It's all been such a whirlwind. I was going to try to sneak in some laundry because I don't have anything to wear for my first day."

"Don't any of the uniforms fit?" Gina asked.

"What uniforms?" Molly asked.

"Mrs. Geld will freak if you're not in a uniform. I suppose she forgot to tell you. They're up in the linen closet. Why don't you take your laundry over and check out the closet? You can see if there is one in your size. Mrs. Geld keeps an assortment of them up there for when she brings in extra help for bigger parties. In the meantime, I'll whip us up a snack and the boys can come up with a blender of some rum concoction," Gina smiled at Molly, adding, "Don't worry. We won't stay long."

Molly wasn't used to such quick friendships and felt a bit awkward to be suddenly immersed in these familiar relationships with staff members. Never the less, she did what Gina said and went over to the linen closet in the main house. When she got there, she saw that indeed there was a row of freshly pressed chambermaid dresses. Each had a large G monogrammed on the left breast. She also noticed the drawers of linens labeled "Blue Room, Yellow Room, Green Room," all neatly packed with different sets of matching linens and towels. She'd have to be careful to keep it all organized after doing the laundry, and it was clear that there would be a lot of it to do. She also saw a row of monogrammed bathrobes. She supposed that each guest bathroom was to be supplied with them. Molly had installed art in wealthy homes and had done catering jobs back in Seattle, but never had she been privy to such excessiveness, and especially not for merely a summer home.

Molly took a size eight dress from the closet and headed back down to the cottage. Nathan, Gina and Stew were already seated with drinks in hand.

"Stew makes the best rum cocktails," Gina said, reaching for a glass from the bar. Without asking whether Molly would like one, she poured a glass and handed it to her.

"We live in Key West in the winter," Gina explained. "Stew's the tennis pro down at the Turley Club so he's just up here for the summer. Ever since we got together, I've been following him south in the winter. We're like two little love birds." Gina bent over and gave Stew a big kiss.

Nathan reached his hand out to give a toast. "Here's to another summer," he said.

"Here! Here!" Nathan, Gina and Stew toasted in unison, they clinked their glasses and took a drink. Molly, who was a bit dumbfounded by the extreme comfort these strangers were showing in front of her, stumbled forward and added her glass to toast last. "Cheers," she said. Then she feebly added, "Thanks for the drink."

"Nathan says you're out here from Seattle. Does it really rain there all the time?" asked Stew.

"It doesn't rain so much as drizzle," Molly answered.

"Why did you come out east?" Gina asked.

"I've got some family business to attend to."

"Did someone pass away?" Gina asked.

"Gina," Stew said disapprovingly, gently punching her on the shoulder. Then he turned to Molly. "I'm sorry, Molly. Gina's had a few of these cocktails already. She's not usually this rude." Stew apologized though he did think that Gina could at times be a bit too blunt.

"I'm sorry," Gina said. "It was just the way you said 'family business.' Stew's being polite; actually, I can be way too nosy. To tell you the truth, nothing ever really happens on the island and minding other people's business is what we often end up doing. Forget I said it. Really, I'm sorry."

"Don't worry. It probably did sound a bit odd," Molly said. For a moment, she almost told the whole story about why she was really there, but she wasn't quite that familiar with these people yet. She decided to change the subject.

"Is there anything in particular I should know about Mrs. Geld?" Molly asked.

"Just keep everything looking organized. Also try to be as invisible as possible while her guests are in the house and she'll be happy," Gina answered.

"How long have you been working for her?" Molly asked

"This is my fourth year," said Gina.

"Fifteen for me," Nathan joined in.

"Nathan is a real islander," said Gina. "The rest of us—we're just a sea of characters who come and go like the tides. Nathan, however, stays on the island year in and year out."

"I don't see what's so odd about that. It's my home." Nathan objected.

"I'm not saying it's odd," Gina explained. "I'm just pointing out that you'll probably always be here."

"Well, I'm afraid I'll just be here this one summer," Molly added.

"Don't be so sure," Gina said. "There is something about this island. Like the tide, it draws you back in. I thought I'd only be here a year."

"What about Benilde?" asked Molly. "She'll be back by next summer, I'd imagine."

"I don't know. I haven't heard from her to be honest." Gina didn't really care too much for Benilde and she was glad for a replacement. She liked the look of Molly. Gina smiled. She stirred her drink and as she took another sip she thought, *Benilde won't be coming back here. I'll see to that.* And then she said to Molly, "I just get the feeling you'll be coming back to this island."

"You must like it here," Molly said, adding "since you've been here a while."

"Every winter, Stew and I say that it will be our last summer up in Maine," Gina continued. "We've been thinking about finding a place where we can settle down and I can open my own restaurant." She glanced at Stew. Obviously, it was a touchy subject between them. "You know, to get married and start a family." Stew hadn't recalled any conversation with Gina about finding a place to settle down or her opening a restaurant. He did recall a few conversations about babies, but he tried to forget those.

"We're young yet," Stew said in response, putting his hand firmly on Gina's thigh as if to ask her to change the subject. "Besides, there are so many things to consider about choosing a place to settle down. It's a bit overwhelming."

"If you like it here, why don't you open a restaurant on the island?" Molly asked.

"It's been tried many times before. With a three-month season, it's a bit rough to keep a place going. Plus, it's not really the kind of place you want to raise a family."

"My sister's kids are doing just fine," Nathan interjected, with a look of insult.

Gina, who often seemed to be a bit of a snob to Nathan, didn't bother to apologize. Nathan knew her tendency to say things the way she saw them, regardless of who it hurt.

"I just meant it isn't a place Stewart and I would want to raise a family. We're not islanders."

Nathan didn't see what that had to do with anything, but he didn't want to argue. He knew from past experience with Gina that it could turn into a very long and twisted debate. Gina had her views about people and their socio-economic position in life. Nathan, on the other hand, didn't see how people were so much different from each other at the end of the day.

Molly turned to Nathan. "Do you have children?" she asked.

"Nope. I haven't found anyone who liked me enough to marry me." Nathan replied.

"That seems hard to believe." Molly hadn't meant to say it but the words seemed to come of their own accord.

"I meant, no one who I liked enough to marry, liked me," said Nathan. His blue eyes twinkled at Molly in response.

Nathan, Stew and Gina sat back then, sipping their drinks in silence and immersed in their own thoughts. Molly, noticing that their glasses were close to empty, and not wanting a second round to start up, broke the silence.

"I don't want to seem rude, but if everyone has finished up their drink I really need to get some rest if I am to be of any use tomorrow."

"Of Course," Gina said, as she got up and gathered the glasses to be washed. "Let's let the poor woman get some sleep. Then she turned to Molly. "It was wonderful to meet you and I look forward to working with you this summer. We'll see you up in the kitchen in the morning."

"I'll see you in the morning. And thank you for letting me know about the uniform." Molly stood as Gina and Stew headed for the door with Nathan in tow.

"Molly, I hope this works out for you," Nathan said on his way out. "With the Fourth of July Geld Family picnic coming up this weekend, I suspect that you and I will be taking a ride over to the mainland to pick up all those last minute groceries and final touches."

"I can do that." Molly said, standing by the door as everyone exited. "Thank you again for everything. Have a good night."

As Gina, Stew and Nathan headed to their cars, Gina asked Nathan about Molly.

"Why did you say she was in Maine?"

"You know I don't know."

"You, my friend, are no good. You don't even let me ask the questions."

"You can't bombard the poor woman," Nathan said with a sigh.

"Well, you have every right to ask her questions. You got her a job, didn't you?"

"Yeah, but..."

"But what?" Gina smiled mischievously. "You have a thing for her, don't you?" Nathan blushed in response.

"You do!" Gina said, punching Nathan's shoulder. Then she turned to Stew and jumped up on his shoulders for a ride to the car.

"Our boy Nathan has a crush!" Gina shouted as Stew and she made their way across the parking lot.

"Shhh!" Nathan said. "Your boy nothing. Now keep it down. It was just a matter of timing. We needed some help around here and she needed a job. It worked out well for everyone"

"And you don't know anyone else around here who'd want a good summer job?" Gina asked doubtfully.

"As a matter of fact, I don't." Nathan answered.

Gina and Stew grinned at each other as Stew gently lowered Gina to the ground next to their VW Golf. The vehicle was parked next to Nathan's hand-me-down Saab he had gotten from the Geld's a few summers back.

"I'm glad you picked someone who seems pretty normal," Gina said as they departed.

Nathan got in his own car and headed back to his house. He couldn't believe that his crush on Molly had been so evident. He was a man who did not let his emotions show. This disturbed him. He was particularly annoyed that it was Gina, the biggest mouth of all, who had been the one to notice. He made a mental note to be sure to seem indifferent to Molly when he was anywhere near Gina.

CHAPTER TWO – The New Job

olly didn't sleep much that night. She got up when the sun rose and dug around in the kitchenette until she found coffee and a French press. Then she sat in the overstuffed chair that Stew had sat in the night before, sipping her coffee. She turned the chair around to face a large window that looked out at the Geld's private pier. There was a small rowboat tied up at the dock and three other boats on nearby moorings—one was a sleek wooden sailboat, another, a larger motorboat, and the third, a larger sailboat. *This must be the fleet that Nathan looks over*, she thought. She was still amazed by such wealth. Molly sipped her coffee as she watched the tide slowly lap over the seaweed and rocks that blanketed the shore. *Mark your calendars crabs*, she mused to herself, remembering last evening's incoming tide. Again, the seaweed rose slightly above the rocks as the water came in and then back down as the waves receded. It seemed to Molly that the rocks were breathing. Molly sighed along with them.

Molly had waited on people all her life, so she did not think it would be a problem keeping house for the Geld's. What worried Molly most was the fact that her daughter lived next door. Eventually, there would be no avoiding meeting her. Worse still, she would need to explain how she came to be the next-door neighbor's housekeeper. *Electra really should have stopped after she found her father*, Molly thought. Anything after that discovery would be a disappointment. Molly wondered if Jimmy had thought of her again after hearing from their daughter. And she still wondered if he and Electra had already met. Maybe Jimmy was here on the island right now, having also been summoned by Electra. This thought brought to Molly its own particular kind of horror. It made her angry to think that Jimmy would have a chance to meet Electra when he had been the one to suggest she get rid of the baby all those years ago. *He has no right to meet her*, Electra thought with anger and resentment.

Molly loved to swim, no matter what the temperature, so she decided to take a quick dip before dressing and heading up to the house in hopes that the cold ocean water would wake her up and snap her out of her foul mood. She hadn't thought to pack a bathing suit (after all, it wasn't a vacation she was going on) so she found a pair of shorts and a t-shirt and headed for the beach. It was a brisk morning. As Molly crossed the lawn, she noticed that the morning dew was still shaped like perfect cobwebs. Molly wondered if there were invisible spiders in Maine that existed only at sunrise. As she stepped from the lawn to the beach, she quickly slowed her gait, giving out a slight yelp as a sharp rock dug into her foot.

The swim, which was more of a dip, was indeed refreshing. Between the cold water and two large mugs of coffee, Molly was wide awake as she donned her new uniform and headed up to the house for her first day of work. Just before she entered the house, she heard a bird song she had never heard before. She felt as though the bird were saying hello just to her.

"Hello, Molly," Gina shouted out from the kitchen window. "I saw you coming in from a swim when I pulled in the driveway this morning. You sure are brave."

"It felt good," Molly replied as she entered in through the side of the house. "Say, do you know what kind of bird that is out there singing?"

"Oh that's a white throated sparrow. Sweet, isn't it?

"Yes, sweet is exactly it," Molly answered with a slight sigh as she smoothed out the apron on her uniform.

"I see you found a uniform that fits. You know, I'm going to have to call you a bitch. I can't believe how good you look in it. Please tell me you swim every morning and exercise two hours every day and that you're not naturally that slim."

Molly was not used to any women speaking to her so directly and she was not sure how to answer. She just stared at Gina in response, slightly irritated that she had broken the spell of her peaceful morning. *What kind of a woman would use that word so early in the morning, even in jest?*

Gina realized she had made Molly uncomfortable and quickly changed the subject to house-matters.

"Mrs. Geld is out in her Japanese garden doing her yoga. You have at least one hour to tidy up her room. If you have any questions, you'll know where to find me."

"Right," Molly said, as she headed from the kitchen back up the stairs. When she got to Mrs. Geld's bedroom, she pulled back the drapes, made the bed and wiped down the tiles in the bathroom. The room looked spotless. She wasn't sure what else to do so she headed back down to the kitchen.

"Help yourself to anything you like out of our fridge. If there is anything special you like just be sure to mark it. I have a sharpie pen hanging on the door. Benilde used to keep her cereals and things she ate in the first cabinet so I suppose you could use that. I'm making Mrs. Geld a poached egg if you'd like one."

"No thanks. I'm fine." Molly was not particularly hungry. Her nerves were still getting the better of her appetite.

"So, you're from Seattle?" Gina asked, moving swiftly around the kitchen collecting what she needed for Mrs. Geld's breakfast tray.

"I've been living there for about fifteen years."

"What do you do out there?"

"To pay the bills, a lot of odd jobs like this one actually. I've been trying to make it as an artist."

"What kind of artist?"

"An unsuccessful one, I'm afraid," Molly answered.

Gina laughed, though she quickly realized by Molly's serious expression that it hadn't been meant as a joke.

"What are you doing out East, if you don't mind me asking?"

"I came to see someone," Molly said.

"A boyfriend? An Internet affair? Who?" Gina asked, with a little too much excitement.

"Nothing like that. I have a daughter who lives out this way."

"Would I know her?" Gina asked. Just then, Mrs. Geld came in, interrupting the conversation.

"Gina," Mrs. Geld began, "Can you bring my breakfast out to the front porch instead of the garden this morning?" Then she looked over at Molly as though she had seen her in her kitchen every day for years. "Molly, I'll write up a list of the things I need help with today. I'm afraid it will be long, with the party coming up this weekend."

Gina pulled together the breakfast tray and took it out to Mrs. Geld while Molly nibbled on a piece of toast. She wondered about the contents of the list.

"She must have gotten started on that list last night," Gina said as she came back in the kitchen and handed it to Molly. "I guess we'll all be very busy today, but I would love to chat some more soon."

Molly reviewed the list very carefully. She was to vacuum all the rooms and also make sure that they all had fresh flowers, including the bathrooms. There was a checklist that looked like a menu that needed to be filled out for each room to be sure everything was set properly. It seemed to Molly that this household was run better than most five-star hotels. Among the chores was a trip to the mainland with Nathan to pick up supplies for the party. Molly felt a bit like a school girl when she realized that she was looking forward to the joint task with Nathan. She also took care to change out of her maid's dress and wear her most flattering jeans.

Nathan was waiting at the dock promptly at 11:00. Molly wondered what *his* list looked liked and she imagined 'pick up housekeeper for mainland shopping at 11:00' was on it. Nathan was driving a fast motorboat that she hadn't noticed by the dock that morning so she figured he must have arrived by water.

"Good morning," Nathan said, admiring Molly's long hair shining in the sun. "Do you have something to clip your hair back with? It'll be a windy ride and most of the ladies like to tie their hair back." Molly's hair was thick and slightly wavy so she was able to wrap it around her hand a few times and tie it into a knot.

"That's funny. The only other woman I've seen do that is our neighbor, Electra. She's got thick hair just like yours. I almost thought you were her for a moment."

Molly realized that the whole time since she arrived in Maine she had never given a thought to the fact that Electra might look like her. She wanted to ask more questions about Electra but instead she asked, "How long is the ride over to the mainland?"

"It's just about 20 minutes, but you might want a sweatshirt or jacket." Nathan noticed that she was just wearing a t-shirt and jeans. "Hold on. I might have something for you on the boat." Nathan pulled out a sweatshirt from under the driver's seat. Molly thanked him and wrapped it around her waist in case she'd need it.

"Well, we better get going. I have the list and it's pretty long," Molly said. "I hope you can show me where some of these shops are."

"Knowing Mrs. Geld, you'll also need some help carrying what she has on that list." Nathan said. Then he asked Molly to untie the line and jump into the boat.

"How do you like the job so far?" Nathan asked once they were settled in and had been riding for a while.

Molly turned her head toward him, feeling the sea breeze tingle her face. "To be honest, it feels more like a vacation than work so far. But, then again, it's only been a few hours."

"Aside from some of these weekend parties, the pace is pretty slow so you'll have lots of free time," Nathan said, almost adding that she'd have time to do her 'stuff.' He wasn't the prying sort, however, so he didn't mention it.

"Do you know how many people Mrs. Geld is expecting at this Fourth of July Picnic?" Molly asked.

"Well, her son B.J. will be up and he is bringing a couple of friends from school. B.J. always brings friends, but never a date. Poor boy has been hopelessly in love with that neighbor I told you about, Electra, practically his whole life. Of course, she is always invited to the parties, but she hasn't always shown up since her Dad died." Nathan thought about Mr. Richards and Gabby, B.J.'s step sister, and how much their deaths in New York had reaffirmed his belief in simple country living. Nathan hated crowded places, and he was certain under no circumstances would he ever go to a big city like New York. Molly wondered about what Nathan meant about Electra's father dying, but before she could ask he continued to answer her question about the picnic, "Besides Electra, there will be a few more neighbors, so I'd say we'll have two house guests in addition to the Geld's and then about ten others."

"Wow, with this list I thought it was a party for fifty people," Molly said, thinking about the statement that Electra would be there and still wondering about the father who had died and if she was dating B.J. her employers son.

"Is Electra in love with B.J.?" Molly asked.

"Now that girl is a mystery. You can see why B.J. pines for her, but I don't think that he has ever even asked her out. They've known each other their whole life, grew up playing tennis and sailing together. I think the closest he ever got on the romantic side was a quick kiss at a Spin the Bottle game when they were teenagers. I must have heard that story a thousand times."

"Why is she a mystery?" Molly asked, again not having meant to talk about Electra, but being unable to resist her curiosity.

"I don't know. There's just something about her. She is not like the other kids. She's so serious. Her mother left her when she was only ten." Molly's heart sank a moment at the mention of this news. "It happened at one of the Geld's parties back in Manhattan over the holidays. Electra's mother met some independently wealthy baron from Europe. He quickly whisked her mom away to Europe." Nathan remembered the endless gossip sessions on the Geld's boat that following year about how heartless Electra's mother had been. "Electra was never invited to go with her mother, and so she stayed behind with her father Mr. Richards, the Geld's good friend and neighbor. He was an investment banker. His family owned the house next door to the Geld's here on the island for two generations. After his death, Electra inherited it."

"What do you mean she inherited it?" Molly asked curiously.

"Electra was his only living relative, so she inherited everything—his company, the house here and their townhouse in

Manhattan. Electra's father had been in one of the Twin Towers that was struck during the 911 airline crash. Sadly, he was not someone who was ever recovered. At the time it happened, Electra was studying music at Julliard. It was devastating to her, as I am sure you can imagine. She spends almost all her time here now. I think she must have dropped out of school. She still plays piano, but only at night. I don't know if she does that because she thinks no one will hear her or if she is just lonely at night. It's hard to imagine such a beautiful creature being lonely. I've come up from the docks in the morning and found B.J. all wrapped up in a blanket on a lawn chair sitting next to her property. I think he stays up all night listening to her and then falls asleep."

"She's my daughter." Molly couldn't hold it in any longer.

"Who's your daughter?" Nathan asked, confused.

"Electra. She is who I came to see."

"You've lost me," Nathan said, slowing the boat down slightly to better hear what Molly had to say.

Molly could not believe she just told Nathan, but she needed to explain it to someone. "Electra was adopted by the couple you just told me about. Of course, I didn't know who they were at the time, nor do I now. One day not too long ago, I got a letter from her."

"Wow," Nathan said, unsure what else to say.

"I didn't mean to say anything to you. Can we keep it between us, just for a while until I can figure out what to do?"

"So I take it you haven't seen Electra yet."

"No, I haven't."

"That is really weird—you taking a job right next door."

"It's not weird. It's just a very big coincidence."

"Wow," Nathan said, bringing the boat back up to speed.

Nathan and Molly were silent for the rest of the ride, thinking about the big coincidence they were both a part of suddenly together.

After they tied up the boat in the harbor, Molly handed her list to Nathan. He offered to go with her to show her the shops and help with the bags. They were breaking for lunch when Molly brought up the subject again.

"I was eighteen. I didn't want to give her up, but my uncle convinced me it was for the best. If I could have known back then that she'd have all this, I suppose I wouldn't have felt as bad." Molly stared out onto the water. She suddenly realized that, while Electra was clearly well off financially, her adopted family situation was not exactly one hundred percent successful.

"What happened to the father?" Nathan asked after they had been eating for a while.

"We broke up. Like I said, I was eighteen. It was back in Boston. I'll tell you the whole story sometime, but right now we better head back so that I can get all this stuff put away before cocktails. I understand that Mr. Geld, B.J. and his guests will be expected this afternoon."

"Yes, and Electra will be expected at the lobster picnic tomorrow. So if you need to talk to someone before then you can call me."

"Does she look like me?" Molly asked, thinking if they look too much alike, it would be best not to get too close to her at the party.

"As a matter of fact, you don't look all that much alike. Her hair is thick like yours, but it doesn't have as many curls and it's not as dark. The other thing is she has got huge blue eyes and dimples." Nathan stopped the description at that. While Molly's question had been innocent enough, he knew that if he kept talking, he could soon be led down a dangerous path he didn't want to go.

Enough had been said, however. Molly was certain Electra looked more like Jimmy. She remembered the way he used to swing his hair away from his face when he played guitar and when he turned to the crowd as he performed, smiling with those big blue eyes and that heart-stopping dimple. Molly chuckled a little realizing that both she and B.J. had a teenager's infatuation for the O'Conner blue eyes and dimples.

Then she thought how strange it would be for B.J. to learn that his new housekeeper is the mother of the girl next door. And imagine what Mrs. Geld would do if she finds out. Her socialite ties would all be undone.

Nathan watched Molly as she collected up the bags of groceries, several in each hand and started to head back towards the docks.

"Let me help you with those," Nathan said reaching out to help her. Nathan had never met anyone as unpredictable as Molly. She seemed so shy and quiet and then suddenly out of the blue she tells him she gave her baby up for adoption. He wasn't sure what to make of it. He found it very strange that he sympathized with her because he did not approve of any mother giving away her own child. He could not figure out why he was so drawn to this woman as he followed behind her ready to help her with anything she might need from him.

CHAPTER THREE – Back in Boston

I t was St. Patrick's Day when Jimmy O'Conner received the letter from Electra.   As long as he could remember, Jimmy hadn't been alone on St. Patrick's Day. He puttered around his townhouse feeling lonely and bored. As he passed his front hallway, Jimmy picked up a stack of mail sure that there would be at least some fan mail. He loved hearing from his fans.

Jimmy lived in Boston when he was not on tour. After making it big, he had moved from a studio just outside of Boston in Jamaica Plains to a swank townhouse in downtown Boston that was on Marlborough Street near the public garden. He had never married and, surprisingly for someone with his fame, had only had few girlfriends. He had never been lonely though in his old studio with its mix-and-match furniture and art from friends. However, since he had an interior decorator furnish and decorate his new townhouse with the finest furnishings from all over the world and art placed on the walls by artists with whom he had never met, he somehow felt very lonely at home. He thought maybe this was because he was getting older and he had no one to share his home with. At any rate, the fan mail and a little Bushmill's whiskey usually made him feel better. It was, after all, what he had sacrificed so much for. Jimmy opened the last letter and began to read:

"Dear Mr. O'Conner, My name is Electra. I have looked up my biological parents and I have reason to believe that you might be my biological father. I was hoping that if you are, in fact, the father of a daughter who would have been born on July 6, 1985, at Brigham and Women's Hospital in Boston Massachusetts, that you would be willing to meet me. I have not, at this time, been able to trace Molly Callahan, but do have on record that she would be my

*biological mother. Enclosed is my address. I hope to hear from you.
Respectively, Electra Richards*

Jimmy hadn't thought of Molly for years. However, her face was still very clear to him. And those green eyes—they were like cats' eyes. He remembered how he sometimes thought he could hear her purr when they slept side by side. He felt a pain in his gut. That young girl he remembered was so beautiful. He had treated her poorly, he knew. He himself was young. Hadn't he been hurt as well? Another wave of regret washed down his throat as he swallowed another sip of whiskey. He had been twenty-two and barely of legal age to play in bars. She said she was not quite yet twenty-one. Later, he learned that she was barely eighteen.

Molly's uncle owned an Irish pub a few doors down from the club where he played. That was how they had originally met. He often went to the pub for dinner. They served a stew that reminded him of his Mum's back in Ireland, and Molly always waited on him with a pretty smile. He loved to flirt with her and watch her blush. She was so innocent and so clearly enchanted with him, even before she knew he played in a band. This made her the perfect girl for him. It was one of those attractions that inspired poems and songs. In retrospect, it was probably best left to the imagination, unspoiled by reality.

He remembered the night she had seduced him. She had begged him to bring her backstage so she could hear him play just once. After the show, she had said she wanted to thank him by inviting him after-hours for a pint of Guinness. On that night, she had offered him a few pints and a few shots of Bushmill's. Then she had also offered herself. She had been frightened and he had too much to drink. In the end, however, he had been unable to turn her down.

After that night, Molly had transformed from the perfect girl to the perfect woman. Jimmy couldn't stop thinking about her. They saw each other as often as they could. She started to sleep over at his place and going to his shows as his girlfriend. Thinking back, Jimmy knew that he had never since experienced such an exciting and intensely passionate time in his life, not even when his latest band's album turned Platinum. Back then, life was full of promise. The tastes of love and success were on the tip of his tongue—and they drove him wild.

Back in his upscale apartment, Jimmy poured himself some more Bushmill's and took a healthy swig. Then he sighed out loud. Nothing tasted quite as good as desire. He continued to think about the days of Molly and his first band, Flip Coin.

Everything seemed to be going so well. He and his band were getting more gigs and Jimmy had felt for sure that he was falling in love. Then everyone suddenly seemed to change. Mark Page, the drummer he founded the band with, announced that he was going to have to quit. Mark had taken a full-time job after he graduated from college. With all of the additional gigs the band had been getting, and the fact that he had gotten married and he and his wife were expecting a baby, Mark explained that he just couldn't keep up with everything. Jimmy didn't understand. The point of starting the band, Jimmy thought, was to get more gigs. It wasn't even about making it big, it was about being able to support themselves with their music. It wasn't supposed to be the second job.

Jimmy confronted Mark about why he was giving up the band. All that Mark had to say was that the band had been a fun hobby, but that the hobby was taking up too much of his time. The fact that Mark called the band a hobby stung Jimmy deeply. Jimmy didn't plan on working at his day job painting houses forever. He planned to be a full-time musician. It was what he was good at and it was what made him happy. He wondered if Mark had always planned on having an office career, a house in the suburbs and a family. Or maybe it all changed because of Kate and the baby.

Jimmy had told all of this to Molly. She consoled him and told him that she had always believed in him. She was sure he could find another drummer and she convinced him that Mark had not been mocking him. Sometimes people's priorities change or maybe Mark just didn't have the strength or the determination he had, she said. Jimmy shouldn't fault him for that. He remembered feeling so relieved that he had a woman who was able to make him feel better, someone who really understood him. They made love that night. Remembering the sensation of it still made him tingle all over. It had been their last night together. It was a moment in Jimmy's life where he truly felt as if it was full tide and he was in a safe harbor. Then, just as sudden as the tide had come in, it started to recede. He remembered the exact moment it happened. It was after they had made love and they were lying in bed. Her head was on his shoulder and he was stroking her hair. He was just about to tell her that he loved her. Instead, she spoke. With each word, the tide receded a little further.

"Do you remember when I said that people's lives sometimes change?" she began.

"Yeah," Jimmy had replied.

"Losing my virginity to you was the best way my life could have changed."

"I was your first?" Jimmy asked, surprised.

"Of course. You did notice, didn't you?" Molly suddenly lifted her head up and rested it on her hands so that she could look him in the eye. Jimmy realized he had made a big mistake by what he just revealed. In the confusion of the moment, however, he continued anyway.

"It was great, but I was a bit drunk."

"You do remember our first time, don't you?" Molly asked, clearly hurt.

"Of course I remember," Jimmy was uncomfortable with being stared down. He sat up in bed, forcing Molly to sit up as well. They were no longer looking at each other. "I just don't remember all the details. You're the one who gave me the whiskey. Anyway, it's worked out well, so why the worries?"

"Why the worries?" Molly had started to sob. "Why the worries? Because, Jimmy O'Conner, that was the most important night of my life. And now yours." She paused. Then she said, in a very steady voice. "We made a baby that night."

"We what?" Jimmy asked. "But I remember asking you if it was okay and you said yes."

"I meant that I was ready."

"Bloody hell! I thought you meant it was okay because you had birth control. Jesus, why didn't you tell me?"

"I just found out," Molly replied. "I was going to tell you sooner, but you were so upset about Mark quitting the band because of his baby and all."

"So now you think I'll quit the band and play house with you?"

"No, of course I don't want you to quite the band. I just want us to be together."

"We were together. Jesus Molly, I've spent every free moment of my time with you. Why did you have to go and do that?"

"I didn't do anything. It just happened."

"It doesn't just happen. You lied to me." Jimmy got up and put his jeans on. He started to pace the room.

Molly leaned forward, sobbing. "I didn't lie. I thought it was okay," she had said with desperation.

"How could you think it was okay?" Jimmy asked her incredulously.

"I don't know. I just love you so much, it seemed like it should've all been okay. It seemed like a natural part of our love."

"A natural part of our love?" Jimmy asked, exasperated.
"How is not telling the person you are having sex with that you're not on birth control something you do to someone you love?"

"But you never asked," Molly sobbed again.

"I did ask Molly. I didn't realize that I would have to spell it out for a twenty year old. What the hell business do you have seducing someone without some kind of protection? It's not like it 'just happened' that night. You knew what you were doing. And you knew I loved it. I thought you were sexy and sweet. I can't believe that you would be so stupid. And then you continued lying to me. Were you trying to get pregnant?"

"I'm not twenty, Jimmy. I'm eighteen." It was all Molly could say.

"Then you're a bloody ignorant eighteen year old."

"What about the baby?"

"What about it? It's not mine. I didn't agree to a baby. You're going to have to get rid of it."

"Get rid of it?" Molly asked in shock, as though she had actually thought Jimmy would agree to keep it. "How could we get rid of something that was born out of love?"

"Born out of love? Molly, listen to yourself."

"Were you just with me because of the sex?" Jimmy couldn't believe how irrational Molly was being.

"Yeah, I guess it was just sex." Jimmy remembered saying. "And now it's over." He had left Molly and the apartment that night without telling her he loved her.

"Oh, Molly, I did love you," Jimmy said as he finished off his whiskey. After that night, he remembered not being able to believe how suddenly everything had changed. However, those changes seemed to propel him forward and give him momentum to make some decisions on his own. His bass player at the time, Tony, told Jimmy that he was thinking about trying out New York. Tony said he had a cousin who could get them some day work as well. Jimmy went to the pub several times after that looking for Molly, but she was never on duty. Molly's uncle scared him so he thought he should just leave her alone until she was ready to call him. She never did try to call him so he thought maybe it had all been a mistake. Maybe she was just late and she got her period, but was still mad at him. Two months later she still hadn't called him and he left for New York.

A couple of years later, when he and his band had a gig in Boston, Jimmy went to the Irish Pub looking for Molly again. Her uncle had told him that she was in art school and only worked on the weekends. Jimmy had gigs over the weekend and never got a chance to go back to the pub to look for Molly. He thought about getting her phone number or sending her a letter, but those options just didn't seem right. Somehow, he had to see her. He wasn't sure if she'd talk to him and he wasn't sure exactly how he felt about her. The next time he returned to her uncle's pub to look for her, however, her uncle said that she had moved to Seattle with a boyfriend.

He couldn't believe that she had actually had the baby—a daughter—and that this daughter, who would be the age he was when it all happened, wanted to meet him. Her letter stirred some emotions inside him that felt unfamiliar, but somehow welcoming. Jimmy pulled out a sheet of paper and began to write.

Dear Electra, By the way, I like your name. I think you may be correct in thinking I am your biological father. One can never fully understand the choices that we make in life, but I am glad you made the choice to learn about your birth. I don't know the reasons why you tried to reach me, but I have arranged for a room for you at the Ritz-Carlton in Boston. If you would like to meet in person, then please check in next weekend, and we will meet for dinner at 7:00. If this time does not work for you, but you would still like to meet, then change your reservation and I will be notified. Respectively, Jimmy O'Conner.

Jimmy had become fairly drunk with all the reminiscing he was doing that night. He picked up the phone and dialed information for Topsfield, Massachusetts.

"Do you have a listing for Mark Page?" he asked the operator. He got the number. Kate answered the phone.

"Hello Kate, Jimmy O'Conner here."

"There's no mistaking that accent. What a surprise. How are you?"

"I'm grand. How's the family? Is your man at home?"

"We're all good. In fact, Mark is with our son Matthew in Boston tonight. They're celebrating his twenty-first birthday."

"On St. Patrick's Day?"

"Matthew was born on St. Patrick's Day, if you can believe it. Do you remember? I was pregnant the last time I saw you."

"Of course. It was a fertile time for us all."

Kate realized then that Jimmy was drunk. She didn't want to get into a discussion about why her husband had quit his band over two decades ago.

"I've got Mark's cell phone if you'd like to try to give him a call," she said quickly.

"Thank you. Just let me get a pen to write with." Kate could hear Jimmy fumbling around in the background. He wrote the number down on the back of the envelope he had addressed to Electra and thanked Kate for the number. Just as Kate was about to hang up the phone, Jimmy asked her a question.

"Are you happy, Kate?"

"Yes, very," she answered.

Jimmy had the good timing of calling Mark at the very moment the band that was playing at the Purple Rose bar in downtown Boston had taken a break. It was still a bit difficult to hear each other, so Jimmy and Mark had a short conversation. Before it ended, Mark had invited Jimmy to join him and Matthew at the Purple Rose for a beer. It had been so long since Jimmy had just met someone for a beer. He decided to join them. It was already 10:00 pm and he knew that most people at an Irish bar on St. Patrick's Day would already be fairly drunk. If anyone made a fuss about him being famous, he'd just say that he gets it all the time. He would tell people that he only looked like himself. As it turned out, no one even noticed as he joined Mark and his son at the bar. It was amazing how Matthew looked so much like Mark.

"You're a spitting image of your dad." Jimmy had told him.

"Yeah, but we're nothing alike at all," Matthew slurred in reply.

"I see. Well, for starters, you don't hold you liquor as well as him. Remember those days after a good gig?" Jimmy gave Mark a friendly punch.

"Oh God. Barely," Mark replied with a laugh. "It's hard to believe that we were Matthew's age back then."

Matthew stared at Jimmy, then back at Mark. "You played in a band, dad? You guys are pulling my leg. What's your real name? You look a lot like Jimmy O'Conner from Quarter Moon. That's a band by the way, Dad."

"Your father is an excellent drummer, and I am who I look like. But let's not be drawing a lot of attention to that right now, okay? Let's drink a toast to your birthday."

They drank a toast and then a few more. Jimmy and Mark talked about the old days while Matthew tried to memorize every thing they said. Matthew noticed that Jimmy started a lot of sentences with "you know yourself." This made it difficult to follow what they were saying since Matthew himself did not know.

"Did my father tell you that I write reviews for bands?" Matthew blurted out when there was finally a lull in the conversation.

"No, he didn't. Do you play as well?"

"I wish. I guess that's why I write about guys like you. Well, not really guys like you. I write about guys who wish they were you. I can't believe I'm having a drink on my birthday with Jimmy O'Conner." The last part of what Matthew said was overheard by the next table and suddenly they were surrounded. Jimmy placed a hundred dollar bill on the bar and motioned for Matthew and Mark to follow,

"Come on; let's go out to my car. We'll never get another bit of peace here tonight."

"I'm sorry." Matthew said, stumbling behind Jimmy. "I shouldn't have said your name so loud."

"It's okay. It was getting too loud in there anyway," Jimmy said once they were out of the bar. Out on the street, Jimmy's car and driver appeared magically. They all hopped into the back of the limousine. Jimmy pulled out a bottle of Bushmill's and three glasses. Matthew's father turned his son's glass over.

"I think that might be enough for him tonight," Mark said.

"Come on dad. It's my twenty-first birthday."

"Then it's settled." Jimmy turned the glass back over and filled all three. He and Mark clinked glasses as Matthew slumped down into the seat. Matthew started to mumble something and then he heaved forward and vomited all over the seat next to Jimmy. Jimmy asked his driver to stop and he opened the door. He pulled Matthew by his collar so that he was leaning out of the car.

"Are you all done or is there more?"

Matthew mumbled again, threw up a couple more times and then said he was okay. Jimmy pulled him back into the car, covered over the vomit with some magazine pages and then told Mark to join him up front. Leaving Matthew slumped over in the back seat, they asked his driver to take them straight back to Jimmy's townhouse.

"How about we take him up and let him sleep this off a bit on the couch?" Jimmy said when they got to the townhouse. "We'll get the car cleaned up and in a little while, I'll have the driver take you back home."

"Jimmy, I am so sorry. This is my fault. I shouldn't have let him drink so much."

"No worries. You know yourself. It happened to us a few times at his age. Come on, help me get him upstairs."

Jimmy and Mark helped Matthew into the apartment. They put him down on the sofa in the living room and Jimmy put a blanket over Matthew as though he had been putting children to bed for years. Then he said, "It's hard to believe we both have kids the same age as we were when we were in Flip Coin."

Mark looked over at Jimmy with surprise. "You have a kid?"

"Yeah, her name is Electra."

"I'm confused. I read in the magazines that you never married."

"Well, technically I have a daughter about the same age as your kid. Realistically, I have had a daughter for about five hours."

"Now I am really confused."

"Do you want a beer?"

"I think I've probably had enough."

"You know yourself. I'm going to have a beer." Jimmy got a bottle and they both sat on stools at Jimmy's bar in his den. "Does this bar look familiar?"

"Can't say that I recognize it."

"Do you remember that Irish Pub in Somerville where I used to go to all the time? It was near Jammers, where we played back in the 80's?"

"Of course. Now I remember the place." Mark took another look at the bar and ran his hands across its smooth surface.

"At one point, the place was for sale. When I found out the person was buying it to build condos, I bought the bar. I figured it was the only thing left from that love affair I had long ago. Do you remember Molly?"

"Molly?" Mark asked quickly remembering the name.

"That's right." Jimmy answered with a sigh.

"You were crazy about her. What ever happened to her?"

"We broke up just after you left the band."

"You two seemed inseparable. I would have thought it would have lasted longer."

"She surprised me by telling me she was pregnant. I was pretty freaked out. I told her she had to get rid of it, and that pretty much broke us up. I tried to see her again, but she didn't seem to want to have anything to do with me." Jimmy remembered going back to the pub after their fight and seeing Molly peek from behind the kitchen door as he sat at his favorite table, hoping to see her and talk to her about what happened."

Mark was about to say he could understand why Molly had been upset with him for telling her to 'get rid of it.' He thought it must have been frightening to a girl of Molly's age and disposition. Mark recalled that Molly was a very shy girl and he thought at the time quite naive. "So what happened? Did she tell you she was going to have the baby anyway?" Mark asked instead.

"I never did talk to her. Not long after she told me, I moved to New York."

"So that was it? You just moved away without finding out what happened to the baby?" Mark was shocked that even his old buddy Jimmy would be that uncaring.

The way Mark put it, Jimmy realized it sounded a bit weak on his side that he would have moved without insisting on speaking with Molly or God forbid even her uncle. "Now, that you put it that way. I guess I really should have asked more questions. I just figured that if she was really going to have the baby she would have told me. " Jimmy scratched his forehead. He decided that he ought to at least let Mark know that he did try a few more times to see her. "I tried to see her again when my band played in Boston, but her uncle was pretty determined to keep me away. The last time I went looking for her, he told me she moved to Seattle with a guy."

Mark didn't feel too much sympathy for his friend, and wasn't surprised that the uncle had tried to keep him away. He could not imagine doing anything like what Jimmy had done to Molly. When Kate had told him she was pregnant, he had also been a little shocked, but he could only remember telling her that he would support her no matter what she decided to do. When she wanted to keep the baby, he had preferred they get married. He was glad that Kate had, though at first reluctantly, agreed. "Well, I 'm sorry that happened," Mark finally said.

"Yeah, you know yourself. I thought about her from time to time. I guess Molly's one of those that you never forget." Jimmy grabbed a handful of nuts he had out on the bar, chewed on them for a bit, and then continued, "I had no idea that she gave birth to our kid, though, until I got a letter from this girl who claims she is ours."

"So, you just got a letter from someone out of the blue? Are you sure it's your kid?" Mark was still trying to absorb the news.

"Well, the timing makes sense. The girl says she looked me up after getting information from the adoption agency and she knew Molly's name. Her name is Electra"

"What about Molly. Did she look up Molly?"

"She said she hasn't been able to find Molly yet."

"Wow. That's a big surprise," Mark said staring at his old band buddy thinking about how different their lives had turned out. "So are you going to meet her?" Mark asked, curiously.

"Yes I am," Jimmy said putting his beer down on the counter and putting his hands up in the air he added, "Can you believe it?"

CHAPTER FOUR – Fourth of July

When Nathan and Molly arrived back on the island and had secured the boat onto the Geld's dock, they carried the party provisions they had gathered on the mainland up to the house.

"Let me help you," Gina said, as she ran down to meet them on their second trip up to the kitchen. "B.J. and his friends arrived on an earlier ferry so Mrs. Geld is rushing around in a tizzy."

"Should I change back into my uniform?" Molly asked, taking Nathan's sweatshirt off and putting it under the driver's seat compartment. Gina noticed this and winked at Nathan.

"Yes," Gina said to Molly. "Why don't you change and I'll help Nathan with the last of the bags. I've already prepared some appetizers so you could fix everyone a drink once they all come downstairs."

Molly quickly went to change at the cottage. In her rush, she hadn't thought to close the blinds. Nathan caught a glimpse of her topless silhouette as he carried the final bag up to the house. It was an image he would never be able to forget. He was completely smitten and very much confused by this woman who appeared out of nowhere and had somehow become a piece of the puzzle of his life. Her presence was fitting into the most unexpected places in his heart.

When Molly arrived at the house, she saw Mrs. Geld leaning over the staircase railing on the second floor.

"Thank God your back," Mrs. Geld said. "Our guests are just finishing up with their baths and will be down on the sun-porch any moment now. Please make sure that everything is set up at the bar. I don't know what everyone is drinking this season. Last year, it was Cosmopolitans."

"And this year it is Mojitos, mother." A young man appeared behind his mother.

"Mojitos?" Mrs. Geld said, perplexed. "What's in that?"

"Rum, mint and lime, mother. It's a Cuban drink."

"Oh dear. Well, keep those away from Nathan,"

"I'd sooner tell a sea man to live in the mountains than to take his rum away."

The young man kissed his mother and headed down the spiral staircase. He walked straight up to Molly.

"Hello, I'm B.J.. Mother told me that you will be taking Benilde's place this summer."

Molly, digging into her recollection of Upstairs Downstairs, curtsied and kept her eyes down. This formality was apparently unnecessary with B.J., who slipped his arm around hers as though he were about to swirl her around in a ballroom dance.

"Let's you and I go see about those Mojitos. Do you know how to mix one?"

"Yes. They're quite popular in Seattle now as well. But perhaps you could watch to make sure I make them the way you like."

"Splendid." B.J. continued to lead Molly out to the bar on the sun- porch.

Next to a tray of appetizers that Gina had prepared was a container of fresh mint. Molly suspected that Gina never forgot a single detail about the likes and dislikes of her employers.

She mixed up a Mojito and handed it over to B.J.. The young man was extremely self-assured; probably more so than any young man Molly had ever met. She could not imagine him having trouble asking any girl out.

"How is it?" she asked, nodding to the drink.

"Now that is a Mojito!" B.J. said, placing his glass back down on the bar. Then he smiled at Molly. "You look very familiar. Have you worked somewhere else on the island?"

"No, this is my first time here," Molly said.

B.J. was about to ask more about Molly when his friends, Hugh and Meredith, made their way out to the sun-porch.

"What an amazing view!" Meredith commented. The young woman looked as though she had walked straight out of a Talbot's catalogue. She was dressed in green slacks with a matching green and pink blouse. Her bobbed blonde hair was pulled back with a green headband. Molly imagined that Mrs. Geld must have looked a lot like Meredith when she was young. Meredith also brought a whiff of perfume with her. She was very petite, especially in contrast to her boyfriend, Hugh, who was wearing a pair of Nantucket Red Chinos with a whale belt. Molly didn't imagine that Hugh needed the belt, as he had a fairly impressive stomach that was tucked in with his monogrammed, Oxford shirt.

"Would you like a Mojito to go with the view?" B.J. asked.

"I'll have a Chardonnay please," Meredith answered.

"A Mojito sounds good to me," Hugh said in a deep lockjaw accent.

"Are all those boats moored out front yours, B.J.?" Meredith asked.

"Would you expect anything less from B.J. Geld the Third, darling?" Hugh said, raising his glass. "Here's a toast to B.J.!"

"Cheers!" they all said in unison as they each settled into a wicker chair.

"I love this fabric," Meredith commented, taking an extra pillow and putting it behind her back. "It's so cheerful. I never know how decorators are able to mix the pale striped patterns with bright floral so exactly and pleasingly."

"Truly a mystery to me," Hugh said, mocking her.

"You men take all this stuff for granted," Meredith said. "What would you do without a woman with a good sense of design?"

"We'd hire a designer," B.J. said with a shrug. "At least that is what my mother did."

"Are you saying I have no decorating sense?" Mrs. Geld asked as she came in to the sun-porch.

"No Mother. I'm saying you have the exquisite taste to hire someone who can capture your own flair. After all, it takes a certain decorating sense to hire the right decorator."

"I don't know why we sent you to business school, B.J.. We should have sent you off to be a politician."

"No talk of politics on the weekend. Your usual gin and tonic, Mother?" B.J. said, getting up and heading back over to Molly to fetch his mother her drink.

"What type of gin?" Molly asked, after B.J. had placed his order.

"Bombay Sapphire, and make it strong. That woman needs to relax," B.J. said in a whisper and with a conspiratory grin. After B.J. had given his mother her drink, they talked about their plans to play tennis and golf the next day. The appetizers were still sitting by the bar when Gina came out and tapped Molly on the shoulder.

"Don't forget to serve them the food. We don't want them all drunk before dinner. I put a lot of work into it."

Molly, embarrassed that she had forgotten about the appetizers, quickly made the rounds. Hugh started piling them onto his napkin before anyone else, as though this might be his only chance for food. As she stood waiting for him to choose the last of his appetizers, Molly saw Nathan pull up to the dock in the motorboat they had gone to the mainland in. She assumed that the man he was helping off the boat was Mr. Geld. He walked up the lawn toward the porch with the same self-assuredness Molly noticed in his son. Was it the security of the money that gave them that confidence or was it inbred in their genes? She wondered if they were suddenly transplanted to the city with no money if they would stoop their shoulders over and shuffle their feet. Her thoughts were interrupted as Hugh suddenly bellowed out to her.

"I'm good for now, honey, but bring that tray back soon," he said. "This sea air makes me hungry."

"Everything makes you hungry, dear," said Meredith, who had only taken one appetizer and was still nursing her first Chardonnay. Molly noticed that Meredith said this to her boyfriend as though they had been married for years. She imagined they probably would be some day. Molly couldn't imagine two people with less imagination and wondered if all of B.J.'s friends were like them. He seemed to treat the two as though they were props—a couple to sit on his mother's sun-porch and chatter away, keeping her occupied while he daydreamt about Electra. Molly thought for sure that B.J. must be very different from Hugh and Meredith to appreciate a girl like her daughter. Molly had been thinking of the things that Nathan had told her that afternoon and had already imagined her own version of Electra. She could not imagine, however, ever having the nerve to introduce herself to her. Mr. Geld entered the sun-porch looking like an older version of James Bond. Molly nearly started shaking a martini for him.

"He'll have a double bourbon on the rocks," Mrs. Geld said to Molly.

"These are my friends, Meredith and Hugh," B.J. said to his father. Hugh stood and shook Mr. Geld's hand. Molly brought Mr. Geld his drink and noticed that he sat down without so much as giving his wife a peck on the cheek.

"I'll have another gin and tonic," Mrs. Geld said. "And bring that tray back around."

"Now that Nathan's back, let's have him take us out for a sunset sail before dinner," B.J. said, rounding up his friends in order to leave his parents alone. He liked to imagine that his parents would soften up to each other if he left them alone. Ever since his step-sister Gabby's death, his parents had been distant to each other. This disturbed B.J. deeply.

"I'm going to run up and get a warmer sweater," Meredith said, placing her unfinished wine glass down. Hugh guzzled the last of his cocktail and headed down the lawn to the dock with B.J..

"That's one hot housekeeper," Hugh said, slapping B.J. on the back. "You could have a nice summer treat, if you know what I mean."

"Come on, Hugh. She's twice my age. And she's the housekeeper for Christ sakes."

"That didn't stop you from taking a little taste of Benilde."

"That was different. I was drunk and it was a big mistake. Jesus, it's the only time I've done anything like that and I don't think it will happen again. I wished I hadn't been so foolish."

"I saw that new housekeeper staring at you. These women know it's just a summer thing. I think you should go for it," Hugh snickered with a slight snort.

"You're such a pig! How does Meredith put up with you?"

"Trust me, man—that girl let's me do whatever I want. She has one goal in life and it is to get my Grandmother's diamond ring by Christmas. Until then, you get the picture."

"That's really sad man. Where's the romance?"

"Some of us are more pragmatic," Hugh replied. "Speaking of which, shouldn't we bring some booze for the boat?"

"Trust me. Nathan keeps that covered."

"No rest for the weary, mate. We need you to take us out on *The Promise*." B.J. shouted out to Nathan as he approached him seated in an Adirondack chair down by the dock.

"You know how to sail," Nathan replied without moving.

"Sure I do, but we need a Captain." B.J. said pulling Nathan up out of the chair.

Just then, Meredith appeared, looking as though she had dressed specifically for a sunset sail. She wore kakis, a striped sailor's shirt with an Irish knit sweater draped over her shoulders and boat shoes.

Nathan took a look at her and knew he was going to be bored out of his mind sailing with B.J.'s friends. Nathan was very close to B.J., but he never much cared for his friends. He knew it was his job, and he didn't like to disappoint B.J., so he went along as the four of them embarked on one of his famous sunset sails.

Back at the house, Molly wasn't sure if she should stay at the bar or leave Mr. and Mrs. Geld alone. She finally decided that a quick trip to the kitchen to consult with Gina would be the best course of action.

"It will be a couple more hours before they eat. Why don't you take a break?" Gina recommended. She was watching the evening news on a small T.V. in the kitchen.

"Okay," said Molly. "I guess I'll go back to the cottage and watch for the boat to come back."

Molly went down to her cottage and sat in her new favorite chair facing the water. She thought about Nathan and how she had told him about Electra. *Why had she opened up to him like that*? She thought back to when she had met Nathan down on the beach. It was odd that she had been so sad when he turned to leave. For some reason, she was drawn to him, not so much sexually, but as the friend that she had been searching for her whole life. She concluded, one more time, that he was probably the most peaceful man she had ever met. She suddenly felt the need to soak that sense of serenity into her own soul. She wanted him to tell her that it was okay if she didn't meet Electra. Molly closed her eyes for a moment and fell into a deep sleep until there was a knock on the door.

"Molly, it's Gina." Molly woke with a start and jumped up to greet Gina.

"I guess I must have fallen asleep," she said, groggy-eyed.

"I'm sorry to wake you. Everyone is back and we're ready to serve. I set the table for you."

"Thank you. I didn't sleep so well last night."

"It's okay, but you better hurry. I need to get back to my sauce," Gina said, turning to go. Molly ran behind her.

In between courses at dinner, Molly sat with Nathan and Gina in the kitchen. Gina had prepared extra food for them. Molly was starting to think this was the best job she ever had.

"Is everything ready for the big picnic tomorrow?" Gina asked.

"I hope so," Molly answered.

"Don't worry. People mostly drink beer and wine and everything is served on paper plates. Nathan's the one with the most work, getting those lobsters going," Gina said.

"Are you much of a pyro?" Nathan asked Molly.

"What do you mean?" Molly asked confused.

"The first step to a lobster bake is building a bonfire on the beach."

"It's actually a lot of fun," Gina said. "Stew is going to come and help. We'll have our own party."

They finished up their dinner and Molly cleared the last of the desert dishes.   Nathan started to head out the door. Before he left, he turned to Molly.

"Don't worry," he said. "Tomorrow will be fine."

Molly knew he was talking about Electra. She finished up the dishes, thinking about how soon she would see her daughter in the flesh.

Molly headed down to her cottage to turn in. As she walked down the path away from the house, she heard the faint sound of a piano. *Electra*, she thought. She changed directions and walked towards Electra's property. She stopped, startled, when she saw Nathan sitting stretched out on the lawn.

"It's not only B.J. who stays up to listen to her. Come and listen and you'll see why. Her music gets into your soul and stirs things up."

Molly sat down next to him. She was shivering and before she even noticed, Nathan had put his jacket over her shoulders.

"Don't be nervous about tomorrow," Nathan said.

"I am nervous," Molly said. "I came all this way, but I don't think I can meet her—not like this."

"Well, then—it's okay to be nervous," Nathan said, confirming Molly's belief that this was a friend who would always know what to say.

"Why is it okay?"

"I understand. That was all I meant. Look, I don't know how I would feel about meeting a grown person for the first time and telling them that I was their father.   It would be starting a relationship with a need to apologize. That can't be a good feeling."

"I hadn't thought of it that way," Molly said. She realized that Nathan wouldn't always say the right thing, but at least he was honest.

Nathan leaned over and gave her a gentle hug.

"Don't worry. Electra's a lovely girl. Don't tell her who you are until you're ready."

"What if I am never ready?" Molly asked returning his hug.

"Don't think about that now," Nathan said, and as Molly sunk deeper into his chest he stroked her hair. Nathan wanted nothing more than to take away the fear and sadness that he felt flowing through Molly. He was happy that she had not shied away from his hug, but instead seemed to get even closer to him. Nathan wondered what Molly was thinking, but he didn't dare to interrupt the moment or the atmosphere of Electra's ethereal music that seemed to be very calming to Molly.

Molly thought she should pull back a little from Nathan, but it felt good to be in his arms. When he stroked her hair it reminded her of a comfort she could not quite remember. She wondered if maybe her mother or father had done that when she was a little girl. She felt suddenly very sad that she could not remember her parents. She understood why Electra might want to know her, but she couldn't stop worrying that Electra would think of her as a disappointment. Nathan continued to hold Molly as they listened to Electra's enchanting piano.

They were both taken by surprise when she started to sing soprano in French. Neither one of them knew what the words meant, yet they somehow spoke directly to both of them. Nathan watched as the full tide started to recede and the music stopped. Molly had fallen asleep in Nathan's arms. He carefully picked her up and carried her down to her cottage. As he placed her on her bed, she awoke for a moment.

"I'll see you tomorrow," he said, and left her to go to sleep.

The next morning, Molly was grateful for the extra beds and bathrooms to clean. The work left her no time to think about the picnic and Electra, and the morning flew by. At lunchtime, Nathan came up to the house where Gina and Molly were eating and asked them to call Stew so he could help with the bonfire.

Molly helped them to gather wood to add to the fire. With each rise in the flames, her anxiety increased. Once the fire was grand enough for Nathan, who admitted that it was actually a little higher than it needed to be, Molly was dismissed from her duties with the bonfire so that she could carry on with the table set up. Per Mrs. Geld's careful instructions, Molly put red, checkered tablecloths on the picnic tables that Stew and Nathan had carried down to the beach. Each table had a centerpiece of daisies and wildflowers that she had collected on a walk around the property. She also set out the tools for cracking the lobsters and hand painted bowls for throwing the discarded shells. After she was done, Molly stepped up onto the lawn and inspected the scene. *This is going to be the most elegant picnic I've ever seen*, she thought.

Molly was quite pleased with herself and hoped that Mrs. Geld would be pleased as well. After a few more moments, she turned her attention away from what she had created and went to find Nathan. He had said that he needed her help in setting up a path of Tiki Torches to light the way from the house to the beach and dock that night.

B.J. and Hugh came down carrying a large cooler full of beers. Meredith followed them, wearing a pair of white pants with little lobsters embroidered on them. If anyone could keep a pair of white pants clean at a beach lobster bake, it would be Meredith. Molly wondered if she was the kind of girl that Mrs. Geld had in mind for B.J. to marry. Maybe that was why B.J. invited the couple—simply to make his mother happy. B.J. and Hugh cracked a beer and stood over the fire. "You need some help Nathan?" B.J. asked.

"Not right now. In a little while, you can help gather some seaweed to cover the coals so they don't burn the tarp that we'll use as a cover to steam everything."

"Sure thing, Captain." B.J. and Hugh kept watch over the fire as though they had a very important part in the lobster baking process. Meredith sat on the corner of one of the benches facing the ocean. Molly asked if she would like a glass of wine.

"My goodness. It's not even five yet," she said. "I'll wait a bit, thank you."

Molly and Gina made trips back and forth from the house to bring chips and dip, corn to cook with the lobster, and an assortment of appetizers Gina had prepared in the shape of lobsters and boats.

Molly wondered if Mrs. Geld let Gina be creative or if Gina had received a list that detailed what shape the appetizers had to be in.

Nathan gave the signal it was time to collect the seaweed. B.J. and Hugh collected the seaweed, watching with boyish excitement each time a crab was uncovered how it scuttled sideways. The boys complained about how hard they were working, but Nathan just laughed at them and told them to keep it coming.

Soon some of the neighbors started to arrive. Once the flames had died down, Nathan and Stew raked the coals until the flames had completely died out. First they covered the coals with a layer of seaweed that the boys had collected, then a layer of clams, followed by a layer of lobster. Finally, they placed the corn, still in their husks, in the pit. After the layers were complete, they covered the whole thing with a tarp. Molly thought it was the most efficient cooking method she had ever seen. Mesmerized as she was with the whole process, she missed the moment when Electra walked across the rocks towards the gathering. She looked up just in time to see a young woman talking to B.J. by the waters edge. The figure nearly took Molly's breath away. Electra seemed to be every bit what Molly had imagined. She was like an angel and almost seemed to hover above the rocks. Nathan, who had been keeping an eye on Molly, saw this interchange. He walked over to Molly.

"That is Electra," he whispered. Mrs. Geld was calling to Molly to go to the house and fetch something, but Molly couldn't hear. She was completely frozen in the moment, seeing her daughter for whom she had made the journey for the first time. She could not have imagined that this was anyone that would be her own flesh and blood. She was suddenly flooded by emotion. Her daughter looked a lot like Jimmy.

"Molly, did you hear me?" Mrs. Geld was losing her patience. "We need those salads!"

Nathan, who was still watching, answered for her. "I'll help her get them," he said, and tapped Molly on the shoulder. Dazed, Molly followed him up to the house.

"How are you doing?" Nathan asked her once they were in the kitchen.

"I'm okay, just a little in shock. She is so beautiful."

"You are too." Nathan said. Molly did not notice his comment.

"Was it the salad she wanted us to bring down?" she asked, confused by this simple instruction.

"Yes."

"I didn't expect her to be so ... so beautiful," she said again, still awe-struck.

"What did you expect?" Nathan asked.

"I don't know. I've never thought about how she looked. At least not until yesterday when you said she didn't look like me."

"Let's be clear, Molly," Nathan said. "The fact that she doesn't look like you doesn't mean that you are not beautiful."

"Nathan," Molly said, looking him straight in the eye. She knew she had to be clear with him on this point. "You have probably been the best friend I have ever had, even though I have only known you a couple of days. But if you are looking for more than that, I need you to know I have nothing to offer. Honestly, I have nothing."

Nathan, who could only disagree with that statement, replied, "Molly, you can count on me to be whatever it is you need me to be. If you need me to be a friend, then that is what I am. Now, are we ready to go back down?"

"Yes, and thank you. Thank you for being the friend you are." Molly answered sincerely as she handed him a couple of the salads to carry.

When they arrived back at the beach with the salad, the crowd of invitees was complete. Mrs. Geld was moving from person to person, making sure she checked in with everyone and said her pleasantries. Mr. Geld was sitting by himself in the Adirondack Chair down by the dock where Nathan had been sitting the day before. Molly noticed that he didn't talk to anyone, but rather just seemed to be surveying his property. When the lobsters were ready, everyone took a seat at the table. Molly made the rounds, making sure that shell bowls didn't get too full, that there was plenty of butter for dipping and that everyone had enough wine or beer. When everyone seemed fairly settled in, Gina instructed Molly to go up into the kitchen where she had set up a table for them to eat. Nathan and Stew were in the kitchen already, digging into the clams. Stew was telling Nathan how one of the wives told him that she wanted to sign up for private tennis lessons and then gave him a wink and patted his butt.

"It's really quite humiliating," Stew said.

"You know you love it." Gina countered.

"I don't."

"Then why are you telling us about it?"

"So Molly will know who to cut off from the booze."

"See what I told you, Molly? Nothing much happens here except dramas like these. Speaking of drama, did you see B.J. make a beeline for Electra? Who wants to bet that this is the year they finally get together?"

"Ah, come on Gina. Leave the poor boy alone, "Nathan said. He was sympathetic to his crush on Electra, and hated how Gina always butted into other people's business.

"Molly, how do you like the lobster bake so far?" Gina asked.

"It's nice," Molly answered, though she could only pick at a few clams and didn't even have a lobster. She was much too preoccupied with Electra to even think of eating.

"You know, I better go back and check on the tables," she said, leaving the kitchen.

Molly was refilling Mrs. Geld's wine glass when she heard Electra, who was sitting on the other side of the table next to B.J., speak about Jimmy. Her heart sank.

"If you will excuse me for a few moments, I'm going to go over to my house and check my voice mail," Electra said. "My father is supposed to call me after his show. He's due to arrive tomorrow."

After Electra had left the table, Mrs. Geld turned to her son.

"That poor girl. She knows her father is dead. Has she had too much to drink?"

Mrs. Geld shook her head. "It's such a pity what has become of Electra. She doesn't even leave the island in the winter. She must be cracking up."

"No, mother. She is not cracking up. She meant her biological father."

Molly, who should have been moving on to another table, lingered behind Mrs. Geld. She strained to hear the rest of the conversation. Did she hear that Jimmy would be on the island tomorrow?

"What do you mean, dear? Electra was not adopted," Mrs. Geld said.

"Yes, she was. She told me all about it when she decided to look up her birth parents. She found her birth father this year, and she went to Boston to meet him last spring."

"Electra left the island?"

"Yes, she did."

"Darling, this all sounds absurd." Mrs. Geld took a sip of her wine and looked at her son square in the eye.

"Why would she make something like that up?" B.J. answered her stare. "Anyway, her real father is Jimmy O'Connor. He's a rock star."

"Just listen to yourself. Suddenly Electra was adopted and her real biological father is a rock star?" Mrs. Geld asked her son, irritated that he hadn't outgrown his boyhood crush on Electra. Mrs. Geld certainly didn't want her only son to be involved with a woman who she believed was clearly emotionally disturbed. When B.J. did not answer her she asked, "Don't you think the Richards would have told her that she was adopted? Why we've known Electra since she was a tiny baby. Mrs. Geld did recall thinking it odd that she had never seen Mrs. Richards pregnant, but then again she had announced the baby in the winter. She was certain Mrs. Richards would not be the type to adopt a child. *Not after she had just left the poor child behind. Clearly she had not been the one to want a child. Poor Electra had no maternal role-model. She was not the right kind of girl for her son.* "You need to take those rose colored glasses off and see her for who she is. Darling, I'm afraid the girl is ill."

"She's not ill mother. It's true. Electra told me that she discovered a note that Mr. Richards had written along with his will, apologizing for never telling her that she was adopted. It said that he meant to. But after a certain point, he just couldn't do it."

Mrs. Geld did not want to hear any of the fiction she believed her son was being told, and wanting to make her point that she did not approve of his affection for Electra said, "B.J., I asked you to invite that girl because it's always been a tradition for the Richards to come to our gatherings and she has been coming to them since the two of you were little babies." Mrs. Geld paused for a moment thinking about the days when the Richards were still together. Mrs. Geld had always admired how attractive Mrs. Richards had been, but she had been appalled when she learned that the woman had left her husband with a small child. She could only imagine the emotional trouble that must have caused the girl. And then the tragedy for her father to die so young. She felt pity for Electra, but she wanted a girl with a little more stable background for her son.

Mrs. Geld turned her attention to Molly. "Oh, you're still here? Can you see if Nathan is ready to do the fireworks?" Molly was still in shock from hearing that Jimmy was expected to call Electra. She did not move at first. Then she turned and ran towards the beach to look for Nathan.

When she found him over at the bonfire, she told him what she had heard and her concerns that Jimmy might be planning to visit. Nathan didn't like the idea of Jimmy showing up any more than Molly. "Oh. That will be awkward," he said, really thinking of it being awkward for him. His feelings for Molly were getting stronger.

"Yes, it will be more than awkward. I don't know if I ever want to see him again, but I do know that I want a chance to meet Electra before I see him."

Nathan took a breath of relief when he heard that Molly didn't want to see Jimmy, and said, "Well, if you need me to help introduce you to her just let me know. You might want to stand back right now though. These are pretty intense fireworks. Mrs. Geld doesn't skimp on celebration."

"Right. The fireworks," Molly had completely forgotten about them. "Mrs. Geld sent me to tell you that they are ready for them to begin."

Nathan set off an impressive round of fireworks, but it was hard for Molly to concentrate as she kept a constant eye on Electra's house to see if she was returning. Afterwards, many of the Geld's guests left while the rest went up to the house for a port. Eventually, only B.J., Hugh, Meredith, Gina, Stew and Molly were left on the beach. Hugh was telling a long-winded story about a ski trip he had taken the previous winter when B.J. said he was going to go next door and see if everything was all right with Electra.

B.J. arrived at the Richards' place and gently knocked on the large, brass knocker. When no one answered, he let himself inside the door.

"Electra," he shouted, as he entered the entryway. "Where are you?" He found her sitting in the den. She was staring straight ahead with the phone on her lap.

"Electra, what is it?" B.J. asked, alarmed.

"It's Jimmy," Electra said.

"What about Jimmy?"

"I just got a voice mail from some guy named Matthew. He said his dad and Jimmy are friends. And he told me that Jimmy is in the hospital. Of course, I called him back immediately. He said that while Jimmy was performing at Orpheum Theatre in Boston that he just collapsed on stage."

"I'm so sorry Electra. Is he going to be okay?"

"I don't know."

"He was probably just exhausted. Maybe it was heat stroke. It's been scorching in Boston lately." B.J. paused a moment. "Electra, does Jimmy do drugs?"

"No, he doesn't do drugs. He drinks his Irish whiskey, but he doesn't do drugs. At least, I don't think so anyway. I just can't believe this is happening. I barely got to know him." Electra let out a sob.

"Maybe we can call the hospital he was sent to and find out how he is. Do you know where he went?"

"It's Mass General in Boston. And I've already tried but no one knows I'm his daughter. They won't let me through to the doctors. They think I'm just some fan."

"Why don't you call this Matthew guy back and ask him?"

"I did that too. All he knows is that he was taken to Mass General. Matthew said he would try to reach Jimmy's manager to find out more and he offered to pick me up from the airport if I wanted to fly to Boston. I'm going to get the first flight out of Rockland."

"Do you want me to give you a ride over in the boat?"

"You don't have to do that."

"I want to take you. Be down at the dock by six am and we can go."

"You don't want to be up at six am after the big party tonight."

"I'll be fine." B.J. walked into the kitchen and found some chamomile tea in a cupboard.   On the way over to her house B.J. had been thinking about telling her his feelings for her. He wanted a chance to let her know before she became too distracted with the excitement of seeing her biological father. Once he heard that there was bad news, he knew it was not the right time to tell her. He knew the most important thing was making sure that she was OK. It was too soon since her adopted father died for another tragedy. B.J. was very worried about Electra. He started the kettle.

"What are you doing?" Electra called out from the den.

"I'm getting you some tea."

"You really don't have to do all this," Electra objected.

"You'd do the same for me."

"Would I?" she asked.

"Remember when I was twelve and I broke my collarbone riding my bike too fast?" asked B.J..   "Do you remember who brought me homemade chocolate chip cookies every day?"

Electra blushed. "I just wanted you to get better so that I could beat you at tennis again."

B.J. came back into Electra's den with a cup of tea. "Very funny but I don't believe it. I think you did it because you are a very sweet person. Did Jimmy say anything to you about not feeling well when you met with him?"

"That was one of the reasons he was going to come to the island – to get away and relax a little. He said he had been feeling fairly worn out lately and I told him that this is the best place to do nothing but relax. He was planning to stay for two weeks. "She sighed deeply. "I've been writing some songs for him to hear. This just can't be happening."

"I'm so sorry, Electra. Have you seen him any other time other than when you went to Boston?"

"Just in Boston. You know I hate to leave the island these days and he has been so busy."

"What was it like when you met him in Boston?" B.J. asked handing the tea to Electra and sitting down.

Electra put her feet up on the Ottoman and leaned back; taking a sip of the tea that B.J. brought her. The warmth of it soothed her nerves and she thought back to the first time she had met her real father. The meeting seemed unreal, like something that had happened in a movie.

"I met him at the Ritz, which was exciting in itself," she began. "He had reserved a table for us in a private section and when I arrived, he was already there waiting. He smiled at me and right away I knew where I got my dimples." Electra smiled as if to illustrate the dimples. She took a sip of her tea and slightly sighing, said, "I still feel bad because he got up to give me a hug, but instead I reached out my hand for him to shake. Can you imagine how cold I must have seemed?"

"I'm sure he knew you were just nervous."

"Well, it didn't seem to bother him. He sat back down and maintained his smile while he ordered a bottle of champagne." Electra was quiet for a moment as she put her tea down on the table and silently recalled the scene, and then she continued. "He asked me all about where I had grown up and about my adopted parents. I told him about how mother had left and then about father dying." Again, Electra paused as she reached for a throw blanket that was draped over the edge of the couch and smoothed it out across her lap, and she continued. "He told me that he was sorry to hear about my father, but that he was so happy I had contacted him." Electra gently touched a broach she had received from Jimmy on that first meeting and said, "He gave me this broach that had a picture of a woman inside it. It is of my grandmother. 'You have a family now,' he said. Then he asked if I had met my biological mother yet. He seemed genuinely interested in that point."

"What did you tell him?" B.J. asked wondering if Electra had given any thought to her biological parents meeting again.

"I told him that I was still waiting to hear back from her. And I asked him when he had last seen her."

"I doubt that he would have seen her if they gave you up for adoption," B.J. added.

"Oh, I know. I didn't expect that he would have seen her in many years. I guess I was just fishing for more information about her."

"What did he say?"

"He told me that they had a fight the day that she told him about being pregnant with me, and that he hadn't spoken with her since that day."

"Wow, that's pretty crazy. Did he leave her because she was pregnant then?" B.J. asked.

"I wondered that myself. Actually, Jimmy told me that he tried to talk to her several times after the fight, but that she wouldn't see him." Electra remembered how Jimmy had put his hand on her shoulder and told her that he was really sorry he didn't try harder to find out what happened with her mother, and defensive to Jimmy, Electra added, "He moved away without knowing that Molly had me. I guess Molly's uncle was pretty hostile to him and didn't really help him get in touch with her."

"That seems strange that she was hiding from him or wouldn't tell him what happened with the baby."

"Yeah, it seemed strange to me. I kind of got the feeling maybe there was something wrong with her. Jimmy seemed to be over compensating when he told me about her." Electra shifted her legs on the Ottoman to get more comfortable and continued, "I think he was worried, since he had never heard from my mother that maybe I wouldn't either. It seemed like he went out of his way to say how wonderful she was—as though he were trying to make up for her not being there. I asked him to tell me more about my mother. He said that we actually had a lot in common, her and me. Her parents had died in Dublin in a car accident when she was very young, so she had been an orphan as well. Can you believe that?" Electra asked B.J. and without waiting for his reply she continued, "My whole life, B.J., I thought I was an ordinary WASP from Manhattan. It was quite interesting to find out that I'm actually 100% Irish!"

"That's cool," B.J. said. "I think we're part Irish on my Dad's side.

"Well, I like the idea of being Irish," Electra said and then added, "I wish that I had an accent like Jimmy. It's wonderful to hear. I wonder if my mother, Molly, also has an accent."

"Did you say your mother's name is Molly?" B.J. asked. He had been following the story closely, but that information had taken him by surprise.

"Yeah, Molly Callahan. I told you I wrote to her at the same time as Jimmy. But I haven't heard anything back yet."

"Where does she live?" B.J. asked sitting up and scooting a little closer to the edge of his seat.

"Seattle. When I looked her up, I found out that she is not married and never did have another family, but I don't really know too much more about her. I know she is a painter. I searched the internet and found a couple announcements to art shows in Seattle. I couldn't find her in any galleries though so maybe it's just a hobby."

"Did you say she is from Seattle?"

"Yeah, why do you ask?"

"And her name is Molly Callahan?" B.J. asked wanting to confirm the facts before he jumped to conclusions.

"Yes, her name is Molly. Jimmy confirmed that was her name. I've been wondering if she ever got my letter. I was thinking maybe I should call her, but I thought I'd wait just a little longer. I was thinking maybe I could learn a little more about her from Jimmy when he came to visit." Electra paused and thought about what might be happening to Jimmy. B.J. could see the concern on her face and he said, "Don't worry. I'm sure Jimmy will be fine and he will visit." B.J. said. Thinking about his mother's new housekeeper he added, "And maybe Molly did get your letter and she is planning to get back to you." He was fairly convinced that he already knew where Electra's mother was at that very moment.

Anxious to get away and explore his hunch B.J. said, "Well, you know how my mother is with her parties. I better get back to the house." Before he left he asked, "Will you be okay?"

"Yes. I'll be fine."

"I'll see you at the dock in the morning then," B.J. got up from his seat to leave.

"Those chocolate chip cookies were a good investment." Electra smiled as B.J. kissed her on the cheek and headed for the door. Back on the beach, B.J. found Nathan and Hugh sitting by the bonfire, smoking Cuban cigars.

"Where are the others?"

"Meredith went to bed when the cigars came out. Gina and Stew went home and Molly went down to her cottage," Hugh answered.

"Is Molly coming back?" B.J. asked them both.

"What did I say? I knew you were going to go for it," Hugh said, giving B.J. a sly, sideways glance. Nathan heard Hugh's comment and was not amused. He gave B.J. a disapproving look.

"Go for what?" Nathan asked.

"Nothing. Hugh's deluded," B.J. said.

"Well then, sit down and join us," Hugh said, patting the spot on the log next to him.

"Seeing how you've pulled out the good cigars, here is my contribution" Nathan said to Hugh. He searched through his duffel bag and pulled out a bottle of Cuban rum. The sight of the rum inspired Hugh to begin another story about a "Hemingway-esque" fishing trip he went on in the Caribbean. Nathan and B.J. puffed the cigars and every so often offered a "really" or "wow," though neither of them were really listening to him. Hugh didn't notice this lack of attention, however. After his story was done, Hugh stood up and staggered a bit.

"I've got to go take a piss," Hugh said and disappeared into the bushes.

After a while, he still hadn't returned but neither Nathan nor B.J. cared to find out where he was. They sat sipping their rum in silence. Finally B.J., who had always treated Nathan like a big brother, spoke up.

"Nathan, can I tell you something in confidence?" B.J. asked.

"Sure," Nathan answered.

"I was just talking to Electra. It turns out that her biological father—you know, the one she was talking about earlier—is in the hospital."

"That's too bad. Is he going to be all right?" Nathan said, thinking to himself that he would be glad if Jimmy didn't show up on the island at all.

"She doesn't know yet. I'm going to take her over in the boat in the morning so she can catch a flight from Rockland to Boston."

"You know you don't need my permission to use the boat anymore."

"I know. That's not what I wanted to ask you about."

"Well then, what is it?"

"Electra told me about her biological mother as well. Her name is Molly and she is from Seattle. Electra had sent her a letter, but she hasn't heard from her yet. I was thinking it might just be Molly our housekeeper."

Nathan took a breath. "You are right," he said. "I found that out myself the other day."

"You mean you knew about this and didn't tell me?" B.J. asked, upset.

"Molly asked me not to say anything"

"I need to talk to that woman," B.J. said, getting up from where he was sitting.

"No, B.J.. Please don't say anything, not just yet. This is between mother and daughter. It's best if we stay out of it."

"Best for whom?" B.J. asked. The anger in his voice was evident. "Electra deserves to know her mother is here and hiding out next door to her like some kind of sick spy."

"You said yourself that Electra is leaving for Boston. She has enough to think about right now. Molly wouldn't have come all this way if she hadn't intended to meet her daughter. Give her some time."

"Personally, I think it is a little creepy."

"It's a strange coincidence for sure, but there is nothing creepy about Molly. She is a little lost, that is true, but she is a good person. I felt it the moment I met her. I also need to ask you not to tell your mother about this. I told her that Molly was a friend of Sarah's."

"I'm not happy about any of this, but I won't say anything to Mother. I hope you're right, for Electra's sake."

"Why don't you just tell the girl the way you feel about her?" Nathan asked, changing the subject.

"She's got enough on her mind— you said so yourself."

"Fair enough."

"Well, I better get up to bed. I've got to get up early tomorrow morning for Electra."

B.J. set his alarm clock for 5:00 am. He wanted to be sure to be down at the dock on time. He fixed himself some coffee and then filled a thermos to take for Electra and the boat ride. He was sitting in the Adirondack chair waiting for her when he heard someone approaching from behind. B.J. turned with a smile, expecting to see Electra. Instead, he saw Molly in shorts and a T-shirt, holding a towel. When Molly saw B.J., she stopped in her tracks.

"I hadn't expected anyone to be down here," she said apologetically. "I was just going to go for a quick swim."

"You're welcome to use our pool. The ocean is freezing." B.J. was surprised that anyone would venture into the cold ocean so early in the morning.

"That's very nice of you, but I prefer to swim in the ocean—and to be down here by myself." Molly realized that that last comment probably sounded rude. "I didn't mean for you to go," she quickly added. "I just meant that in the morning it's nice and peaceful down here. Besides, I wouldn't want to make noise that close to the house, especially the morning after a party. What are you doing down here so early yourself?"

"I am taking our neighbor, Electra, to the mainland so that she can catch a plane down to Boston. I think you should know that Jimmy is in the hospital."

"Who?" Molly asked. This comment took her completely by surprise. She hadn't expected B.J. to know about Jimmy.

"I know who you are Molly. Electra told me last night."

Molly stepped a little closer and B.J. noticed her legs had goose bumps. Molly, noticing that B.J. was looking at her legs, wrapped the towel she was carrying around her and sat on the grass next to his chair.

"Electra knows who I am?" she asked in a slight panic. She pulled her hair, which was blowing in her face, back into a knot.

"No. She doesn't know. But she told me about her mother, Molly, and that she had written to her in Seattle. To have someone from Seattle named Molly suddenly appear next door looking for a job has to be more than a coincidence. I guess I just figured it out."

"I didn't plan this." Molly said. "Taking the job with your family, I mean. It just kind of happened. To be honest with you, I didn't have much choice but to take it. I need the money and I also need the time. I don't want to leave yet, not without meeting Electra and telling her who I am." Molly paused, not quite sure what else to say. Then she added, "I guess I had hoped that Electra would understand why I gave her up. Now that I am here and she is, well, next door—it doesn't seem so simple. I hate to say it, but I don't think she's going to be happy to meet me."

"I doubt she feels that way or she wouldn't have tried to look you up."

Just then they both noticed Electra approaching them at a fairly fast pace.

"Are you going to tell her?" Molly asked B.J.. She needed to know.

"No, I won't tell her."

"B.J., I'm sorry I'm a little late, especially dragging you out of bed so early." B.J. and Molly stood. Electra hadn't noticed Molly before.

"Oh, I'm sorry," she said. "Am I interrupting?"

"No," B.J. replied quickly, worried that Electra might have gotten the wrong impression about him and Molly.

"Our new housekeeper was just headed off for a swim when she saw me here waiting for you," B.J. said, being careful not to use Molly's name. He held his arm out to Electra. "Let me take your bag."

Electra swung her knapsack over her shoulder and handed B.J. an overnight bag. Then she followed him to the dock.

"Have a good swim," Electra said, as they left Molly behind them. B.J. got the engine running and Electra pushed off and jumped in the boat.

Molly watched them disappear. She felt ashamed of herself for not having said anything to Electra. She had almost asked B.J. to go ahead and tell Electra who she was, but the timing of it all was off. She made a promise to herself that as soon as Electra returned she would go over to her house alone and tell Electra who she was.

"What's your new housekeeper's name?" Electra asked, once they were on their way.

"You know, it's terrible. I've already forgotten. She has only been here a couple days." B.J. handed Electra his thermos with coffee in it at the exact moment that Electra pulled a thermos out of her knapsack.

"Well, I guess we're both prepared," Electra said, laughing. She took the cup off the top of her thermos and then poured two cups of coffee from B.J.'s. "I'm guessing that Gina stocks better coffee than what I usually pick up at the general store." She took a whiff from B.J.'s thermos and then filled the cups with the steaming liquid.

"It's too bad we don't have some time to water-ski. I've never seen the bay this calm," B.J. said as Electra stared out at the water ahead.

"I don't think I have ever seen it like this either," Electra acknowledged. "Can you slow down? It's so peaceful." B.J. slowed the engine and turned to look at Electra who was sipping on her coffee. He was more than happy to make this time with her last as long as possible.

"I noticed your dad was keeping to himself last night," Electra said. "Does he still blame himself about Gabby being at the Twin Tower?" The engine of a lobster boat passed them, interrupted the silence.

After the boat had gone, B.J. answered. "I don't know if he blames himself, but I know that he is still very heart broken. I think Gabby's death really made him stop and think about his life."

Electra's thoughts turned to Gabby. "I remember the summer before it all happened. Gabby spent the month of August here on the island. One day, she came over to our house with her tennis whites on. She was a little out of breath, as though she were in mid-game when she made her decision about the job. It was as if she couldn't wait to tell everyone and she burst through our front door very excited to see my father. I didn't even know about her getting an offer at my Dad's firm in the Twin Towers or about your father urging her to pursue it to continue the families' legacy of working together. She said she wanted to tell my father personally that she had decided she was going to start her career in New York at his firm. She was so grateful for my father's recommendation. Do you remember the dinner party your mother had for her after that and how we all toasted to her future in New York instead of the West Coast?"

B.J. nodded. He and Electra sat in silence for a moment, as if honoring the memory of Gabby as well as Mr. Richards, who had both died on that fateful day at the Twin Towers. B.J. had spent a great deal of time over the past couple years worrying about his parents. Ever since Gabby's funeral, when his father saw Jasmine, his first wife and Gabby's mother, after many years, he wondered if his dad regretted not moving to the West Coast with Jasmine and Gabby. He also wondered if his Dad regretted his part in urging his daughter to go to New York instead of the West Coast where she had another opportunity closer to her mother Jasmine in San Francisco.

"My Dad has been very sad," he said finally. "He hardly even touches my mother anymore. I wonder if he regrets ever marrying her. Maybe he would have been happier with Jasmine."

"Well, I'm glad he did marry your mother because if he didn't, then my best friend B.J. would never have been born," Electra said. She moved from the side of the boat to give B.J. a kiss on the cheek and sit on the seat next to him.

"Yeah, I'm glad that my Dad married my Mom and had me otherwise, I couldn't be your best friend," B.J. said holding the steering wheel with one hand and putting his arm around Electra's shoulders and giving her a quick hug.

"That was quite a party your mother put on last night," Electra continued, changing the subject. Electra wanted to linger on the hug, but she didn't want to push the boundaries with B.J., and she wanted to be sure he knew that she supported him and understood how difficult it must be for him with his own family's loss, and that she sympathized, Electra added, "I see your mother is more determined than ever to make sure that things run the same as they always have for generations." Electra gave B.J. one of her classic dimpled smiles. "I don't think I've missed a Geld Fourth of July picnic since I was born."

B.J. who always melted when she smiled at him, turned to her and said, "I hope you will be at our Fourth of July lobster bakes for many more years to come." B.J. thought to himself that he would like Electra to be there as his wife. He was a little saddened that his mother didn't approve of Electra and worried that it would scare Electra off someday, as his grandmother had scared away his father's first wife Jasmine. B.J. knew that not everyone understood his mother and her love of being a Geld "matriarch." He hoped that over time Electra might understand her better. B.J. looked at Electra and explained, "My mother is an institution. I know she seems shallow to a lot of people, but she truly loves my father and me. I think she believes deep in her heart that she has saved him from himself by keeping him on track with his family heritage and by being every bit the matriarch his mother had been."

"I remember your grandmother. She was a tough cookie," Electra said thinking how quickly B.J.'s mother had stepped into her shoes. "Your Mother seems to be living up to the Geld standard though."

"Yeah, Jasmine his first wife wanted no part of being a Geld Matriarch. Sometimes I wonder what would have happened to my Dad if he had followed Jasmine to California."

"Well, anyway, we will never really know what happened with our parents will we?" Electra sighed and looked at B.J. thoughtfully. "I think it's wonderful how much you admire your mother."

B.J. was relieved to hear Electra say that. "She can be a pain in the neck, but I really do love my mother. I hope you get to know her better someday." B.J. added, looking for a reaction on Electra's face, but she was clearly thinking about something else. "What about your biological mother? Will you be disappointed if you never meet her?"

"I don't know that I have to meet her. I'd just like for her to reply and acknowledge my existence."

"What if she turned out to be like your adopted mother?"

"If she is like my adopted mother, then she would never acknowledge my existence," Electra answered matter-of-factly. "Right now, I have plenty to think about with Jimmy in the hospital. I wonder if he minds me calling him Jimmy. I can't quite call someone else my dad. Truthfully, it's a bit awkward."

The ride to the mainland had neared its end. B.J. slowed the boat down even further and headed for the guest dock to drop Electra off.

"Will you call me as soon as you find out anything?" B.J. asked as she jumped up on the dock and reached for her bags. "You have my cell phone, don't you?"

"Of course I have your number. It's in my cell phone, and anyway, I know it by heart," Electra said picking up her bags.

"I'm afraid I will be back in New York when you return. I'm so sorry I won't be here to pick you up, but I really do want to know how you are doing."

"I'll call you from Boston," Electra promised as she walked away from the docks. "And thanks, B.J., for the ride—and the talk."

CHAPTER FIVE –The Big Break

It was supposed to be Matthew's "big break" and Jimmy's last show before taking time off to spend with Electra. Even though Matthew had made such a terrible fool of himself in front of Jimmy O'Conner on his birthday back in March, Jimmy had still sent Matthew his agent's card and told him that he could cover his next gig in Boston. Matthew had done a lot of articles about up-and-coming bands so far, but he had never been able to interview someone as famous as Jimmy. He could see the interview being picked up by Rolling Stone or Spin. There was little else Matthew thought about that summer other than the Quarter Moon show he was going to cover.

Four months later, there he was—back stage at the concert at the Orpheum Theatre in Boston. Jimmy's manager had told Matthew that Jimmy would meet him after the show for a quick interview. Matthew was so excited that he had forgotten to pay attention to the band. He loved the Quarter Moons, but he just wanted the show to be over so he could write his long-awaited review.

From behind the stage, Matthew heard Jimmy singing, "Full tide, quarter moon. The moment didn't come too soon." Then suddenly, the saxophone solo that usually kicked in after that instead was absent. The audience was eerily silent for a moment until a groupie in the front of the crowd screamed, "Oh my God, somebody do something!"

There was a lot of confusion and then Matthew saw Jimmy O'Connor, his "big break," being carried out on a stretcher. There would be no interview that night. Matthew was just taking his press badge off when Jimmy's manager approached him.

"Your dad is a friend of Jimmy's isn't he?"

"Yes he is." Matthew answered.

"Can you help me?"

"What do you need?"

"Jimmy was supposed to catch a plane to go visit his daughter in Maine tomorrow and she will be expecting him. I need to let her know he is being taken to the hospital and that he won't be arriving, but I don't have her number. Could you go to Jimmy's townhouse and see if you can find the number? Her name is Electra Richards; it should be a 207 area code."

"I didn't know he had a daughter," Matthew said.

"Never mind about that. Can you do this?"

"What about his cell phone. Maybe it's programmed in that."

"Jimmy doesn't have a cell phone. It's one of his eccentricities. If he needs one, he uses mine and I've already checked it." Jimmy's manager gave him a key to his apartment and directions on how to get there. Matthew, still in shock from seeing Jimmy being wheeled past him, took the keys and walked away.

The crowd that had been quiet when Jimmy had first collapsed on stage had become unruly and there seemed to be a lot of chaos and people trying to get closer to the front. Matthew was having trouble making any progress at reaching an exit and so he put his Press Badge back on and found a security guard to help him navigate his way through the crowd.

When he arrived at the townhouse, Matthew let himself in and looked around for the phone. Once he found it, he scrolled in the digital display for dialed calls that had a 207 area code. When he found one, he hit the dial and a phone rang. Finally, a recording kicked in. You have reached Electra Richards, please leave a message. It was a young woman's voice. Matthew hadn't thought about what he would say so, in a panic, he hung up. Then he called back and left a simple message that she should call him on his cell phone because her father was in the hospital. With nothing else to do but wait, he found the familiar couch where Jimmy and his Dad had laid him down on his birthday and took a seat. It seemed like a very long time before she returned the call. Their conversation was brief. He had agreed to meet her at the airport when the first plane arrived from Rockland, Maine. Matthew spent the rest of the evening nosing around Jimmy's place. He also helped himself to some of Jimmy's whiskey and then fell asleep.

When Electra came through the security gates, Matthew noticed her immediately. There weren't many others coming off the small aircraft. Her beauty and resemblance to Jimmy made Electra stick out from the crowd.

"Electra!" he called out. "Over here!" hearing her name, she hurried over to him.

"You must be Matthew. I'm glad you're here. We got in a little early. Is there any word on Jimmy?"

"Yes, I finally got through to his agent. He said that he suffered a minor heart attack, but that he is stable now. They're keeping him one more day or so to run a few more tests and rest up. I also arranged for his agent to get us in to see him."

"Where's your car?"

"I'm afraid I don't have a car, but we can take the subway. The Green line will take us there. "

Electra was confused. Why would he come to pick her up if he didn't have a car? Instead of seeming ungrateful, however, she simply said, "I'd rather not waste the extra time on a subway. I'll just pay for a cab. Thank you for the news and for arranging for me to see my father. Maybe I'll see you again some time."

"I really better go with you," Matthew said. "It's still not easy to get past the nurses and I'd feel more comfortable knowing I escorted you the whole way." Matthew didn't want to say goodbye to either Electra or the whole experience of being involved with Jimmy's life.

"Okay, but let's get going though," Electra replied, heading out to the arrivals area to flag a taxi.

"You said your Dad and Jimmy are friends?" Electra asked once they were in the cab. "Have you known him long?"

"Our fathers were friends about twenty years ago."

"Were friends?" Electra asked, confused.

"They used to play in a band together, and they hadn't seen each other until just recently. I met him once about four months ago."

"This is odd. My father's agent calls the son of a guy who knew my dad twenty years ago to telephone me about him being in the hospital. Then he sends him to pick me up without a car. What's going on here? Is this some kind of terrible hoax?" Electra was feeling nervous thinking about the possibility that this could all be a rouse.

"I know it is a bit odd, but I was there back stage the other night when it happened. I was supposed to write a story about Jimmy and the band."

"A story?" Electra asked.

"I'm a journalist."

"You've got to be kidding? Did Jimmy's agent really send you?"

"Yes, I swear." Matthew handed her the agent's card. "Call him yourself. He's expecting us at the hospital."

"Why wouldn't a manager send a car?"

"I don't know. It's all been so confusing."

The cab pulled up in front of the hospital. Electra pulled out her cell phone and dialed the agent's cell number. "I'll take it from here," she told Matthew, dismissing him.

"Can I have the card back then?" Matthew asked, worried that he would not see Electra or Jimmy again without it. Electra ignored his request as she spoke to Jimmy's agent.

"Yes, I'm at the hospital now. Which room should I ask for?" she said over the cell-phone. Matthew strained to hear if she would repeat the number. After she had hung up, Electra closed the cell phone and held out her hand to Matthew.

"Really, both Jimmy and I are grateful for your concern," she said. "He is expecting me now, so goodbye."

Matthew shook her hand. "Can I take you to dinner later?" he asked.

"I don't think so. Now, if you don't mind, I'm anxious to see Jimmy."

With that, Electra left Matthew on the curb where the taxi had dropped them off.

After being escorted to Jimmy's room by his manager, Electra greeted Jimmy with more than enough enthusiasm to make up for the reserve she had showed him at the Ritz on their first meeting. She gave him a huge hug and sat at the side of his bed.

"What a fright you gave me!" she told him.

"You weren't the only one I frightened." Jimmy told her. "I was pretty scared myself. I thought I was too young to get a heart attack. Now, not only do I find out I'm in bad health, but I'm old as well."

"You're not too old. It happens to younger people too— younger people who don't take care of their health, that is," Electra said. "I'm so glad you are okay."

"I'm not so keen on being in this hospital, but I'm awfully glad to be alive. You can't imagine all the things I've thought since I've come through. The first day after you find out that you almost died is like the first day of a whole new life."

Electra looked at all the flowers that had been sent to Jimmy's room. In her haste, she hadn't thought to bring anything.

"So what do you think this new life is all about?" She asked.

"I don't know, but I expect I'll be spending some time thinking about it now." Jimmy reached out and put his hand on Electra's thigh. "Electra. I'm so happy you came to see me. You're the silver-lining in all of this. I do know that I want you to be a big part of my new life."

Electra stood up, feeling a bit overwhelmed by the statement. Then she said, "I'm sorry I didn't bring you flowers."

"I'm just so happy to see you. Do you remember the pendant I gave you with my mother's photo?"

Electra reached inside her blouse and pulled it out. "Yes, I'm wearing it."

"Since I met you, I have been wondering if I should tell my mother about you. The last time I spoke to her, she told me that I had broken her heart because I, her only child, hadn't given her any grandchildren. I was thinking about her statement when I heard that my brilliant manager sent Matthew to go get you at the airport." Jimmy paused a moment. "He's writing for the music tabloids," he continued. "I can only imagine who he'll be leaking this story out to and the last thing I want is for my Mum to being doing her shopping and then find out from the Tabloids that she has a grandchild."

"I'll talk to Matthew and make sure he understands he can't say anything."

"He won't understand. I know the type all too well. He'll write the story for sure. Anyway, I promised his dad that his kid would get a story."

"Well, if he is your friend's son then he should respect your wishes and not write a story."

"You'd be surprised when you are a public figure how much it changes personal relationships. Trust me it's better to have someone you know write the story. I make it a point to line someone up to cover stories on me and make sure that I have some input on what they say. That way at least there is some truth in what gets written about me. Anyway, I really think that my Mum should know you exist." Jimmy had been thinking all morning about how he would ask Electra to go to Ireland with him. "I have time between shows. What would you think about taking a trip with me to Ireland and meeting my mother?"

"Wow! That is a big change from taking a rest up on the island. Are you sure you're ready for a trip like that?"

"I know. I feel bad that I am sitting here in the hospital when I was supposed to be with you at your place in Maine. I was really looking forward to that time with you, but at the same time, I really feel that I need to see my Mum. I haven't really spent time with her. And, I need to tell her that she has a granddaughter. If you went with me she could meet you and we would still have some time together like we planned." Jimmy was also thinking about his band. He hadn't told them that he was going to take time off in Maine until just before the concert in Boston. The band members had planned their own vacations over in Europe a couple weeks before the Munich concert and that would leave them no time to rehearse before the show. Jimmy was thinking with his new plan, they could fly into Dublin and have the band meet up there for a few days of rehearsal and then he and Electra could spend the next couple of weeks with his Mum in Sligo.

"I would love to meet your mother, but I haven't traveled in a long time."

"Do you have a passport?"

"I do." Electra answered. "The year before my adopted Dad died he surprised me with a trip to Paris for my birthday." Electra remembered how much fun the trip had been and reflected back on how glad she was to have had that time with him. She started to realize why Jimmy was so anxious to see his mother after his recent health scare.

"When is your birthday?" Jimmy asked concerned that he didn't know it.

"It's tomorrow. B.J. used to tease me that I was a 'delayed firework'."

"Well, that settles it. I 'm taking you on a trip to Ireland for your birthday," Jimmy said wanting to start measuring up as a father. "What about Munich? Have you ever been to Munich," Jimmy asked. He would invite her to go to his concert. Certainly that would be something her adopted Dad could never have offered her.

"No, I've never been to Munich."

"Ok, then. My treat, we'll take a trip to Ireland and then you will travel on first class to Munich and see my band from back stage."

Electra was overwhelmed with the offer, but she didn't feel like she could turn Jimmy down.

"That is very generous of you."

"So you'll go?" Jimmy asked excitedly.

"Yes." Electra agreed.

"We can bring Matthew along to write a story about you meeting my Mum." Jimmy looked over at the flowers on his bedside table and added, "God, I sure hope the boy can write. I guess if that story doesn't work out, he can cover the Munich show." Jimmy was thinking maybe he'd even have Matthew merge the two stories, perhaps introducing Electra on stage at his Munich show.

"I'd love to go to Ireland with you, but I don't know that I want that guy Matthew to come along."

"You don't know my Mum. We'll want someone else there to distract her, trust me." Jimmy would need to layover in Dublin for a few days for rehearsals. He would wait and tell Electra about that later. He was afraid it would be a bit lonely for Electra and had thought it might be good for her to have someone her own age along for the trip. He also wanted whoever was writing the story about them to get to know her. He needed to sell Electra on the idea of bringing Matthew along on the trip.   "She'll be very happy about you. Don't get me wrong, but I have to warn you, with you born out of wedlock, she'll be a little upset with me. I'll need to spend some time with her alone. I was thinking maybe you could coach Matthew and help him with the story. Electra had never had anyone mention her as being 'born out of wedlock' it startled her to hear herself described that way. "What part of Ireland does she live in?" Electra asked not wanting to linger on his previous comment.

"It's on the coast in an area called Sligo. We'll fly into Dublin and then take a small plane from there. It's great country, especially in the summer. Do you like to surf?"

"People surf in Ireland?" Electra asked surprised.

"Where I come from they do." Jimmy answered recalling the time he spent on his board in his teenage years. It was through his surfer friends that he gained an interest in rock music.

"I don't surf but I love the ocean. You know I've spent the last few years on the island."

"I've been wanting to talk to you about that. Listen, I know that you are a musician. Music is meant for other people to hear. It's to be shared. If you've got talent, you can't hide it away up in Ridgeport, playing piano for the lobsters and mosquitoes."

"I don't plan to stay there forever. I just need some time."

"Don't take too long then. Take it from me; you're not going to be young forever."

"Didn't I just say I would go to Ireland with you?" Electra asked as she fidgeted with her pendant. "That is a big step for me." The suggestion to bring Matthew along had not made Electra very comfortable. She was also a little unnerved by Jimmy's comments about his mother.

Jimmy smiled at Electra as she tucked the pendant back into her blouse. "That is great news. I haven't been to see my Mum in a while now. My father died a couple of years ago, and I know she is very lonely. I asked her to move to Boston with me, but she won't have any of that. She's an Irish woman, through and through."

"What was your father like?" Electra asked. "I hadn't heard you speak of him."

"He was a pain in the ass." Jimmy said, in a matter-of-fact tone.

"So you didn't get along?"

"That would be an understatement," Jimmy replied. "He didn't care too much for me."

"He must have been proud that you became so successful."

"Just the opposite. He was the music teacher in our town. He taught all the kids piano, violin and recorder. He always made a point of telling me what a musical failure I was, especially after I started to play in rock bands. He said it was just a bunch of noise and that I couldn't carry a tune to save my life."

"What about your Mum? Is she proud of you?" Electra wanted to get a better sense of what she would be like.

"I don't know if proud would be the right word. She is disappointed that I moved away from Ireland and that I never brought home any grandchildren. She is, however, grateful for my success because my father's music lessons didn't bring in much money. What little it did bring in often got spend down at the pub where he played in the evenings with his friends. I have been sending her money so that she could live a little more comfortably. Now that my dad is dead, I support her completely. She always raises a fuss, but she needs me. I'm all she has right now." Jimmy paused and then took Electra's hand in his. "I've been thinking a lot about what would happen to my Mum if anything did happen to me."

Jimmy stopped and stared out his bedside window for a moment and held Electra's hand a little tighter. "I have a special favor to ask of you."

"Sure, anything," Electra answered though she was a little uncomfortable with Jimmy's serious tone.

"If anything happens to me, I need you to take care of her. You will be all she has. That is one of the things I have been thinking about since I found myself in this hospital bed. I know it is a lot to ask. I have arranged for it in my will so that you will both be well taken care of."

"Of course I would look after your mother," Electra said. She didn't like Jimmy talking about wills. She had enough of that with her adopted father. Electra was interested in finding family not new inheritances. "I only hope that she likes me."

"She will," Jimmy said. "I'm sure of it."

A nurse came in the room and let Electra know that they needed to run some routine tests and that they'd need her to step outside a moment. Electra bent down and gave Jimmy a kiss on the cheek, "I'll be back in soon to talk about the trip," she said before leaving his room.

Electra was not prone to be impulsive and she was extremely surprised with herself for having made such quick plans to jump on a plane and go to Ireland let alone Munich. *B.J. will understand,* she thought to herself as she reached into her purse to give him the update call she had promised when he dropped her off early that morning.

"Hello Electra," B.J. answered right away recognizing her number on his cell phone.

"Jimmy had a mild heart attack, but everything is OK. He is doing really well."

"I'm sure you feel better now that you've seen him," B.J. offered.

"Yes, and actually I have a favor to ask you."

"Sure what is it?" B.J. asked.

"I've agreed to go to Ireland with Jimmy and meet his mother."

"Wow, that's a big surprise. When are you going and how long will you be gone?" B.J. interjected quickly, disturbed by this sudden announcement.

"It will be a few weeks because I am also going to go see his show in Munich. I realize this is very last minute, but what I wanted to know is if you can ask your Mother if she wouldn't mind having her housekeeper go over to my place a few times while I am gone and keep things dusted. She has the key."

B.J. was disappointed to hear she would be away so long and asked, "Three weeks, why so long?"

"It is a long time," Electra acknowledged. "And it is very unlike me to do something this spontaneously. But, I think this is something that I really need to do, and it's obvious that this means a lot to Jimmy."

"What about your birthday?" B.J. asked. He had planned to bring her some flowers and champagne and finally tell Electra about his feeling. It was terrible news that she would be out of town.

"Jimmy is treating me to this whole trip as a birthday present. I couldn't turn him down. "

"Is his health good enough for all that traveling?" B.J. asked not as concerned about Jimmy as much as he was hoping he could change Electra's mind about the sudden trip.

"We may need to wait a few days before we leave, but Jimmy thinks the time in Ireland will be restful for him."

"I thought the plan was for him to rest up in Maine." B.J. reminded Electra.

"It was, but after his health scare I think he is feeling sentimental about going home to see his mother. I was thinking that we'd go up to Maine after the Munich show and maybe I'd even throw some kind of party." Electra added hoping that the mention of a party would appease B.J. He had the same insatiable interest in entertaining as his mother.

"A party sounds great." B.J. was almost more surprised about Electra suggesting a party than he was hearing that she was going out of the country.

"Yes, I thought you would like that idea." Electra said before being distracted by a nurse who had let her know that she could go back in and see Jimmy. "Well, I've got to go," Electra said to B.J. "Thank you for everything and I will call you soon." BJ wished her well on her trip. Once off the phone with B.J., Electra slipped back into Jimmy's room.

"Everything ok?" she asked.

"Yeah, just got poked and prodded, but apparently, I should be out of here soon, "Jimmy said.

"That is good to hear," Electra said with relief.

"So back to the travel plans,'" Jimmy said. "I am going to put you up at the Ritz here in Boston while we wait for me to get the green light. You should check-in today. I will get you the best room sparing nothing for the birthday girl." Jimmy smiled thinking that he would get a nurse to help him order flowers and chocolates to be delivered to her room. "I'll get my manager to take care of the travel plans. He is used to setting travel up at the last minute." Jimmy knew his manager would be relieved to hear that he was changing his plans around and that he could set up rehearsal time in Dublin. He also knew the band would not object to Dublin as a rehearsal spot. Dublin was a magical city for them.

"The Ritz sounds nice," Electra answered fondly remembering their first meeting there. She wanted more than anything to please Jimmy, but she needed him to know that it was a big deal for her to take a trip like the one he was proposing. "It will be fun to go there again. I have to admit, though that staying a few nights at the Ritz in Boston is a little different than jumping on a plane overseas for a few weeks. This isn't easy for me."

Jimmy looked at Electra appreciatively and said, "What can I do for you in return?"

"I'd love for you to still go to my place in Maine and spend a little time with me there. Do you have any time off after your show in Munich?"

"I'll have to check with my agent," Jimmy answered glad that Electra wanted him to spend more time with him. "I think we might. The Munich show is a bit unusual. When we go to Europe we usually plan a whole tour, but this time we're only going to Munich. I'm not really sure what happened. I think the Munich show got booked and then the rest of the schedule didn't work out so we're setting up a new tour date for Europe in November, and the band is going to spend the remaining time this summer in Europe on vacation. " Jimmy was pleased how everything had turned out.

Electra pulled on one of Jimmy's many 'Get Well' balloons. "I hope you can. I'd like to have a party at my house in Maine. I could introduce you to some of my friends, particularly my friend B.J., who is practically family." Electra watched Jimmy's face and then added, "Who knows maybe I will hear from Molly before then and we can invite her too." Electra definitely saw Jimmy flinch at her last comment.

"Now, I told you that I never heard back from Molly, so don't get your hopes up too much about her," Jimmy said with concern in his voice.

"I just meant, if I hear from her. But what do you think about the idea of a party?"

"I like it." Jimmy said enthusiastically.

CHAPTER SIX- Back on the Island

On Monday, Molly had her morning swim and coffee and settled in to what became her summer routine before heading up to the big house to start her chores. When she arrived in the kitchen, she had forgotten that it was Gina's day off. Gina, always organized, had thought to leave a note with clear instructions of what Molly should do in the kitchen in her absence. She had informed Molly that on a Monday after a weekend of entertaining, Mrs. Geld does a juice fast and had left instructions for the different juices and their combinations. In the refrigerator, Gina had placed separate containers for carrots, beets and celery and on the counter; Molly found a beautiful, hand-painted pottery bowl filled with apples and a few pieces of ginger. Per the instructions, after she made the morning juice, Molly left it out on the sun-porch.

Mrs. Geld was not out yet and the whole house was very quiet. Molly wasn't sure if she was in the meditation stage of her yoga or if she had simply decided to sleep in. Not wanting to disturb her in either case, Molly retreated back to the kitchen to fix her own breakfast.

In the excitement and anxiety of the weekend, she hadn't eaten very much. The emptiness of the house gave room for her to notice the emptiness of her stomach. She puttered around Gina's kitchen and used the juicer to make herself some fresh orange juice. There would definitely not be any fasting for her that day. The only thing she had overindulged in lately was fear. Molly used the fancy Nespresso machine to fuel her culinary experiments with shots of espresso. First, she made herself German pancakes and spread them with Nutella and raspberry jam. When she finished eating them, she checked on Mrs. Geld and saw that the juice was still untouched. She checked the time and it was past ten. It was a cool morning and the fog had rolled in. Molly imagined that after such a busy weekend and with the weather the way it was, Mrs. Geld had probably decided to sleep in. Perhaps when all her chores were done, Molly herself would crawl back under the covers and do the same. Until Mrs. Geld came down from her room, however, she'd have to wait.

She went back to the kitchen and was about to clean up from the pancake breakfast when she saw the containers of leftovers from the lobster bake. She decided to make herself an avocado and lobster omelet. She pulled out more bowls and pans and was certain that Gina would be horrified to see her kitchen in such disarray. It had always been a fantasy of Molly's to have a kitchen this well stocked and with plenty of room to create. Her apartments had always been small with closet-sized kitchens. Even if she could have afforded gadgets and a well-stocked pantry, there would have been nowhere to put them.

Molly hadn't eaten so much in a long time. After she finished up her omelet, she sat back, fully satiated. The house was still quiet and she saw no harm in taking a rest before tidying up. Her thoughts turned to the night of the lobster bake. She was thinking about Jimmy. Molly realized that, in her journey to meet Electra, it had never occurred to her that there would be a chance of seeing him again, even though Electra had stated that she had also looked him up as well. She wondered how much Jimmy would have changed after becoming famous and pondered how he might be, but couldn't imagine him any other way than how she had remembered him. He was confident but not cocky and he really knew what he wanted. Another pang of regret swept through her. She felt sorry for not appreciating him for that. Molly had spent years being painfully embarrassed by her naiveté with him. After Jimmy, she had always been excessively cautious about birth control—even though she had still desperately wanted to have a child for years after giving up Electra.

She didn't like to admit it, but it was true that she had spent most of her life bending to the desires of her boyfriends, hoping that things would progress to marriage and that she could start trying to have kids. Molly had never regretted giving birth, but she had always felt uncertain if it had been the right thing to give her baby up for adoption. Her had given her so many reasons why she should, but none of those reasons ever settled easy in her heart. Upon receiving Electra's letter, old questions had begun to come out of the closet. Why had she really given her up for adoption? She had hoped that this journey would answer that question for her once and for all. Molly re-affirmed to herself, that she would, upon Electra's return from Boston, go to her immediately and tell her who she really was. Just as Molly was making this resolution, Mrs. Geld entered the kitchen.

"Good morning, Molly. Thank you for the juice," she said. "I'm afraid I'm a bit off my schedule this morning." Mrs. Geld stopped when she noticed the mess in the kitchen. "What's all this from?"

"I meant to clean up sooner." Molly quickly lied and said, "I was trying a few recipes for days when Gina is off and you or your guests are not fasting. I'm afraid my cooking is getting a bit rusty."

"Oh," Mrs. Geld answered picking up the pots in the sink and examining them. "So what did you make?"

"I made German pancakes and omelets," Molly answered. Mrs. Geld scanned the counters looking for the finished products. "And where are they?"

Blushing, Molly answered, "I ate them already. If you like, I can make more."

"Oh, no dear. My schedule is off but I will stick to the juice program today. I do have a favor to ask of you though."

"Anything. What do you need?" Molly answered.

"This morning, just after I finished up my yoga, I got a call from B.J.." Mrs. Geld wiped her hand across the counter and added, "That boy is so considerate, and he knew to wait until after my morning session before calling." She sighed and then continued, "Anyway, he called to tell me that our neighbor Electra phoned him from Boston. Apparently, a musician friend of hers has taken ill and she is going to accompany him back to Ireland to see his mother."

Mrs. Geld paused a moment before continuing. "Your name is quite Irish, Molly. Are you from Ireland?" Mrs. Geld was thinking maybe being Irish she would sympathize.

"I was born there," said Molly, "but I left when I was very young."

"Oh," Mrs. Geld continued, "Well, Electra hadn't planned on being away long, so she's requested that we look in on her house. I hope you won't mind terribly, but I volunteered your services for a few weeks just to do a bit of dusting." Mrs. Geld took a closer look at Molly to see how she was reacting to the request. "I know it's a bit of an odd request, but we're neighbors, and certainly I'd expect the same of her if we were to be out of town unexpectedly."

Molly was surprised by the request, and at first, she didn't answer.

"I know I should have asked you first, but..." Mrs. Geld started to say.

"Of course. It won't be a problem," Molly said, after regaining her senses. "Did B.J. tell you what was wrong with her friend?" She wondered why B.J. referred to Jimmy as a friend and not as Electra's father.

"No, I don't think so. I didn't ask. I am so worried about that boy. I am glad that I have raised him to be so thoughtful, and he is such a good friend to Electra. I just wish that he would realize that she is not the right girl for him."

"Why do you say that?" Molly asked, trying to sound curious. Instead, the comment came out a bit defensive.

"You don't know her. She was the attractive young lady who was sitting across from me at the lobster bake."

"I noticed her. She was very beautiful," Molly remembered when she had first caught sight of Electra. She paused looking at Mrs. Geld who she knew to appreciate beautiful things. Molly couldn't imagine how Mrs. Geld could not see her son with a woman as beautiful as Electra. "Why don't you think she'd be right for B.J.? I think they would make handsome couple, and can you imagine their children?"

"That's just it. That girl does not know what she wants. She doesn't want to get married and have a family, let alone leave her house. Last year, my son invited her to a party we hosted with several other families from the Upper East Side. Any other girl would have jumped at the chance, but she simply replied that she would not be able to attend. She's practically become a recluse here. Frankly, I was surprised she even showed up last night. Then there's that story about her father. It's just so sad."

"Maybe she's just going through something."

"Oh, yes, she is but it's been several years now. She hasn't even finished up her music degree. There's another thing she can't commit to."

"Nathan told me she plays her piano every night. That sounds to me like she's quite committed to her music. I wish I had the discipline to paint everyday."

"Are you a painter?"

Molly had been thinking about her art career, or lack of it, ever since she stored her paintings away.

"No," she answered. "I thought that I was for a time, but I guess it didn't turn out to be much of a success." She was surprised to hear herself say this truth out loud. It was a conclusion she had been finally coming to grips with twenty years after graduating from the New England School of Art. Going to art school was a desire Molly had before she met Jimmy. She saved her money from working at the pub and also applied and received a scholarship. At the time she told her that she would need to work around her school schedule. Then, of course, she met Jimmy and got pregnant. Her , who knew that Molly wanted to be an artist, insisted that that she should not interrupt her plans for art school because of the baby. He had helped and supported her. Molly felt bad when straight after graduation, she told her that she was going to move to Seattle with a boyfriend from school. Molly thought she should have stayed on and helped him at the pub, but her boyfriend's work had been accepted at a gallery in the Pacific Northwest and she had gone to be with him. She realized that she had sacrificed precious time with her and also allowed her own art career to play second fiddle to her boyfriend.

Not wanting to compete for the same type of attention as her boyfriend, Molly had taken work at a temp agency instead of pursuing an art gallery for her own work. When that boyfriend left her, Molly considered trying to find a gallery to show her work, but never found the motivation until years later when she met Joel on one of her temp assignments. Joel had been impressed by Molly's art degree and her bohemian lifestyle, so in an attempt to impress Joel, Molly had given up a chance to work full time with an assignment at the Children's Theatre. Molly took an evening job as a bartender and resumed her non-obsequious career as an unknown artist, living paycheck to paycheck, while seeking success with a gallery. Molly thought that Joel truly supported her art career and that he valued their life together and was willing to make sacrifices. Molly was shocked when Joel, seemingly out of the blue, dumped her for a lawyer; and moved in with the new woman in her large home in the suburbs. She was further stung by being told that he would not be taking the paintings she had given him because they would not fit the décor of the new girlfriend's home.

Molly was very embarrassed by her life choices, so when Mrs. Geld asked her, "What do you really want?" she simply answered, "I don't know."

"No offense to you Molly, but that is what I'm afraid will happen to Electra. She'll be middle-aged and still not sure what she wants." That particular comment really dug in to Molly, leaving hollowness in the pit of her stomach. "My son will take on my husband's business some day." Mrs. Geld continued to speak as Molly lowered her head. "He'll need a wife who can entertain. Electra has that beautiful home and I don't think she has thrown a single party. She's just not social, that girl. No, she is not the right kind of girl for B.J.."

"Well, they're young," Molly said, trying to change the subject. "Now about that house, is there a key somewhere? I'd be happy to go over there when I'm done here this afternoon."

"I have the key to Electra's house. I will leave it on the front entrance table on my way out. I'm going to play a little golf this afternoon."

Feeling fairly depressed, Molly started her chores slowly, but then found that the cleaning helped to sweep away her negative thoughts and was soon moving through the rooms with a purpose. Once the house was cleaned up, she went down to the dock to take a break. The fog had dispersed and the sun was peaking through blue spaces between the clouds. Molly was lying down on the dock bathing in the sun when she heard the engine of a motorboat approach. The dock started to rock slightly and it felt like she was on a waterbed. Molly sat up and saw Nathan bringing the boat into the dock.

"Getting a bit of relaxation in, 'ey?" Nathan asked, as he cut the engine. With quick, sure moves, he jumped from the boat and pulled the rope around the cleat three times.

"No one is here. Mrs. Geld is off playing golf."

"I told you you'd get some nice breaks during the day. Especially, in July when Mrs. Geld is here on her own most of the time."

"Speaking of Mrs. Geld, she assigned me an interesting new task today," Molly said lifting her head and shading her eyes.

"What's that?"

"Apparently, Electra has decided to go with Jimmy to Ireland. Mrs. Geld wants me to look after her house. I'm assuming that Jimmy was who Mrs. Geld was referring to when she said Electra would be going with a 'musician friend.' "

"Did Electra call her?"

"B.J. called for her. I wonder why he didn't tell his mother that Jimmy is Electra's birth father, especially since Mrs. Geld thinks Electra is having some kind of breakdown and has invented him."

"He probably just didn't want to explain the whole thing, especially since she didn't believe the story the other night. How are you doing with all of this?"

"I don't feel right being in her house without her knowing who I am, that is for sure." Molly said. She confirmed in her own mind that she had to tell her daughter who she was, and she had to do it as soon as possible.

"Do you have her cell phone?" She asked Nathan, "I need to tell her I am here."

"If you're not ready to do that, I wouldn't mind looking after her house for you," Nathan offered. "I keep an eye on it in the winter time or at least I did before Electra started staying on the island year round."

"No, that wouldn't be right. Anyway, it would make Mrs. Geld suspicious."

"How would she know the difference?"

"I don't know. All the same, I am certain that I need Electra to know that I came here to see her, but that things got a bit off track and that I am now working next door."

"If you're sure that's what you want."

"Yes. I wish I had said something when she was here at the lobster bake."

"You weren't ready yet." Nathan said in a comforting tone.

"I might have been if she hadn't mentioned Jimmy. I imagine that he must be okay if they are planning to travel."

Nathan got back in the boat and said, "Why don't you hop in the boat and I will take you over to my place? I have Electra's cell phone number in my desk drawer,"

"You can get to your place by boat?" Molly asked.

"Yeah. It's not quite like these summer homes, but I like it. I live down by the town beach where I first met you." Anxious to call Electra before she lost her nerve, Molly pulled her shorts on and jumped in the motorboat.

"Would you mind undoing the cleat for me while I get her started?" Nathan asked surprised by Molly's sudden motivation to talk to Electra.

Molly quickly jumped back out and untied the boat.

"You waited all this time. Why rush now?" Nathan said as he got the engine running.

"I just think she needs to know before she goes to Ireland. What if Electra tells Jimmy's mother that she had also written to her birth mother and never heard back from her?"

"Why do you care? She doesn't even know you."

"Yes, but she is my daughter's grandmother." Molly said looking out at the water "I don't want her to think badly of me. Back when I still had hopes that Jimmy would change his mind about the baby, I used to imagine going back to Ireland with him to introduce our newborn to the family." Molly sighed at the thought of that memory. "He never wanted to do that with me. But now, that's exactly what he is doing."

"Are you jealous?" Nathan asked.

Molly knew that that was exactly the problem. She was jealous that Jimmy had become a friend to Electra and jealous that he didn't have to be embarrassed about his life. She was jealous that he had a mother for her to meet and family roots and a home still in Ireland.

"Yes, I guess I am," she said after a long pause.

They passed by some very large houses with both sailboats and motorboats docked and moored in front of them. After some time, Nathan started to slow the boat down. As they rounded the tip of the island, he pulled up to a dock. Cutting the engine back, he told Molly to jump out and tie up the boat. Molly threw the bumpers over the side and jumped out. She turned toward the shore and noticed a lovely cottage with wooden shingles that had been seasoned silver by the ocean air. The windows were framed with red shutters that matched the red of the barn that was to the right of the cottage.

"Is this all yours?" she asked. She was unable to hide the surprise in her voice.

"Yep. This property has been in my family for years. For my bonus one year, Mr. Geld gave me stock in a company called Jamster. Then for my bonus the next year he gave me the advice to sell it along with some other stock he had bought me back the 90's. He mentioned something about a "bubble bursting." I tell you, the only bubble for me was the one over my head when I found out what it was worth! Wooo hooo!" Nathan jumped from the dock onto his lawn. "Anyway, I took some of that money and re-did the cottage and then the barn. Most recently, I have been investing in my very special project I am building in the barn. I will show you that later."

Molly was starting to realize there was a lot more to Nathan than she had originally thought. He was one of those people that, on the surface, seemed very simple. As she got to know him, however, she was discovering that he had many aspects of himself that surprised her. She noticed that the lawn was kept very well trimmed and that rosehip bushes bordered the path from the dock up to the house. Nathan saw Molly looking at the bushes.

"They're not only pretty to look at, but an excellent source of vitamin C," he said.

"Leave it to a New Englander to be practical about their shrubbery," Molly said as she arrived at the door to the cottage and waited for Nathan to catch up. She stepped through the door and was amazed to see a spotless and tastefully decorated living room.

"Is there some kind of zoning law on this island that requires everyone to be neat?"

"What's this coming from a housekeeper?"

"I'm really not a housekeeper. I'm a woman of practical trade who happens to be engaged in a project of engineering cleanliness for people who have enough money not to engineer their own. My own home, I'm afraid, is usually in chaos and speckled with a generous amount of dust."

"I'm disappointed to hear that," Nathan said. "Especially after the high level of personal recommendation I provided." He added teasing.

"Sorry to disappoint you. So how did you get to be so neat?" Molly asked truly interested in why he was so neat.

"When you're a sailor, you don't think of leaving your boat until everything is buttoned up. Why wouldn't I do the same with my house?" Nathan smiled and then went in to another room.

"I'll just be a second," he called out. "I'm going to get you Electra's cell phone number." He returned in a moment with an index card.

"Are you nervous?"

"Yeah, but I really need to do this," Molly said, catching sight of his phone. "Can I use it?"

"Sure," Nathan answered, handing her the portable. "It works out on the patio if you'd like some privacy."

"I can call from here." Molly dialed the number and got Electra's voice mail so she hung up.

"Did you change your mind?" Nathan inquired when she returned his phone quickly.

"I got her voice mail."

"Did you leave a message?"

"No." Molly answered with a bit of regret in her voice.

"Do you think that if Electra came back to the island today, you would go to meet her?"

"Yes," Molly paused "I think I would. I wonder if she has already left for Ireland. Do you think her phone will work there?"

"I can't say that I know much about those kinds of things. Why don't you come see what I'm working on in the barn and then give her another try a little later?"

Molly followed Nathan outside. At the barn, he opened the long swinging doors. She saw the finished frame of what looked like about a forty-foot wooden sailboat.

"It probably takes a bit of imagination to see the final result I have in mind," Nathan said. Molly had an appreciation for design and could easily imagine what a special boat he was building.

"It's amazing," she said, walking around the structure to see all its angles.

"Really? You like it?"

"I'm not a sailor, but I can say for sure that it's a fine piece of art."

"Thank you. If you're interested, we could change the part about you not being a sailor. Tomorrow afternoon I will be teaching a sailing class."

"Who do you teach?" Molly asked.

"Mostly little kids, but you're a beginner too, right? Anyway, it will be good to have some adult company, and good for the kids to know that even big people need to learn to sail."

"Who are the kids?"

"A couple of them are my nephews. My sister started a summer kids program, kind of like a day camp except that it's volunteer and the program changes based on who is available to be with them. Do you not like children?"

"I love kids. I used to work for the Children's Theatre in Seattle."

"Children's Theatre—now that is a program they haven't had. Maybe we could volunteer you to set that up this summer." Molly remembered the Children's Theatre and smiled. The little kids dressed up and took their parts very seriously; it was so cute. She would love to do something like that.

"I don't know about that," she said not wanting to over commit, but secretly liking the idea.

"Of course you could. It would be great. Why don't you tell them tomorrow at sailing class and see if they like the idea?"

"We'll see." Molly said. In an act of spontaneity, Nathan put his arm on her shoulder. Then he led her out of the barn and back over to the cottage.

"Would you like some ice tea?" he asked, giving her the phone to try the call again.

"Sure," Molly answered as she redialed Electra's number. Again no one answered, but this time Molly left a message.

'Electra, this is Molly. You sent me a letter in May. I know it has been some time, but I am in Maine now. In fact I am using Nathan's phone, you know Nathan who works at the Geld's? It's a long story, but I am also working in their household. I'm their housekeeper for the summer. I would have liked to explain all this to you in person, but...' With that last half-sentence, the phone beeped with the options to re-record or send. Molly didn't think she could say what she just said again. Even though the message was incomplete, she chose "send."

Then she put the phone down and took the ice tea Nathan had placed on a side table for her.

"I guess that's that," Nathan said, having heard her message.

"She's going to think I'm a crazy person."

"Don't worry. Electra is not a judgmental person. She'll be very happy to know you came to see her. You did the right thing."

"It would have been so much more normal of me to have just knocked on the door when I first got here."

"True, but that's not how it happened. I'm not sorry about it because otherwise we'd probably still be looking for a housekeeper." Nathan blushed as he added, "And also I wouldn't have met you."

They walked together to Nathan's patio and sat down to finish their tea. It felt natural to Molly to be in Nathan's house, as if she had been visiting for years. She took the last sip of her tea and looked at Nathan's profile. He had tipped his head back and was sunning himself like a cat. Molly thought that in a lot of ways Nathan was very much like a cat.

Molly wanted to befriend Nathan, but at the same time, unlike other men she had wanted to know better, she had no expectation of possessing him. She continued to look at him. He had a slightly upturned nose that looked to be in a constant state of peeling and a chin that was neither square nor pointed. It was shaped like the curve of an upturned smile. He had high cheekbones and his sky blue eyes were bordered by tan wrinkles. His hair was always unruly, and he had several curls of blond hair that fell sideways across his forehead. He could feel that she was watching him so he kept his eyes closed. He took this solid look as a good sign.

"If you're done with your cat nap, I'm ready to go back to the Geld's," Molly stated after some more time went by. Nathan, who had not been napping, stood up and took their empty glasses into the kitchen. As the screen door slammed, he re-emerged.

"Sure," he said. "Let's hit the water."

"Thank you very much for letting me use your phone. I really appreciate it," Molly said as Nathan pulled the boat up to the Geld's dock.

"I'm sorry you couldn't reach Electra. If you want, you can try again another day," Nathan replied.

"Maybe. I want to give her a couple of days to absorb the news I just left first, though." Molly was feeling a little uneasy about her decision to leave the message on Electra's machine.

"Let me know if she calls you back," she added, as she jumped out of the boat.

"I will," Nathan said, turning the boat off and cleating the boat line.

"I guess I better get over to Electra's and see about dusting the place."

"Do you want me to go with you?"

"No, I'll be fine."

"I'm going to go clean out the cruiser then," Nathan said, pointing to the Geld's yacht. "If you need anything just come on down to the dock."

"Thanks again, Nathan. I'll see you soon."

Nathan watched as Molly walked away. He liked the way her hips moved. He knew he'd be thinking about her for the rest of the day.

Molly found the key to Electra's house on the front table where Mrs. Geld had said it would be. It was an odd thought to her—having a grown woman as a daughter. To top it off, here she was about to let herself inside her house. Over the years, when people had asked her if she had children, Molly always answered no. Even though she had carried and given birth to Electra and remembered the very early weeks of holding her and feeding her, she had long since separated that experience from the rest of her life. She always thought of having children as something that she very much wanted. Yet she never acknowledged that it was ever something that she did have at one time, even if for a short while.

Molly walked up to Electra's front door. Once again, she was in front of the lion face brass knocker. This time, however, she slipped the key in the door and entered. She wasn't surprised to see another orderly home. She went to the kitchen and looked around in the drawers and cabinets for a trash bag to collect the flowers from the vases. Except for the essentials, Electra didn't have all that much food in stock. Molly noticed that most all the food Electra had was very healthy. Molly went through the house slowly, looking for the vases with the flowers that would need to be removed. She started to pull one bunch out and throw them into a bag. Then she pulled them back out again. They had not yet wilted and were too beautiful to throw away. She put the flowers back in the vase and decided that she would collect them later in the week.

Molly realized that having access to Electra's house had given her the perfect opportunity to learn more about Electra's life. She walked from room to room, looking for any pictures of Electra and her adopted family. Finally, on a table next to her beautiful grand piano, she found a picture of Electra with who she assumed was her adopted father. They were standing on the lawn down by the ferry dock. Electra looked to be about nine or ten and her adopted father was tall and thin with a full head of silver hair. He looked very serious, but also very gentle. The young girl holding his hand was looking at up him. She seemed to be a very happy child and Molly could see that there was a special connection between the man and his adopted daughter. She felt a pang of jealousy as she put the photo down and walked away to explore the rest of Electra's extravagant home.

Molly found her bedroom and instantly noticed a picture of Electra with B.J. on her dresser. They were on the Geld's sailboat. Electra had her t-shirt pulled over her knees and B.J. had his arm around her. It must have been one of those island afternoons where it got cold very quickly. They really do make a handsome couple, thought Molly. She liked B.J. and wouldn't be sorry to see them get together.

Molly knew she was being nosey by looking at all of Electra's things, but she couldn't help herself. She opened Electra's closet and looked through her clothes. All of her clothes and shoes were size 8, the same as Molly. She pulled out a few of the dresses and held them up. She was as envious of Electra's wardrobe as she had been of the Geld's kitchen. In the past, Molly had never really been too concerned with not having many material possessions, but the more she saw of what people like the Gelds and Electra had, the more she thought she wouldn't mind having her own nice things.

"This is for a dinner party next weekend," she said. Molly pretended she was at a fancy dress shop talking to an imaginary store assistant. She hung the dress on the side of the door and pulled out a pair of heels that were stylishly pointed and hand-beaded. She held them below the dress and examined the match.

"I think these will do," she said in exaggeration. "What else do you have in a size 8?"

Molly continued to go through the clothes and picked some to try on. She tried on one of the more casual outfits and wandered around the house. She sat in different rooms and imagined that she lived in Electra's house. Suddenly, a coo-coo clock in the hallway chimed out, making Molly come to her senses. She needed to get back to the Geld's house and prepare more juice for the lady of the house.

Molly was unsure if she was supposed to keep the key to Electra's house. Just to be on the safe side, when she got back she put the key back on the front entry hall table and went to look for Mrs. Geld. She found her on the sun-porch. She was lying down in her bathrobe with cucumbers on her eyes. When she heard Molly enter the room, she took the cucumbers away and sat up.

"Oh, there you are." Molly couldn't tell if Mrs. Geld was annoyed.

"I hope you weren't in need of me. I was over at Electra's," Molly answered cautiously.

"Oh, no. I'm doing fine. I helped myself to some green tea. If you can prepare the beet, apple and ginger juice, it would be wonderful. Also, B.J. mentioned that you like to swim. I just wanted to be sure you knew that you are welcome to use the pool."

"Yes. He told me. Thank you." Molly took away Mrs. Geld's empty teacup and went to make the juice. As she put the veggies through the juicer, she wondered if she should tell Mrs. Geld who she really was. She decided that she would let Electra make the choice. This was her daughter's life she had stumbled into, she reminded herself. She resolved to remain merely the housekeeper until she knew what Electra wanted. She was pretty certain that B.J. would not say anything to his mother. Molly thought again about the photo of B.J. and Electra that was on Electra's nightstand and felt another pang of jealousy. She wished that she had a male friend like B.J. when she was a teenager or any close friend for that matter.

The next morning when Molly headed up to the house for her morning chores she could see Gina moving about the kitchen. Gina seemed to be in a very good mood. She was singing as she prepared Mrs. Geld's breakfast tray.

"Hi Molly," Gina said cheerfully. "Mrs. Geld is going to the yacht club for lunch today, and then off on a boat ride with a friend of hers. What do you say we have a girls' picnic by the pool after we finish up with our work?"

Molly thought it sounded relaxing, and answered, "That would be nice." However, she still had a hard time picturing herself being 'one of the girls' with Gina or any other woman for that matter. Molly didn't really have any close woman friends. As a teenager she had always been too busy working in her 's pub and then after that she was always with a boyfriend. The thought of such female companionship was welcoming, but she couldn't help but feel she was some kind of imposter, and that Gina would soon learn that she was a betrayal to the female gender.

Molly could still hear Gina singing from upstairs when she opened up the laundry shoot to send the towels and sheets down. Molly tried to sing as she finished up with her upstairs chores, but it felt unnatural to her. Molly wondered why Gina, who seemed to be very opinionated, would take a liking to her. Molly tried to think of what she would say to her at the pool. She worried that Gina would be questioning her more about why she was on the island.

Molly gathered the fallen linens and towels and loaded them by color into the washer for her first load. She saw Gina in the garden outside the kitchen picking mint. "For some ice tea," Gina explained as she caught Molly's eye when she walked back through the laundry room door to get back in the kitchen. "It's such a perfect day. I'm totally psyched that we have the place to ourselves." Gina reached into a duffel bag she had stashed in the laundry room and pulled out a bikini.

"Here, I brought this for you. I noticed you've been swimming in your shorts. Anyway, it's never going to fit me. I bought it a couple years ago to inspire myself to do a diet."

"Thank you," Molly said slightly embarrassed. "I've never actually owned a bikini before."

"With that figure, are you nuts? Girl if I were you I'd be flaunting my stuff," Gina said swaying her hips from side to side. "What I'd give to have hips and a flat stomach, let alone long thin legs." Gina was quite petite and by no means a heavy woman. It was just that she was short and the bulk of the weight she did have was around her hips and thighs. "I do have one thing on you though," Gina said putting her tan olive skin arm up next to Molly's white and freckled arm, "I've got the Mediterranean skin and I do tan." Gina started to take her own clothes off as she said to Molly, "Put that suit on, grab a couple beach towels and let's go relax." Once she was completely naked, Gina reached back into her duffel bag and pulled out a one piece bathing suit. Pointing to her thighs, she told Molly, "They say the high cut should make my legs look longer."

Molly was still holding the bikini that Gina had given her. "Well, go ahead. Put it on," Gina said. Molly turned her back to Gina and put the bottom on under her maids' dress and then quickly pulled her dress off and replaced her bra with the bikini top. "It looks great from the back," Gina said, "turn around."

"Ah," Molly said looking down at the bottoms, "I think I need to shave first."

"A little behind on our bikini wax ey?" Gina teased her.

"Yeah, like I've never had one. I'm just going to run down to my cottage and shave. I'll meet you up by the pool. Do you have any suntan lotion though? I'm afraid I will burn like crazy."

"There should be some lotion in the same cabinet where the beach towels are."

Molly opened a drawer next to the shelf that held the beach towels and found all different levels of lotion. She grabbed the highest she could find which was a 30 and told Gina she'd meet her at the pool.

"Wow! I'm glad someone is getting use out of that bikini. You look fabulous. And I mean fabulous." Gina said to Molly who was laying a towel out on a lounge chair.

"Thanks. I hope I put enough sunscreen on though."

"You are shockingly white," Gina teased her.

"Well, I have been living in Seattle and I am Irish," Molly answered.

"I wouldn't recommend you wear a black bikini, but that pale green looks good with your white skin." Gina sat up from her chair and poured Molly an ice tea. "This is what I call the perks of the job," Gina said handing Molly her ice tea.

"So far I really can't complain," Molly said taking a sip and putting her glass back down on a side table.

"So I am sorry I laughed the other day when you mentioned that you were a failed artist. Tell me more about the work you do back in Seattle." Gina said with genuine interest.

"Oh, don't worry about that," Molly answered relieved that Gina hadn't started the conversation by asking why she was on the island. "It must have sounded funny when I said I was a failed artist. I do mostly watercolors and if I can afford the paint sometimes I also do oils. My watercolors are usually landscapes and the oils are abstract."

"Do you show your work in a gallery?"

"I'm not signed to a gallery, but I have had a couple small shows at boutique galleries and there is a tavern where my work has been displayed back in Seattle. I haven't sold enough to live on my art. I'm really not that good."

"Don't be modest. I'm sure your work is beautiful. Maybe you just haven't found the right market yet."

"My work is ok. It's more like I haven't found the right inspiration yet. My technical skills are good. Everyone always comments on that. In fact, a couple times with my watercolors, I've been told they look almost like photos."

"Hmm interesting," Gina said twirling the spoon in her ice tea. "That's sort of the same with cooking. Sometimes people tell me that a certain dish is very good, but it's rare that I get someone telling me that 'they've never tasted anything like it'."

Molly was impressed by Gina's analogy and felt she really understood what she meant. "Yeah, I'd like my work to be recognizable. So that when someone looked at my paintings they would say "oh, that's a Molly Callahan." Molly got up and started walking down the pool steps. The water was like bath water compared to the ocean. Gina joined her in the pool. They treaded water and talked more about cooking and painting and then went back to their lounge chairs.

After sunbathing for a while Gina asked, "Do you have a boyfriend back in Seattle?"

Molly, who had been lying on her stomach, flipped over and got up to take another sip of her tea. "No, actually I just broke up with a guy before I came out here."

"Ah, I get it," Gina said again in a teasing tone. "You're getting out of town for a while."

"Yeah, actually that is a big part of it."

"Oh, and you came to visit some family." Gina added remembering the conversation from the first night.

"Well, that was the excuse for coming," Molly said not wanting to bring up the Electra story with Gina quite yet.

"Oh, I understand," Gina interjected quickly. "There is nothing wrong with taking a road trip after breaking up with someone. "So why did you break up? That is if you don't mind me asking."

"No, that's ok." Molly actually welcomed having someone to talk to about Joel. "He broke up with me. He started seeing someone else."

"Ouch!" Gina said.

"Yeah, well the thing that bothers me the most about it is that he put on this whole bohemian act, and then he left me for a lawyer. He even moved into her big house out in the suburbs." Molly swatted away a fly. "If he left me for a yoga teacher or organic farmer it wouldn't have bothered me so much. I mean of course I'd be hurt, but I guess what bothers me so much is that he wasn't who I thought he was."

"No kidding. What a phony." Gina confirmed in her own mind that was what she loved about her boyfriend Stew. *He might not have exactly the same dreams as I do, but at least with him what you see is what you get, no surprises.*

"I guess it just shows I wasn't as close to him as I thought I was. That is what really hurts." Molly added.

"What did he do for a living?" Gina asked.

"Joel? He was a temp. I actually met him on an assignment we were on together at a bank. We kind of bonded over not wanting to be a part of corporate America. He loved that I was an artist. It's kind of a bummer too because after the bank, I got an assignment at the Children's Theatre. The job had the potential of going full time, but he convinced me to turn it down and do my art full time."

"What did you do for the Children's Theatre?" Gina asked interested.

"I was just doing administrative stuff for pay, but I also helped out with designing the kids' stage and just helping overall. It was a lot of fun." Molly thought back to a production they did of Peter Pan and how much fun she had helping a little boy named Jason with flying across the stage.

"So why did you quit the Children's Theatre job then?"

"Well, one of the parents was impressed by some of the work I had done on the set for their kid and it turned out that she worked in a gallery and was able to get me in on a local artists show. Joel was probably more excited than I was about that. Joel said that it was so much cooler to be an artist and that I really needed to take that opportunity. He encouraged me to spend all my time preparing for the show." Molly excused herself to go to the bathroom. The whole discussion brought back memories of Joel that slowly uncovered painful truths about him. Molly looked at herself in the mirror before leaving the bathroom. Sometimes she looked at herself as though she were looking at someone on the cover of a magazine. The woman in the mirror looked back at her with green eyes and smooth skin. She could see clearly that she was a good looking woman, particularly for her age, but she could only think of herself as being terribly plain. She had trouble associating herself with the woman in the reflection.

"So how did the art show go?" Gina asked when Molly returned from the bathroom.

"It was ok. I sold a couple pieces which was enough to cover a few months' expenses, but I didn't have any other shows lined up after that. It was very depressing and I just wasn't inspired to do much. I thought that Joel's initial encouragement meant that he was prepared to support me, but in retrospect, I think he just liked telling people his girlfriend was an artist."

"Well, it sounds like you're better off without him," Gina said getting up and putting a t-shirt over her bathing suit she said, "I'll be right back out. I'll go get the picnic lunch I promised. Gina came back out with a tray. There were a couple bowls and salad plates. "Voila, some gazpacho and shrimp salad. Both delicious and healthy."

"Wow, thank you," Molly said sitting up and positioning herself so that she could use the side table to eat.

"What about you," Molly started to ask, "You mentioned the other night that you want to open a restaurant."

"Oh, I do. The trouble is figuring out where to do it. It wouldn't work up here on the island."

"So where else have you thought of opening?" Molly asked.

"Well, actually I would love to do something here in Maine. I've also thought about Vermont. The problem is that I just don't see Stew giving up his Key West winter's quite yet."

"So you think the two of you are going to get married?" Molly asked surprising herself that she would ask such a personal question.

"We've talked about it," Gina said pushing aside her gazpacho and sticking her fork into a piece of shrimp. "He tells me he doesn't want to be with anyone but me." Gina dipped the shrimp in cocktail sauce and took a bite. "I don't think he'd mind being married as long as he could keep his same routines. It's been fun going down to Key West with him and then back up here in the summer. Almost like a never ending party, but I'm going to be 35 this year. It's time for me to settle down and get my business going. And I really want a family too. "

"You should tell him," Molly said.

"Oh, believe me I have. He understands what I want, and I know he'd like to give me what I need. The trouble is that he is not ready to give anything up."

"So what are you going to do?" Molly asked interested because she herself had failed to succeed at settling down.

"Well, I'm going to start looking for properties on my days off this summer and if he is serious about being with me and letting me fulfill my dream then he will help me make it happen. I've gone down to Key West for five years now. I think I did my part."

"I've never been to Key West, but I can only imagine that spending the majority of the year down there versus New England must be dramatically different. It seems like it would be a good place for business, and it sounds like Stew has a good job there."

"That's all true. But Key West isn't my vision. I want a quaint New England restaurant with a fireplace and I want to be challenged by the change of weather for seasonal specials. I don't know. I guess it's also hard to imagine a childhood for my children in Florida since my childhood was spent in New England. Stew is originally from Maine so I know his family would be happier if he settled here. "

"Well at least you know what you want." Molly said thinking she wished she were so sure of what she wanted.

"Yes, I do know what I want." Gina said stretching her legs out on the lounge chair. She tilted her head back and closed her eyes.

On a quiet morning a couple days after her lunch with Gina, Molly was finishing up vacuuming in one of the Geld's guest rooms when she paused to look out the window. The angle of the boats moored out front seemed to center the view of a small island in the distance. She thought the image would be perfect for sketching and even better for painting, with the contrasting greens of the lawn and trees and the blue hues of the water and sky. It had been a long time since Molly had felt inspired to paint—and even longer since she had such an impulse to drop everything she was doing and follow her creativity. Usually when she painted, she would sit down in front of a blank canvas and agonize over how to fill it. That morning, however, she couldn't think of anything more she wanted to do than to take what she was seeing out the window and recreate it on canvas. She hadn't intended on painting on the trip, and was even prepared to give her art up for good after the failure of her last show. Molly had been thinking more about her art after her poolside conversation with Gina. She thought maybe she was giving up on her own dream too soon. Molly realized that she had lost her art to Joel. She had allowed it to be something it was not for the sake of impressing him. Molly wanted to reclaim her own vision of what her art meant to her. She found Gina's determination to be uplifting. Molly had a few supplies in her truck. Perhaps she had known all along that she would want to paint again.

When Molly finished her chores, she went to the truck and retrieved her sketchpad, pencils, and paints. She found a spot outside just below the window she had been looking out of earlier. The view wasn't quite the same from the ground, however, so she went back up to the guestroom to set up instead. She made sure to shut the door behind her and then she found a space in front of the window in the bathroom. She used the toilet as her seat and the towel rack as a makeshift easel. Molly had been drawing an outline for a few hours when, from the guest bathroom window, she caught sight of Nathan knocking on her cottage door. She remembered that he had offered to bring her along to his sailing lessons that day. Molly moved her picture to the side and cranked the handle on the window, which opened sideways instead of up and down. It didn't open wide enough for her to stick her head out so she shouted to Nathan as loud as she could, hoping that he would hear her. At first, Nathan wasn't sure where her voice was coming from.

"Do you still want to come to sail with the kids?" he shouted back in no particular direction.

"Yes, I do! Just give me a couple minutes," she called down to him. She wasn't sure why she told him yes since she had been very engaged in her painting. She supposed it had just been a natural response.

"We need to drive there. Meet me up in the driveway and not the dock," Nathan said as he turned to go. Molly gathered all her things and rushed down to her cottage to drop them off. Then she grabbed a sweater and went out to Nathan's car.

"Why are we driving? Isn't sailing that way?" Molly asked, pointing to the water.

"Yes, but where we are going is on the other side of the island. It would take too long to go by boat."

"I thought we passed by it yesterday. It didn't seem far."

"That was the yacht club. It's private. We're going to the town boat club. You don't have to have a membership to learn how to sail there."

When they arrived, a group of island kids of varying ages were gathered on the dock. They all shouted out, "Hello Mr. Potter!" Then one of the boys looked at Molly.

"Are you Mr. Potter's girlfriend?" he asked.

"I'm just a friend," she replied, blushing.

"This is Molly," Nathan said to the kids. "Everyone say hello."

"Hello Molly," they said in chorus.

"She is going to learn how to sail this summer too. And if we do a good job teaching her, she is going to teach us how to do a play. Do you guys want to do a play?"

"Do you mean like Snow White?" one of the little girls asked.

"Snow white is lame," said a boy. "How about Spider Man?"

"I'll tell you what we will do," Nathan said. "Everybody go through your books tonight and next week when we meet, you can tell Molly your ideas. Then we'll let her pick."

"She's a girl. She's going to pick something stupid and girly!" one of the boys said.

"Okay then. I'll pick the play," Nathan said. "Now let's get ready to learn how to turn the boat. Molly, why don't you go with these two," Nathan said, pointing to two boys at the back of the group. "They know how to pull up the sail and get everything ready to go."

Nathan walked over to the boys. "I want you to show Molly how to get the boat ready just like I showed you, okay?" The two boys were excited to be chosen. They nodded their heads and raced each other to get on the boat. Molly reluctantly followed behind a little red head boy with freckles and another toe-head boy with skin as white as hers.

The group had a good afternoon. They took turns going out on the boat and learning how to shout 'Jibe!' and then quickly ducking after pushing the tiller away from the sail. They also learned how to shout, 'Ready about hard to lee!' while ducking as the boat turned a little slower. The children did a great job of showing off for their new grown-up classmate.

"Maybe you could ask Mrs. Geld for Tuesdays off so that you won't have to worry about missing the kids summer camp day," Nathan said to Molly as the two were driving back to the Geld's house from the class. Nathan wanted to be sure he spent all of his days off that summer with Molly. This was the first excuse he could think of.

"That might be a good idea," Molly answered. Then she added, "It was a lot of fun. But, you were quick to sign me up for the children's theatre program."

"Well, you told me you loved working at the Children's Theatre in Seattle. Anyway, I thought it would give you a chance to have a little authority. I imagine it's a bit rough having little kids tell you what to do."

"They weren't telling me what to do. They were reinforcing their recent knowledge," Molly said smiling thinking about how cute the kids had been. It had really reminded her of the days she spent with the kids at the theatre. She just loved some of the silly things kids said. Molly thought again about how she had let Joel convince her to quit the job working with the children. Hadn't he noticed how happy she had been? She knew she needed to start taking better care of doing the things that made her happy. She wanted to be more like Gina. *How had Mrs. Geld described her... Vivacious?*

"So, are you going to do it?"

"Yes, I'd love to keep working with the kids, and I'll do my best to help with some kind of skit. It will have to be something simple." Molly smiled. She looked out the window at the island scenery going by. It had indeed been the most perfect day. She had felt content to be alone and painting in the morning and then happy again to be with Nathan and the kids in the afternoon. For what seemed like the first time, Molly had coexisted in both the world of her own private creativity and that of enjoying the company of others, both on the same day.

Molly realized that she was getting herself more and more attached to island life. She worried that if her conversation or eventual meeting with Electra did not go well, that it would be tough to break away.

CHAPTER SEVEN – Trouble Overseas

.J. was daydreaming about Electra when her name popped up on his cell phone. It startled him with its loud ring.

"Hello B.J.! This is Electra. Can you hear me?"

"Yes, where are you calling from?"

"I'm in Dublin. We just arrived this morning. I was having a Guinness with Matthew when I noticed that I had a new message on my cell phone. I thought it might be you so I listened to it. You're not going to believe who it was."

"Slow down. First of all, you don't drink beer."

"I don't. I'm having a Guinness," Electra laughed.

"Are you drunk?" B.J. asked. "And who is Matthew? I thought you were there with Jimmy."

"Jimmy is here. It's a long story. Matthew is the son of the drummer from Jimmy's first band in Boston. He's a journalist and he came along to do a story on Jimmy. I was against the idea at first, but Jimmy has been so busy doing interviews and always being whisked away by his manager that I'm glad Matthew came along." Electra winked at Matthew who was standing next to her.

"How old is he?" B.J. asked, concerned.

"He's our age. You'd really like him. I've invited him to the island in August for my party. Anyway, you haven't asked who the message was from."

"I'm sorry. I'm just not used to hearing you sound this way."

"What way?"

"All giddy."

"I'm just a little excited. I was so worried when I left the island, and now it seems that things are all falling into place," Electra took her free hand and reached for Matthew's hand as she continued to tell B.J., "The message was from Molly, my birth mother. She did come and she is on the island now. She is at your house as a matter of fact." Electra paused a moment and then asked B.J. in a non accusing but curious way, "Did you know about any of this?"

B.J. was still taken aback by the news that Electra was traveling with another young man. After a few moments, he composed himself enough to speak.

"Yes, I knew," he said.

"Why didn't you tell me?" Electra asked.

"She asked me not to tell you. She wanted to tell you herself," B.J. said, remembering that it was really Nathan who had asked him not to say anything to Electra.

"I suppose it is better this way. What is she like?" On her end of the receiver, Electra excitedly squeezed Matthew's hand.

"Did you notice the woman who was serving with Gina on the night of the lobster bake?" B.J. asked

"Oh, my God. I do remember that woman. I had a strange feeling about her. I just can't believe that was my mother!" There was a break in the conversation and B.J. could hear Electra telling the news to someone he presumed to be Matthew. B.J. couldn't quite hear the rest of what Electra was saying, but he definitely heard a man's voice in response.

Who was comforting Electra and why did she sound so happy? B.J. thought in desperation. He had not anticipated her meeting someone else, at least not so soon after venturing off the island. The night he went over to her house after the lobster bake, he had thought about telling her his feelings as everyone suggested he should. Then she got the call about Jimmy and he didn't think it was the right timing. He wanted her to be ready, but now she was traveling around Europe with some drummer's son.

"Electra, are you there?"

"Yes. I'm here. I was just telling Matthew about how I've actually already seen her. Does she know that I am traveling?"

"Yes, she does. I told my mother to ask her to go over to your house to keep it in order until you return."

"That is weird having her cleaning my house."

"I can tell her not to go, and get someone else."

"No, she might get offended. Listen, will you be going to the island this weekend? Can you tell Molly that I want to speak with her? Or maybe you could call her and ask her to ring me again. Tell her she can call from my house."

It was only Tuesday morning when Electra had called. B.J. had planned to go to the island that weekend, but he quickly decided that he would go sooner. He needed the excuse to call Electra back. He absolutely had to make sure that this Matthew guy was not making the moves on Electra before he had a chance to tell her how he felt.

"I hope you can reach me tomorrow before we go to Sligo. We're leaving in the afternoon. I'm not sure if we can get phone reception once we're there," Electra continued, "but we'll only be there for a couple of weeks and then we're going to Munich. The Quarter Moons have a concert there." *A few more weeks was much too long for her to be gone*, B.J. thought.

"How is Jimmy? Will he be okay to play?" B.J. asked, thinking they might change their mind about the concert in Munich.

"He seems fine, and he is committed to do the concert in Munich," Electra answered to B.J.'s disappointment.

"Are you sure it's a good idea so soon after the last concert?" B.J. asked trying to sound concerned for Jimmy.

"He'll be fine. He promised to take it easy in Sligo. He says his Mum will spoil us all rotten and we can be lazy. It's on the water, so I imagine we'll just relax in the sun and maybe go to a pub for a Guinness."

B.J. hardly recognized the way Electra was talking and he couldn't stand the thought of her being on what sounded like a full fledge vacation with some other guy.

"I'm glad you called. You know I'm always here for you," B.J. said, hoping to remind her of their long history together. "Also, I'll actually be going up to the island today so I can call you tomorrow morning with Molly on the line?"

"You're the best, B.J.. Talk to you later."

"I love you," B.J. said. But she had already hung up.

B.J., who had been getting ready to leave for work when Electra called, paced around his Manhattan apartment. He needed to get up to the Island. His father would object for certain, but he knew that it was absolutely necessary to get Electra back on the Island sooner than later. He thought to himself that Molly owed him one. He could have told Electra who she was and he hadn't. He'd remind her of that. Maybe Molly could convince Electra that she needed to come back, that she needed to see her mother sooner. After all, hadn't she traveled all that distance just to see her? He really needed to get Molly talking to Electra and get Electra back to Ridgeport where she belonged. Maybe, B.J. thought, he could call the house and get his mother to put Molly on the phone. But how could he explain that he needed to talk to Molly? B.J. confided in his mother about many things in his life. He had told her about Benilde. He couldn't have her thinking he had made such a mistake again. Electra's secret about her mother was one thing he could not share. There was no way around it. He needed to get to the island and speak directly to Molly.

B.J. called into the office and let his secretary know where he'd be and left his apartment to catch a taxi to the airport. He would think of something to say to his father later.

Nathan was in his barn working on his sailboat when he got a call from B.J.

"Nathan. It's B.J.. I need to ask you a favor. I need you to pick me up this afternoon over in Oakharbor."

"It's only Tuesday. I thought you and your Dad wouldn't be here until Friday?"

"I'll tell you about it later," B.J. said. "I'm going to be working from Maine for the rest of the week."

"I'm surprised your Dad doesn't do that more often."

"Well, he won't be too happy that I'm doing it, but I don't have to visit with my customers in person as much as he does. I have all the lower level accounts at this point so I do most of my business over the phone. He'll be upset because of what it will look like to the others in the firm, but I'll get my work done. I really need to get to Maine, Nathan."

"I know you love it here, but why the rush?"

"Like I said, I'll tell you when I get there."

"You know it is my day off, but for you I'll do it." Nathan said with a slightly sarcastic tone. He loved B.J., but hated being interrupted on his day off. "What should I tell your mother about your early arrival if she asks? She won't like you skipping out of work any more than your father."

B.J. had already been thinking about potential excuses. He told Nathan to tell his mother that he had some research to do on a portfolio of companies for one of his new clients and that he needed privacy to get this done in the time that the new client had requested. This was partially true because he did, in fact, have such a project with a new green fund he was setting up.

"And Nathan, do you think you could bring Molly with you?" B.J. asked, knowing that it was a strange request.

"OK. I think you're in luck because today is her day off as well. " Nathan answered; glad to have an excuse to invite her. "But why do you want her to come?"

"It has to do with Electra," said B.J.. "See you soon," B.J. hung up before Nathan could ask about Electra.

Nathan could see Molly working on a painting as he approached her cottage. She was facing the window, and when she saw him she waved him in with her paintbrush.

"Nice painting," Nathan commented looking at her work. She was doing a watercolor of the Geld's sailboat *The Promise*.

"Thanks. I was sitting here reading this morning when I noticed the angle of the boat on the mooring was just perfect for a sketch." Molly put her brush in a water jar and wiped her hands on a cloth. "That was early this morning," Molly sighed, "I've been at it ever since, but it feels really good."

"I hate to interrupt your work, but I have a favor to ask."

Molly realized she had forgotten about the kids' sailing class. "Oh my God what time is it? I'm so sorry I forgot about the class."

Nathan had also forgotten, "Oh, shit. The class. Can I borrow your phone?"

"You know I don't have a phone in the cottage. Where is your cell? Molly asked.

"I'll be right back. It's just in the boat. I need to call my sister and see if she can cover." Nathan shook his head as he turned around and headed quickly out the door and back down to the dock. *I cannot believe I forgot the sailing class,* Nathan thought to himself as he pulled his cell phone out of his windbreaker pocket and dialed his sister's cell phone number. *My summer routine has been seriously interrupted. I don't know why I am letting myself get pulled into all this drama.* Nathan had a frown on his face as he waited for his sister to pick up his call. He wasn't sure what he would do if she were not available. He was pleasantly surprised when Sarah told him that she could take his place with the kids. Nathan quickly shifted thoughts from the kids' class back to Molly. Nathan was fairly sure she would agree to go with him once he told her that B.J. wanted to speak with her about Electra, but when it came to Molly he could never be sure what to expect.

Nathan walked back up to Molly's cottage. He was swinging his arms by his side and looking very intent.

"So, what happened to the class?" Molly asked as he got back inside.

"It's no problem, my sister can cover."

Molly had packed up her paints and set the easel in the corner. "Well, I'm ready to go, but where are we going?"

"B.J. asked me to go pick him up in the mainland. We have a few hours yet, but I wouldn't have made it in time if we did the class."

"But it's your day off."

"I know, but B.J. sounded pretty distraught. He also requested for you to go along with me. I guess he has something to tell you about Electra."

"Is she ok?" Molly asked concerned.

"He didn't say." Nathan looked over at the painting that had been set aside. I'm sorry I didn't mean for you to just drop everything. I was just frazzled when you reminded me about the class. Why don't I make it up to you and take you out for a bite to eat on the mainland while we wait for B.J.?"

"Actually, that would be nice," Molly answered. It had been a long time since anyone had taken her out to eat, and she had been so absorbed in her painting that she had not stopped to eat.

Molly was quick to get aboard the motorboat and once they got started Nathan was driving faster than usual. Ten minutes into the ride, Molly tapped Nathan on the shoulder and then clasped her hands around each elbow to show that she was cold. Nathan opened the seat cabinet and pulled out his extra sweatshirt for her. It was starting to feel very comfortable between them.

After they tied the boat up, Nathan took Molly's hand and led her to a restaurant that had a porch overlooking the docks.

"Let's eat here so we can look out for B.J. when he arrives." Nathan suggested.

"OK," Molly agreed. It looked like a nice place and she was certain that with it being on the water, they would have lobster rolls which she had already decided on.

As they ate their meal, Molly and Nathan discussed what it could possibly be that B.J. needed to speak with them about. It must be about Jimmy, they decided. Maybe he had fallen ill again. Nathan tried to get Molly to talk more about Jimmy. He wanted to gage her current feelings for him, but instead Molly changed the subject.

"I wonder how your sister is doing with the day camp?"

"Oh, the kids love her. I'm sure it's going well," Nathan said still feeling bad that he had forgotten about it. They talked about the kids and some potential ideas for a play that they might do. Nathan was glad to see a shift in Molly. She seemed so much more relaxed. He on the other hand felt very uneasy. They were finishing up a couple pieces of apple pie that Nathan had insisted on when they saw B.J. walking down toward Nathan's boat.

Nathan got the check and they rushed down to meet B.J.

"So, what is it B.J.? Is Electra okay? Is it Jimmy?" Molly asked excitedly.

"Everyone is fine." B.J. explained. "Electra called from Dublin. She said Jimmy has been busy with interviews and the band. She told me that she got your message and she is very excited to speak with you. I would have called, but I wasn't sure how to get you on the phone without my mother asking why I needed to speak with you."

"You could have called me," Nathan said. "I'd have gotten Molly on the phone for you." B.J. considered this for a moment and realized that Nathan's suggestion would have been possible. He hadn't thought of it, and anyway, somehow he knew that he needed to explain all of this to Molly in person. He needed her to understand how important it was for Electra to come home soon and not stay away until August.

"It's too late to call Electra now," B.J. explained, his voice urgent, "but we need to call her first thing in the morning. She said that they are leaving for Jimmy's mother's place in Sligo in the afternoon which would be morning here. You're up early to swim, right Molly?" B.J. asked in a tone that was more of a statement than a question.

"Yes, we can call first thing in the morning." Molly said. "I don't know what I will say to her, though."

"Tell her she needs to get back and that you've traveled all this way to meet her," B.J. said.

Molly was sure she would tell her no such thing. "I will tell her that I am looking forward to meeting her, but I cannot tell her to change her plans." Molly was actually glad for the additional time to enjoy her newfound life on the island before having to meet Electra.

"Why not?" B.J. demanded. "She asked you to change your plans. Or were you planning to drive to Maine this summer anyways?"

"She asked to meet me, but she never asked that I come to Maine. I was the one who decided to drive clear across the country."

"You could still ask her," B.J. objected.

"I know you like the girl," Nathan said, "but why the hurry? She'll be back in a few weeks."

"Why the hurry?" B.J. said, raising his voice, "I'll tell you why. When she called to tell me that she got your message, she also told me that Jimmy had invited along another man our age named Matthew Page. She said that their fathers had played in a band together years ago."

"Mathew Page?" Molly repeated. *I wonder if that is Kate and Mark's baby. She was pregnant before me. He'd probably be a few months older than Electra.* Molly's thoughts turned back to the days of the Flip Coin band.

Nathan did not like this person turning up from Jimmy and Molly's past any more than B.J.. "So what's the deal with Matthew and Electra?" he asked. "Do you think they're together?"

"That would be weird," Molly chimed in.

"Don't even say it," B.J. said. "They can't be dating. But I tell you, I have never heard Electra sound the way she did. Hopefully, she is just happy to hear from you and happy that Jimmy is okay. I mean, don't get me wrong. I want her to be happy, just not with another man."

"Hey, mate, we told you to tell Electra how you felt about her the night of the lobster bake," Nathan reminded him.

"I hardly thought she would be taking a trip to Europe with this Matthew fellow a week later. I was going to say something after she got back from visiting Jimmy in the hospital. Then I tried to tell her on the phone when she called from Dublin, but she had already hung up."

Nathan had never seen B.J. so undone. "I'm sure she is just excited about hearing from Molly and about Jimmy being okay and going to Ireland with him," Nathan said, hoping to make B.J. feel better.

"She only just met Matthew, right?" Molly asked.

"As far as I know," B.J. answered.

"Then she's hardly going to run off and marry the guy. Don't worry about it," Nathan said.

"We'll call first thing in the morning," B.J. reminded Molly. He was very worried about the Matthew guy, and nothing anyone could say would calm him down.

When they got to the island, Mrs. Geld was very surprised to see B.J.. However, she seemed to buy into the excuse that he needed to work in a quiet place. They all went to bed early, although B.J. hardly slept a wink.

At six am, he knocked on Molly's door. She was already up and making coffee. She opened the door to let him in and asked if he would like some. B.J. accepted the mug that Molly had just made for herself. As she was fixing a second cup of coffee, B.J. dialed Electra's number on his cell phone. From the kitchen, Molly could hear that B.J. had reached her in Dublin. Molly's heart started to pound. Finally, B.J. handed his phone to Molly. He seemed to be very shaken up and had a concerned look on his face. Molly took the phone from B.J., her own hands shaking.

"Hello Electra," she began and then cleared her throat. "This is Molly."

"Hello. Thank you for calling." Electra's heart started to beat very fast and her hands were suddenly clammy. She thought she might just drop B.J.s cell phone. She wiped her hand on her pants and then put the phone closer to her ear.

"Did you get my message? I'm sorry it got cut off. You must think I'm a crazy person." Molly said. She had sat down and was tapping her foot at a furious pace.

"No," Electra started to say and then corrected her, "I mean Yes, I got the message, but no, I don't think you're a crazy person." Electra had in fact been wondering if Molly was a little crazy. There was a short silence and then Electra added. "I'm sorry that I left the island so quickly and missed you."

"It's my fault that we didn't meet." Molly said and then asked nervously, "When will you be going back to Maine?"

"I don't plan to be back for three weeks. Matthew and I are going with Jimmy to meet his mum." Electra paused for a moment. "I guess that would be my grandmother," she continued. "Then we're going to Munich for a show."

"Oh," Molly said. B.J. was pacing around and motioning with his hands for Molly to say something more about wanting to see her sooner. Molly couldn't bring herself to ask Electra to come sooner. The call was hard enough for her to do. Instead she said, "I think that B.J. would like to speak to you again. Should I put him back on?" Molly didn't wait for an answer before handing the phone back to B.J.. "I'm sorry," Molly whispered to B.J. as she handed him his phone back.

"When did you say you're coming back?" B.J. asked straight away.

"Not for a few weeks. I told you that when I called you from the hospital," Electra reminded him.

"I know. I just thought now that you know about Molly being here, that you might have considered coming home sooner."

"Well, I can't really. You're not going to believe this, but I sat in a rehearsal and Matthew convinced the band to have me sing with them. You know back up vocals. I usually just sing classical and opera, but we kind of improvised. My singing gave some of the songs a whole new sound that the band really liked." Electra smiled and thought about the afternoon when she and Matthew were listening in on one of the band's rehearsals. She remembered how Matthew had given her a little push and told her she should sing backups with the band. She had thought he was crazy at the time, and she wasn't even sure how he got her to just step up and start singing with them. *Matthew definitely has an ear for music.* Electra thought to herself and then continued telling B.J., "Anyway, it's pretty amazing, but the band asked me to sing backup for their show in Munich. The weird thing is that it totally feels natural. I mean, I'm not even nervous thinking about it. I do want to meet Molly, but I'm' sure you can imagine this is a pretty unique opportunity. Maybe you could put Molly back on the phone. I want to let her know that I do feel really bad about not coming back sooner."

B.J. reluctantly gave the phone back to Molly.

"Molly," Electra said very sincerely, "I feel very bad about how long I will be gone after you went all that way to see me. But it sounds like you'll be on the island for the summer now that you've taken the job at the Gelds."

"I hope you don't mind that I did that?" Molly asked wondering if Electra was trying to tell her something.

"Oh, no. I guess it's a little weird, but it's going to work out well." Electra was very preoccupied with the excitement of being with Matthew and singing with the band that the full impact of the fact that her birth mother whom she had not yet met was spending the summer as a housekeeper for her neighbors.

"I'm glad you don't mind. The Geld's are very nice people. And you are very lucky to have a friend like B.J.," Molly added.

"Oh, speaking of B.J.," Electra said excitedly. "I have some good news for him.

"I met the keyboard player, George, in Jimmy's band. He is amazing and very good-looking. He saw a picture of me and B.J. that I have in my wallet." Electra didn't quite confess that she had taken it out of her wallet to show George. Electra continued telling Molly "George, was immediately smitten, and so I told him I'd introduce him to B.J.."

"Why would you introduce the keyboard player to B.J.?" Molly asked Electra. She was confused.

"You know, because B.J. is gay."

"Why would you think that?" Molly asked, putting her hand over the mouth of B.J.'s cell phone. With her hand muting the receiver, she whispered to B.J..

"I think you need to talk to Electra," she said softly to the distraught young man. "She wants you to meet George, the keyboard player of the Quarter Moon's. B.J., she thinks you're gay." B.J. grabbed the phone away from Molly and spoke in a voice Electra had never heard before.

"You what? Why would you think that? Electra, I'm not gay."

"It's OK B.J., Benilde told me last summer," Electra stammered. "I was telling her how I had always been a little in love with you. Then she told me that you were gay."

"And you believed her? Why would you believe her?"

"Why would she tell me that you were gay if it wasn't true?" This situation had gotten far worse than B.J. had ever anticipated. He was not used to being so out of control of his emotions.

"She must have been jealous," B.J. said.

"Why would Benilde be jealous?"

"It's a long story, but let's just say we fooled around once last summer. I didn't have sex with her or anything, but she got the wrong idea. It was a huge mistake on my part. I don't even know how I could have let it happen. You know, it's not like me to do anything like that. I tried to tell her the next day that it was a mistake. She was very insulted and thought that I was rejecting her because she was a housecleaner. I told her that that had nothing to do with it and that I was already very much in love with someone else. She pressed me to tell her who it was because she didn't believe me, so I told her. Electra, I told her that I was in love with you."

Electra could hardly believe what she just heard. "You told her you were in love with me?" Electra asked tentatively. "Why would you say something like that?"

"Because I was in love with you. And I still am in love with you."

"You're in love with me?" Electra asked. "This is a bit of a surprise."

"Listen, I am happy that you are having a good time," B.J. said. "This wasn't the way I wanted to tell you. Do I really seem gay to you?"

"I don't know. Why wouldn't I believe Benilde? Think about it—you never bring any girlfriends to Maine. And I've never seen you with a girl in New York either. I don't think I ever even heard you talk about another girl."

"Did I ever tell you about a boyfriend?"

"No, but I just thought maybe you hadn't told your mom yet and you didn't want anyone on the island to know. You know, your mom wouldn't be the easiest person to tell something like that to, with all her traditions. You also had your frat brother—what was his name?— David, stay with you last summer. I guess I just assumed he was your boyfriend. But, anyway, if you were in love with me why were you fooling around with Benilde?" Electra could not in the least bit picture B.J. hitting on someone.

B.J. realized that he was still in a bit of a corner. "I don't know why something happened with Benilde. It was a mistake, apparently a bigger mistake than I could have known. I'm really sorry I had to tell you this way. I hope that you can believe that it's true. I really do care about you."

"Is that why Benilde is gone?" Electra asked.

"No. She got over it. Her mother is really ill. I also think she was tired of being away from home so much. I'm sorry that I didn't tell you last year before all of this happened. I know you have a lot on your mind right now and you did on the Fourth as well. That was why I didn't tell you then. Plus, I just always imagined a more romantic way of telling you, but now I wish that I had said something sooner."

"It certainly comes as a surprise."

"Maybe you can think about me, about us, just a little bit, Electra." There was a silence on the other end as Electra took in all that B.J. had just told her. B.J., not being able to stand the awkwardness that had suddenly fallen between them, changed the subject.

"Speaking of surprises, you mentioned that you were considering making an announcement about your birth parents at the party you're planning in August. Do you want us to tell my mother about Molly?"

"Hmm. I'm not so sure that is such a good idea. Maybe, you should wait."

"OK. I'm not so sure that Molly is going to want to meet Jimmy. You might want to talk to her about that."

After hearing that last comment, Molly reached out for the phone and took it from B.J.. "Electra, I am very much looking forward to meeting you," Molly said quickly. She looked at B.J. with panic on her face. "But I also need to say that I would like to request some time to think about whether or not I should meet Jimmy if you bring him to Maine later this summer." Molly tapped her foot as she thought about what to say next. She had no intention of meeting Jimmy again, but she did not want to upset Electra. "It's been a long time, and maybe some things are best left alone." It was all Molly could think of to say. She wanted to tell her how long it took for her to get over Jimmy and that she simply couldn't face him, but the words just would not come out.

"Let's be glad that we have all found each other," Molly continued. "Things are working out very well for me here. Also, I won't tell Mrs. Geld who I am. It will be awkward, but probably the best thing to do." Molly thought about her job and the money she'd have at the end of the summer. And she thought of Nathan and how he had helped her gain the courage to call Electra. She didn't want to upset how well things had been going for her personally if there was no need to do so.

"I am looking forward to meeting you when I get back," Electra said. "We'll have so much to talk about. It means so much to me that you have opened up this part of your past. I had a wonderful life with my adopted dad. I can tell you all about him. He was a very special person."

Molly wanted to say that she could see that from the photo she saw of Electra and her father, but was careful not to let Electra know that she had been snooping about her house.

"I'd love to hear about him," Molly said, although she wasn't really sure that she wanted to hear about the person who had taken her place as a parent to her daughter.

Electra knew she was pushing her luck by saying what she said next. "Jimmy really wants to see you, Molly. I understand that you need to think about it, but I just thought you should know how he feels." Of course, Molly had wondered for years about what Jimmy had thought about her, but she still didn't want to see him. She was just too embarrassed about how she had behaved and what a failure she had made of her life since she had last seen him.

"Thank you for letting me know," she told Electra, "I think we all have a lot to think about before we rush into too many things."

B.J. furrowed his eyes at Molly's last comment, thinking that he didn't want Electra rushing into anything with Matthew. Frantic to say something more to Electra, B.J. took the phone from Molly. "Think about what I said." He told Electra. "I mean about my feelings for you. I do love you very much."

"I will B.J.. We'll talk before I return. I have to go now though. Bye."

Electra's mind was spinning in a million different directions as she clicked her cell phone off and rejoined Matthew who was sitting nearby in the hotel room busy reading the most recent edition of Spin Magazine. Electra could tell by how absorbed he was that he hadn't been paying attention to her call and she was greatly relieved not to have to explain anything to him just yet.

"Well. That's an interesting start to the day." B.J. said to Molly.

Molly looked at B.J. sympathetically and said, "Don't worry she only just met that Matthew guy."

"I wished I hadn't said anything about Benilde." B.J. knew it had been a mistake to tell Electra. *I suppose it serves me right for letting anything happen with Benilde*. B.J. thought to himself. "The ironic part is that I think I partially did it because my frat brother was here visiting and he really thought that Benilde was the cat's meow. Back at school, he was the ladies man." B.J. told Molly, "I don't know, maybe in my pathetic way I was trying to show off to him— you know a macho thing, not a gay thing. To think that all the while, Electra thought he was my boyfriend. The only thing more depressing than that is my job. Speaking of which, I better start working."

B.J. put his coffee cup in the sink. Molly wanted to ask him why his job was depressing. She was under the impression that he was wildly successful. Instead, she simply said "good luck" as he retreated from her cottage to go start his work day in his Dad's study.

Molly rinsed out the mugs from their morning coffee. She felt relieved to have a few extra weeks before she would meet Electra, and she was pleased by how easily Electra had spoken to her. It was nice that the first step in meeting her daughter had taken place over the phone. She realized that she should have called from Seattle first, but she was glad that she didn't. She would have never ended up with her job at the Gelds or living in the cottage. She also would have never met Nathan, Molly thought with a smile. Just then, Nathan pulled up in the motorboat and as he got to her cottage door he knocked lightly and spoke her name "Molly," Nathan called out to her. She liked the way her name sounded with a Maine accent. It made her feel like someone who belonged, like a local.

"Coming," Molly yelled back, and went to let Nathan in.

"Hello!" he said as she got closer to the door.

Nathan was happy to see that Molly was smiling. He had been worried that she might have been upset by the call to Electra.

"Have a seat on the sofa," Molly said as she let him in the door. Nathan preferred to sit on the stool at the kitchen bar, but he took Molly's direction and sat down on the sofa.

"Did you and B.J. get through to Electra?" he asked.

"Let me get the coffee started and then I'll tell you about it," Molly said, putting the kettle, which was still warm from her coffee with B.J., back on the stove. Nathan settled in to the couch as Molly once again spooned coffee into the single serving French press. When it was ready, Molly brought the coffee over to Nathan. She sat down in the overstuffed chair next to the sofa and recounted the conversation she and B.J. had with Electra.

Nathan took a sip of coffee and then stretched his legs out. He hadn't put his coffee cup back down yet, when Molly got to the part about Electra telling Molly how she thought that B.J. was gay. Nathan spilled some of the coffee on the sofa as he shook with laughter.

"Electra thought B.J. was gay?" He asked Molly. Still laughing, he placed his coffee cup on the table. As Nathan settled back into the couch, he noticed that he had spilled the coffee on the couch.

"Sorry about that," he said.

Molly, who hadn't noticed the spill at first, jumped up and went over to the sink to get a dampened sponge. She ran over and tried to soak up the coffee, worried that it would permanently stain the Geld's sofa.

"It's not funny," she said, wiping up the spill and blotting it dry with the paper towel. "Seriously, the poor boy was devastated."

Nathan thought it over a moment. "Was it last summer that Benilde told Electra B.J. was gay?" he asked

"I think so. Why?"

Nathan crossed his legs and wiped a stray curl away that had fallen from his forehead into his eye.

"Last summer, B.J. had one of his old fraternity brothers here for a couple of weeks. Electra probably thought he was a boyfriend." Nathan chuckled again then continued. "I don't know what they do in those frats, but those boys get pretty tight. I could see how Electra might have gotten the wrong idea." Nathan took another sip of his coffee, careful to return it to the table quickly.

"That poor boy has the worse luck," he continued. "The same frat brother is apparently working at the company where B.J. really wanted to work." Nathan had heard the boys talking about their jobs and was himself a bit surprised to learn that B.J. had turned down the job of his choice to work for his father.

"You mean B.J. didn't really want to work with the Geld Group?"

"He graduated top of his class at Harvard Business School. Don't get me wrong. The Geld Group is a good company, but he could have gone anywhere."

"The Geld's company must be pretty good to afford all this," Molly said, pointing to the boats docked outside and to the big house on the hill.

"Well, let's you and me both hope that the Geld's can really afford all this. I have to admit, I worry sometimes about the day they won't. The new folks that come to this island bring their own help— and from God knows where. It's the old families like the Gelds you want to work for. They know how to treat their employees."

"You really enjoy working for the Geld's don't you?" Molly who had been thinking a lot herself about how much she was enjoying her job asked.

"I do. What about you?"

"I do too." Molly said wiping her hand across the wet spot on the sofa, making sure that the stain was gone. "I like it a lot actually. I just worry that I'm going to do something wrong and fail at my job. And I worry about what the Geld's will think of me when they find out why I am really here." After Molly said that, she realized that, once again, she was exposing her vulnerable side to Nathan. And once again, it felt safe.

Nathan sensed that Molly was feeling comfortable with him and quickly asked her about her plans for the next day.

"Would you like me to pick you up after you finish with the house tasks tomorrow morning? I can take you on a picnic" he said. "I have a spot in mind that I think you're going to love. It's so beautiful; you may want to bring your sketch pad."

"That sounds wonderful." Molly answered thinking about how nice it was to spend time just relaxing with Nathan. "Mrs. Geld has already mentioned that she is going to the yacht club for lunch so I should be able to get done by noon."

"Perfect. I'll meet you down at the dock at midday."

B.J. went straight to his father's study after leaving Molly's cottage that morning. He was glad to get back to work as it took his mind off of Electra and Matthew. As far as B.J. knew, his father only made use of the study to smoke cigars and drink port, but it was set up with every essential of a working office. It was far more productive than being in the office where B.J. was constantly being interrupted. He had a new client of considerable wealth who wanted him to set up a green fund. B.J. knew that the only way for the Geld group to compete with the larger firms was to have a niche, and having a client with deep pockets and a press worthy name, he thought would be a good start.

B.J. worked steadily for the next few days researching renewable power sources, biodegradable plastics and eco restoration companies. The bottom line didn't look too promising on the majority, but he was pleased to find a few worth tracking. On

Friday, his mother informed him that he needed to pick his father up from the mainland and that he should use the time to talk to his father.

"I think you should talk to your father on the ride back," she told him. "He's not too happy that you left the office—even if you have work to do. It doesn't look good to the other junior associates. You can't be taking advantage just because your father is the President."

B.J. wanted to tell his mother that the other junior associates thought his father was a joke and that they knew that it was, in fact, B.J. who was pulling the firm up by its bootstraps. He didn't want to ruin her image of his father, though. He also wanted to get the speech over with sooner rather than later, so he said nothing.

When B.J. pulled up to the docks in Camden, his father was just getting out of a taxi. As he docked the boat and was walking up the ramp, B.J. looked up at his father and noticed that one side of his shirttail was hanging over his belt and his clothes were rumpled. He could not recall ever seeing his father looking so disheveled. B.J. knew immediately that something was wrong. He grabbed the sides of the railing and quickly stepped up the ramp, which swayed slightly with each step. Soon he joined his father on the street.

"Let's get a beer before we head back," his father said. "I need to talk to you."

Mr. Geld led B.J. over to a table in the corner of a deck bar.

"I know. I'm sorry. I should have asked your permission before taking off from work," B.J. said apologetically.

"Yes. You should have asked before you left, but what I need to talk to you about is a more serious matter. I had wanted to avoid telling you and I trust that you will keep this from your mother. But I need your help."

"Sure Dad. What do you need?"

"You know that Richard's Investment Bank has been one of our most important accounts, and since Electra's father died and his partner, Larry Johnson took over running the firm, they have been pulling their clients out of our funds." Mr. Geld stopped to take a sip of beer.

That should not be coming as a surprise since you have been losing their client's money for years, B.J. thought, as he also took a swig from his frosty mug.

"The Richards family and ours have done business together since our grandparents went to college together," Mr. Geld continued. "We've already suffered some very major losses over the past few years, and we absolutely have to get that partnership back on track." Mr. Geld paused again and chugged the rest of his beer. "What I am trying to tell you, son, is that we are in very bad financial shape. Your mother does not know about this, so I trust you will keep this between us." B.J. had never had a conversation like this with his father and was completely unequipped about how to respond. He also wondered how his father could possibly think he was unaware of the company's financial situation. He had graduated top of his class at the B school.

"Why don't you just tell her and ask her to spend less money?" he eventually said.

"What you need to understand, B.J.," said his father, "is that when you live the way we do, saving a few bucks here and there is not going to make a big difference. Our company, and our lifestyle, is built on a complex infrastructure. There are a lot of people who expect that infrastructure to remain in place. It's not a choice, B.J.. It's a responsibility."

"Okay," B.J. said, thinking to himself that it was about time his father took notice that The Geld Group was not the hottest thing on Wall Street. Instead, he tried to be sincere.

"What do you want me to do, Dad?"

"First of all, I need for your mother not to know a thing about this. I don't want her worrying." B.J. took note that he was repeatedly making the point for him not to say anything to his mother. Taking the opportunity to let his father know that he did not approve with how he had been so cold to his mother in recent years, B.J. said, "I think what would be best for mother is if you could be together with her more. You know, like you were before Gabby died."

"That is why I need your help," Mr. Geld replied. "I don't want to be like that with your mother. I've just been so worried these last few years. I thought things would work out and get better. Your mother commented about how I have not been myself. She too thought it was because of Gabby, which of course in the beginning it was. But now with the business deteriorating, I've even been too stressed to..." Mr. Geld stopped in mid-sentence, remembering that he was talking to his son. "I guess at first the excuse was convenient, but now it's gone on too long," he continued. "I do love your mother and I've never regretted my choice not to go with Jasmine when she gave me the ultimatum about moving west and then later left me and took Gabby. I would have loved if Gabby could have stayed behind with me, but I was young. I was your age in fact. Can you imagine raising a baby on your own and trying to keep the hours at the office that we do?" B.J. wondered to himself what his father meant about "hours at the office" when he had never seen his father work longer than an eight- hour day. Mr. Geld sighed. "It wouldn't have worked even if I tried," Mr. Geld said, staring out at the docks. "No, I don't regret that Jasmine took Gabby west. I only regret losing her so young," Mr. Geld paused again and cleared his throat.

"She's gone and I know that," he continued. "I need to do what is best for your mother and for you now. Your mother, unlike Jasmine, has always believed in me. I need to make sure she is always taken care of financially. She's never known a life without money."

Mr. Geld put his arm on B.J.'s shoulder. "This is going to sound a bit strange, but I have a very specific request." B.J. leaned back a little away from his father's reach.

"As it's not a big secret that you have always been in love with Electra, it shouldn't be too difficult a thing for you to do. I need you to ask her to marry you." B.J., who was about to take a sip of his beer, put it back down and stared at his father in disbelief.

"She is the largest share holder of Richards Investment Bank and she has the deciding vote. If you married her, you could make the right decisions and get our family partnership back on track."

"First of all, I cannot believe what you are asking me," B.J. said, truly amazed that the best business plan his father could come up with was for him to marry Electra. Then he continued, "And second, you may be asking me a week too late."

"What do you mean?"

"She is off in Ireland falling in love with someone else right now." B.J. said wincing at the thought of Electra spending time with Matthew.

"She was just here the other night." Mr. Geld replied.

"I know. I was actually planning to tell her how I felt that night, but she had other things on her mind. Now she is in Ireland." B.J. shook his head. "Anyway, Dad, even if that were not the case, I'm not going to marry someone so that the firm can get a few clients back." B.J. knew the next statement was disrespectful, but he was very irritated by his father's current state, "Dad, do you really think that is all it will take to turn things around?"

Mr. Geld had waved the waitress for another round of beer. "I don't know what to tell you, son. The Richards Investment Bankers once accounted for eighty percent of our business. It started slipping away slowly. I didn't notice so much at first because I was still very distracted with what happened to Mr. Richards and to Gabby." Mr. Geld recalled the days after the conclusion of their death and how he felt a piece of him had died as well along with them. He had been too depressed to think of anything but his sadness. Then he had watched his wife carry on as though nothing had happened. He resented her at the time. Later he realized that she was doing what she had to do, which was to keep their life together. He loved his wife and would do anything to make up for all the time he lost.

"I don't know how we can replace the percentage of the business we have lost," he continued. *Having one partner account for 80% of the firms business was never a good idea*, B.J. thought as his father continued. "I met with The Richards Group recently and they are voting on whether or not to drop our funds all together. But they need a sign-off from Electra. I just thought if you married her, she would put you in charge since she is not interested in the business."

"Dad, again, I cannot believe what I am hearing. You can't tell me that your solution to growing the Geld Group business is to have your son marry Electra Richards. I seriously think that you have lost it." B.J. stood up and started pacing. "I told you when I first agreed to join the firm that what we need is a new set of funds. We need to create a niche. I am working on those. Why did you take the meeting without preparing for it? We could have prepared something to let them know what we have to offer"

"But you love her."

"Dad. Stop this. It's insane."

Mr. Geld pulled out a flask from his coat pocket and took a few swigs before finishing his beer.

"B.J.. I am not a brilliant businessman. To be honest, I have no idea how I ever graduated from college. I have run the company into the ground." B.J. never thought he would hear his father fess up to his lack of business skills. Strangely, the confession gave him a new sense of hope.

"Dad, you need to get yourself together." B.J. grabbed the flask from his father. "And what are you drinking like this for? I hardly recognize you. If I could marry Electra, I would do it tomorrow. But the point is, I've made a disaster of that situation and according to you, you have made a disaster of the company. So we're just going to have to find a way to get our dignity back. I'll help you Dad. We will rebuild the Geld Group."

The waitress came back with a couple more beers. B.J. dismissed them and asked for the check.

"I'm sure mother is waiting, so we need to leave. We'll work things out. I'm glad we had this talk." B.J. realized that he was starting to sound more like the father talking to his son instead of vice versa.

When they arrived home, B.J. helped straighten out his father's clothes and walked with him up to the house. Molly saw them walking up the lawn, Mr. Geld slightly staggering. She knew immediately that something was wrong and went up to the house after them. Mrs. Geld entered the kitchen in her usual flurry when new arrivals enter the house.

"Gina, Molly, Mr. Geld is here. Can you meet us out on the sun-porch?" she said breathlessly.

"Something is not right," Molly said to Gina. "I saw B.J. walking up with Mr. Geld, and he looked drunk."

"Mr. Geld doesn't get drunk very often," Gina responded.

"He was definitely drunk," Molly said.

"You go out and see what you can get for him and I will follow with some cheese and crackers."

"I'm not offering him another drink," Molly said.

"Just go,' said Gina with a wave of her hand. Molly went out to the sun-porch and resumed her position behind the bar.

"I'll have a gin and tonic," Mrs. Geld said, "and pour my husband bourbon."

B.J. walked up to the bar and whispered to Molly, "Water it down okay?"

"Sure," Molly answered. "Can I get you anything?"

"No, I'm good," B.J. answered. He felt as though at this exact moment he had crossed a threshold from being a boy to a man. Suddenly, he felt the burden of responsibility. He was not prepared to let anyone down. He watched his mother sipping on her gin and tonic, staring out at the ocean. He wondered if she noticed that her husband was half undone and just chose to ignore it or if she was so programmed for routine that this Friday evening cocktail with her husband was like any other to her.

Molly realized that she had a lot to learn about marriage and the life of the privileged. She went to the kitchen to let Gina know that the Geld's were ready for supper. Gina immediately bombarded her with questions.

"Is he really drunk? What's going on?"

"Everything is fine. He's just a little drunk. I guess he and B.J. had a father son happy hour together," Molly lied, not wanting to start this gossip with Gina. "Is dinner ready? I think they are ready to eat." Molly added.

"Sure. Just give me a couple minutes," Gina said. Molly went back on the sun-porch to let the Geld's know that supper was ready.

Mrs. Geld was not there and B.J. was pulling his father up by his shoulders.

"Come on Dad. Let's just get you to bed," B.J. said, as he got him standing. When Mrs. Geld arrived back to the sun-porch, only Molly was standing there.

"B.J. told me to tell you that Mr. Geld is not feeling well," she said. "He is going to skip dinner. B.J. will join you momentarily in the dining room."

"Oh," was all Mrs. Geld said. She finished her gin and tonic, put her glass down and headed for the dining room. "I do hope that he hasn't picked up some bug in the city."

Molly cleared Mr. Geld's place from the table and let Gina know they only needed two entrees.

"Something odd is going on around here," Gina said as she dished out a couple plates. "I have something I want to ask you, if you don't mind sitting with me after we're done serving."

Molly had wanted to disappear down to her cottage, but it had been a while since she talked to Gina, and she didn't want to seem ungrateful after all the help Gina had given her by ignoring her when she needed to talk. "Sure. I have a feeling they'll be quick with their meals tonight anyway."

After the table had been cleared and Mrs. Geld had retired upstairs to check on her husband; and after B.J. was back in the den working on his project, Molly and Gina set a place for themselves in the kitchen.

"Let's not let this good meal go to waste, get out a couple plates for us." Gina said to Molly.

Molly wasn't particularly hungry, but she got the plates and sat down at the kitchen counter. "How have you been?" Molly asked Gina, "We've been on opposite schedules the past few days; I haven't seen much of you."

"Pretty good. It's quiet here when the Geld's don't have company. Stew has made friends with the chef who cooks over at the Golf Club dinning room, and we've been hanging out with them a bit. You'd like the folks down there. Of course the food's not as good as mine." Gina said as she took a few bites of the roasted lamb she had prepared for the Gelds and then washed it down with a little wine. She then blurted out what she wanted to speak to Molly about, "You're not going to break Nathan's heart are you?"

"No, of course not. What makes you say that?" Molly asked and then added, "We're just friends."

"Well, I know Nathan and I have to say I think he is a bit smitten with you, so I hope you take it easy on him."

"Really, I would never hurt Nathan," Molly said pouring herself a little of the wine that Gina had out. "Is this OK?" Molly asked filling half the glass.

"Oh, don't worry we've got a whole case of the stuff. Have as much as you like?" Gina said watching Molly carefully pour the small amount in her glass.

"So I have something else to ask you, which may be a little more delicate, but I feel it is my responsibility to say something," Gina said looking Molly in the eye.

Molly was always a little unnerved by Gina's directness and she shifted uncomfortably in her stool as she asked, "What's that?"

"Well, we kind of had a late night a few nights back up at the Golf club. To be exact we were up all night partying. I thought I'd stop by here on my way back to take some food out to thaw." Gina stopped talking, but continued to look at Molly and then she said, "Hell with it. I'll just come right out and say it. I saw B.J. coming out of your cottage very early in that morning."

Molly gasped for a moment, completely unsure how she should handle it and she replied, "Oh, it's not what you think."

Gina raised her eyebrows and then asked, "What should I think?"

"B.J. was down at my cottage to call Electra in Ireland. We phoned early because of the time difference and because he had something urgent to talk to her about."

"OK, but why does he need to make the call down in your cottage. You don't even have a phone down there." Gina commented her voice still disapproving.

Molly stammered, "Really, it was nothing like what you're thinking," Molly repeated without really answering Gina's concern.

"Stew said I should just keep my mouth shut, but it can't lead to anything good. Trust me."

"Pour yourself some more wine and I will tell you why B.J. and I had to call Electra together, but you must promise that you will keep what I tell you a secret from Mrs. Geld."

Gina poured both of them wine and listened intently while Molly told her the whole story of how she was Electra's birth mother. When Molly was finished telling her, Gina said, "Wow that is a crazy story. When I first met you, I didn't think it was going to be you who spiced this season up with gossip, but wow, you've really taken the cake with that story."

"I almost told you the whole story that first night when you all came over to meet me at the cottage."

"Yeah, I'm sorry I was pretty nosy and pushy that night." Gina smiled at Molly and said, "I just had a good feeling about you, and I wanted to know more."

Gina paused and then very firmly said, "But, I still meant what I said about not breaking Nathan's heart."

"I'm more worried about it being the other way around," Molly confessed to Gina.

"You don't need to worry about that. Nathan is a good man."

"Oh, I know he is a good man. What I am worried about is him getting to know me better and finding out that I'm not such a great catch. It's been my experience that a lot of guys like me at first because of my looks, but then," Molly stopped talking and picked up her glass of wine and twirling it around without drinking it she added, "then they find out how screwed up I am and they run for the hills."

Gina sympathized with Molly. She was good at outwardly showing a ton of confidence, but she also worried all the time that others might question her. It was one of the reasons she liked being with Stew. He wasn't the type to question. He was more happy go lucky although she was becoming increasingly concerned about that attitude and how Stew might never want to settle down. Gina realized that there had been a bit too much silence since Molly's last comment and she quickly said, "I'm sure you're no more screwed up then anyone else. It sounds like you've had some hard choices to make. I don't know what I would have done if I were in your shoes."

"Well, I'm certain that you wouldn't have chickened out like I did when I first arrived on the island and didn't go through with knocking on Electra's door."

"I wouldn't assume that. To be honest with you, I find Electra a little intimidating. She can be very aloof. B.J.'s mother is so against the idea of him and Electra, but personally I think they're a perfect match. They're both so.." Molly waited for Gina to finish the thought and when she didn't say anything more asked Gina, "so what?"

Gina looked back at Molly thoughtfully and said, "That's just it. It's hard to put words to how those two are. It's like they're very powerful and to be envied like a God and Goddess, but then it's also like they're both just so sweet, like they're angels. I don't know, but I think they make a good match."

"I do too." Molly said half of her feeling protective of them and the other half feeling envious of how they obviously belonged together.

"Well if you need to talk, I am here for you," Gina said smiling at Molly. "I'm sure as the day when Electra comes home gets closer, you will be very nervous."

"Thank you." Molly said with gratitude. "I really appreciate it. You have been a good friend." Molly smiled back at Gina and then asked, "So, have you found any properties for your restaurant? Have you talked to Stew about staying in New England?"

"Yes, and no," Gina answered. "I found a perfect property on the mainland, but I haven't found the right time to talk to Stew about it." Gina knew that he would not want to give up his Key West winters, and she wasn't quite ready to have the conversation she knew was inevitable, and that would most likely result in having to make a decision between her dream and him. As much as she loved Stew, Gina had realized the evening they stayed up all night partying at the Golf club that he was not and may not ever be ready to settle down with her in New Engand, or perhaps anywhere.

"I'd love to hear about it," Molly said sincerely.

"Well, it's an old colonial with a large front porch," Gina answered picturing her future restaurant. "I'm thinking the front porch could be outdoor seating in the spring and summer. I'd open up the whole first floor and section off part of it for the kitchen and then use the upstairs for a living space. The place is run down, but I can already picture the whole thing. In fact I was going to offer for you to hang some of your watercolors for sale. The one I saw you working on would look great. I need some kind of boat scene for above the fireplace mantel." Gina had in fact already been thinking of asking Molly if she wanted to be her roommate for the winter.

Molly remembered dragging her unsold paintings from the tavern in Seattle, but this time thought that perhaps the new paintings she was working on might be perfect for Gina's restaurant. "I'm very flattered you would think of that," Molly said truly impressed that Gina had thought to include her in her vision. It was particularly gratifying to Molly that someone she thought of as so confident and together would even consider counting her in. "That gives me motivation to finish the paintings I've started and even start new ones." Molly spoke a little faster with enthusiasm.

Gina put her hand on Molly's thigh and looking her in the eye, said, "I told you I like working with you. It's refreshing having someone around who I can relate to."

Molly could not imagine how Gina could relate to her. She thought of herself as being completely different, but she didn't want to interrupt Gina's thoughts or have her change her mind about the paintings in her restaurant so she did not inquire further about why Gina could relate to her.

CHAPTER EIGHT – The Picnic

The next afternoon, Nathan arrived at the dock promptly at noon for his picnic date with Molly. She was waiting with a duffel bag at her side.

"What's in the bag?" Nathan asked.

"Lunch," Molly answered.

"I told you that I was taking you on a picnic," Nathan said, holding up his own basket.

"I guess we'll have a good selection then," Molly said, wondering about the contents of Nathan's picnic basket. As they rode in the motorboat, Molly noticed when they passed by Nathan's dock. They rounded the island and continued on. It was a beautiful day and they had already passed a couple other motorboats and a large schooner. "Beautiful boat," Nathan commented as the large watercraft glided by.

"Yeah, Molly replied. "Where are you taking me?"

"It's not far. It's a surprise."

It was fairly choppy out and Nathan carefully navigated the motorboat around the waves. He was standing firm, holding on to the steering wheel, and Molly was glad for the cushioned seat. She was slightly mesmerized by the light dancing on the tip of the waves. She looked at Nathan and saw the same light in his eye and felt the peace she had observed in Nathan the first time she met him at the town beach. It made her feel calm and safe. Nathan knew Molly was looking at him and he felt certain that that day would be the day their friendship had a chance to bloom into something more.

Molly saw a small island come into sight. Nathan slowed the boat down and then shut the engine off all together as they neared the shore. He threw an anchor over the side.

"I noticed you're not afraid of the cold water, so we'll just wade in from here," Nathan said as he pulled out a small inflatable raft and blew it up. Molly took off her shoes and shorts and stripped down to the bikini that Gina had given her. She was in front of Nathan and as he caught sight of her bare back, he dropped the raft and the air started to whistle back out. Nathan quickly picked the raft back up and re-inflated it. Tossing it in the water, he jumped down next to it. After a quick yelp because of the cold water, he asked for Molly to hand down her duffel bag and his picnic basket. Balancing the bag and basket on the raft, he slowly walked to shore. Molly watched as he picked up the basket and gingerly made his way across the rocks up the beach. She could not remember ever having anyone be so romantic toward her. She was usually the one doing something thoughtful for someone else—and it was usually for someone who did not appreciate the effort. Nathan pulled a blanket out of the basket and laid it down further up the beach where there was a slightly sandy area.

"Come on up," he yelled out to her. Molly jumped in the water without even flinching. Then she joined him on the beach. He was placing a fourth stone on the corner of the blanket when she bent over and kissed him. It took both of them by surprise. Molly quickly stood back up and pulled a couple towels out of her duffel bag and laid them on top of the blanket. Then she sat down on one of them. There was a brief silence and then Nathan sat down next to her.

"That was very nice, thank you," he said.

"It's just such a perfect day, and I'm feeling so happy. Thank you for bringing me here."

"It is a beautiful spot," Nathan said. Neither one of them moved. A silence fell upon them. The quick kiss had stirred other desires for them both. Molly's kiss had been sweet and innocent. She hadn't meant to do it and was far too shy to try it again. Nathan knew that if he kissed her, it would not be quite so innocent. He felt waves of desire flood through his body and was unable to stop himself as he bent toward her, trying for a similar sweet kiss. He kissed her lightly at first and then, brushing her hair away from her face, gave her another kiss, this time slower and more inviting. Molly leaned closer to Nathan as he put his arm around her and pulled her toward him.

Molly thought about Gina's comment the night before. She didn't want to hurt Nathan. It felt good to be with him, and she was stirred by his passion, but she hadn't expected anything like this to happen. She was afraid that if she let things go further, that it would interfere with the friendship she had with Nathan.

Nathan felt Molly tense up as he held her closer and kissed her. He wanted her so much it was hard to pull himself back, but he didn't want to take her if she wasn't ready.

"How are you doing?" Nathan asked Molly as he pulled back from kissing her and instead gently rubbed her cheek.

Molly was out of breath from the previous kisses, and her head was spinning as her mind told her to stop and her body told her to let go. She couldn't think of what to say and so she reached again for his mouth and kissed him.

This time Nathan could not restrain himself. Molly's kiss for an answer was all the permission he needed. Nathan responded to her kisses and then turned so that his knees were on either side of her. He continued kissing her mouth and then slowly moved down her body, switching back and forth between grasping and kissing first her breasts that had come free from the bikini top, and then her hips and stomach that rose to meet his caresses and kisses. Molly had stopped thinking altogether and just absorbed the pleasure of his touch.

After they had finished making love, Molly and Nathan lay on the blanket. Nathan was holding Molly and she had her leg wrapped around his.

"I've never done that before," Molly whispered to Nathan.

"I don't think that is quite an accurate statement," Nathan said knowing they were both adults and that she did in fact give birth to a child.

"Well, of course, I've done that. What I meant was that I have never done it like that."

"Well, that was really good so you can do it like that any time you like," Nathan gently slid his arm which was around Molly's waist and squeezed her butt.

"What I'm trying to say is that," Molly started to say with a little fear in her voice.

"Shhh. Don't say anything," Nathan cuddled her a little closer.

Molly obeyed and let him hold her until it was getting near time for them to get back to the house.

Molly spent the next few days doing her chores at the Geld's with thoughts of both Nathan and her upcoming meeting with Electra on her mind. She was pleased that, at least over the phone, Electra did not seem to mind that she was working as a housecleaner for the Gelds. Molly was also glad that she would have some time in case Electra changed her mind about any of what they had talked about. Or, she thought, if she herself got cold feet and couldn't follow through with the meeting. At least with a few more paychecks, she might have enough money to get back to Seattle. Molly took another sip of her coffee and shook her head, both in response to the fact that the coffee had gone cold, and to her own defeating thoughts of going back to Seattle without meeting Electra. She had done the first step. She had spoken with her daughter. There was no turning back. Molly also reminded herself of the generous bonus Mrs. Geld had offered her to complete the summer.

Looking out her window, Molly saw Nathan pull up to the dock. She opened her kitchen window that faced out toward the dock and shouted down, "How about coming up for a cup of coffee?"

Nathan waved back at her. Molly noticed the smile that had swept across his face and she thought of their first kiss when he took her on the picnic. Again, she realized that she would find it very hard to just pick up and go back to Seattle. She remembered when she said to herself that Ridgeport Island would be a place that she would like to stay. Molly watched Nathan walk up the path towards the cottage. *Nathan is a man I would like to stay* with, she thought.

Molly settled herself on the overstuffed chair while Nathan took a seat on the couch. This time he was careful not to spill his coffee.

"I just wanted to thank you for taking a chance with me," Molly said and then added, "I don't just mean with the job recommendation, but also as a friend."

"That's not chance, that's luck getting to be your friend." Nathan said smiling. Patting the seat next to him on the couch he told her, "Come sit next to me."

Molly obeyed, getting up from her chair she sat down on the sofa and curled up next to Nathan. "Nathan," she started to say and then paused.

"Yes?" Nathan responded putting his arm around her.

"About the other day on the picnic," Molly was thinking about how much she had enjoyed it, but she wanted to let Nathan know that she was also very frightened. "You told me not to speak."

"I'm sorry," Nathan quickly replied rubbing her shoulder just a bit and then added, "I know you had something to say. I'm sorry I didn't let you speak. It was all so perfect, I was afraid you might be telling me it was a mistake and to be honest, I just wanted that one day to stay as it was in case it was all we ever had."

"I thought it was perfect too. That is what I was trying to tell you." Molly wasn't used to her boyfriends being worried about their future; she thought *worrying about the future is my neuroses.* "What I was trying to tell you," Molly said looking into Nathan's eyes before continuing, "I'm scared."

Nathan squeezed her tightly, and said "Don't be scared. There's no reason to be scared." Nathan looked Molly in the eyes and added, "I love you. I love you very much."

"That's what scares me," Molly said, her eyes slightly tearing as she kept looking at Nathan. "It's only been a few months since Joel broke up with me, and to be honest that still really hurts." Molly could almost see waves of empathy pouring from Nathan and enveloping her like a blanket. She felt as though she was being held in a safe place and she let open her own floodgates of emotion and tears.

"Shhh," Nathan comforted her. Molly continued to sob thinking to herself how her crying on Nathan's shoulder was exactly what she was afraid of doing. She was worried that once Nathan finally realized what a basket case she was, he would not be so interested in her, but she couldn't stop. She was crying so hard that she began to hyperventilate.

Nathan wanted only for Molly's pain to cease. He hated the thought that some man could have hurt her that much. He couldn't understand how. He rubbed her back, "Shhhh, try to take a deep breath. Slow down. You're going to be okay," Nathan took slow deep breaths and instructed Molly to breath with him.

Molly slowly recovered. "I'm sorry she said."

"There is no need to be sorry," Nathan said sincerely. "Do you feel better?" he asked draping a blanket around her shoulder.

"Yes, I do." Molly answered, thinking it odd that she did in fact feel much better and to her surprise, not as mortified as she thought she would feel for having cried like that in front of someone else.

CHAPTER NINE - The Request

After speaking with Molly and B.J., Electra slipped her cell phone back in her purse and went down to the hotel lobby. They were finally on their way to the airport to meet Jimmy's mother. Jimmy's PR firm had been informed about Electra and the plans to have her sing backup vocals in Munich. They advised Jimmy that the story about him reuniting with his daughter should be run after the show so that he could do a surprise introduction on stage. Matthew would write the concert review and then back flash to the introduction. Jimmy had read some of Matthew's past stories and he was relieved to discover that the boy could actually write. A few of the stories he had written about lead singers and guitarist from start-up bands back in Boston had reminded him of his own start. It had been a gut reaction back at the hospital in Boston to invite Matthew along on this trip and he was very pleased with how it had been working out. Matthew was so enamored with the band and the music that he somehow seemed to draw Electra into the excitement. Jimmy was impressed by how it had been Matthew's idea to have Electra sing backups. He had also noticed the developing relationship between Matthew and Electra, and was glad to see her look so happy. He was also more than happy to see how easily Electra fit in with his band. He could see she was a natural entertainer. Jimmy hoped that, if everything went as he had planned, Electra would join the band and take them to the next level they were striving to reach. It was true that they were successful, but Jimmy felt they lacked a certain depth that he was sure Electra would fulfill with both her music and her vocals. He also could not ignore the enormous impact of the human interest story of his daughter searching for him. It impressed him that Matthew saw this potential and this gave him great respect for the boy. Jimmy mused how his old buddy Mark had passed on his music genes to his son and how, perhaps in an indirect way, they were still partners, coming up with new ideas for the band.

Just as Electra was about to step back into the lobby, her cell phone rang again.

"Hello," Electra said, slightly out of breath, hoping it was Molly again. She wanted to apologize to her. She thought that maybe she had pressed too hard and too soon on the topic of Molly meeting Jimmy. She also wanted to ask more about how Molly ended up working at the Geld's. She was starting to feel a little uneasy about the situation.

"Electra, this is Larry Johnson. Where are you?" It was her adopted father's business partner at the Richards Investment Bank.

"Hello Mr. Johnson. I'm in Ireland. It's a long story."

"You didn't dial in to the board meeting yesterday. We haven't been able to reach you."

"Sorry about that. You know I trust your decisions."

"Glad to hear that. This one is rather important, however. We need to have your signature on something."

"What is it?" Electra asked.

"I don't know if you are aware of it, but the Geld Group Funds have been losing us money for some time now. We've pulled out most of the accounts that have been affected, but we are motioning to pull all our clients out and dissolve the partnership. I know it is a sensitive issue given the history of the two firms, but we need to do what is best for Richards Investment Bankers and our customers."

"Larry, The Geld Group and Richards Investment Bankers have been partners since my Dad and Mr. Geld's parents went to college together. The Geld Group financed the founding of my Dad's company. You know my father left me the company for a reason. I have to think about what he would want. I need some time."

"Electra, with all due respect, your father was a businessman. He would want what is best for the company and for our clients."

"There must be some other solution. I need to catch a plane right now. Give me a couple days and I will call you back."

"Really, Electra, this is the right decision. Go to the hotel business office and just send in your approval. You shouldn't have to worry about this kind of stuff. You said yourself that you trust me."

"Larry, I have to go. I'll be in touch." Electra hit the end key and shut off her cell phone. As she did, Matthew and Jimmy were rolling their suitcases past her and through the lobby towards the entrance.

"The car is here. Where are your bags?" Jimmy turned and asked Electra.

"Over there," Electra answered pointing to a corner where she had left her bags.

The bellman overheard their conversation and whistled to another bellman inside. They had Electra's bags wheeled out and in the limo in a matter of minutes.

"Who were you talking to?" Matthew asked with a tinge of jealousy, wondering if it had been B.J.. Electra had told him a little bit about the surprising conversation where she learned that B.J. was not gay and Matthew had been troubled ever since.

"A guy named Larry Johnson. He was my Dad's junior partner and he has been pretty much running the business since my Dad died," explained Electra. Then, since Jimmy was listening in, Electra added, "I meant my adopted dad."

"What did he want?" Jimmy asked.

"He wants me to vote on something. Actually, it's a bit disturbing."

"What is it?" Jimmy asked, concerned that Electra was feeling troubled.

"It's complex, but the gist of it is that they want to dissolve the partnership between my adopted dad's company and the Geld Group. You know our neighbors in Maine?"

"Why would they want to do that?"

"Apparently, their funds have not been doing well. It's a business decision, they say. However, when my Dad died, he left me the company for a reason. Even though I don't know much, well, really anything, about business, he left me controlling shares of the company with a specific wish that certain things remain in place. The partnership with the Geld's was one of them."

"I'm sure that your Dad would want you to overlook that if it was jeopardizing the company," Matthew chimed in, thinking that dissolving a partnership with the Geld's would be a good thing for him. He didn't like Electra talking to B.J. Geld. She had seemed a bit removed since the last conversation she had with him. He couldn't hear what she was saying, but Matthew saw Electra look at him as though she had something to hide.

"Matthew, you don't know a thing about this so you really shouldn't give your opinion."

"Excuse me. I'm just trying to help you out." Matthew still didn't want to see Electra showing so much concern for another man. B.J. was a businessman and he stereotyped them all, including his father and his grandfather, as boring and selfish.

Jimmy looked back and forth between Matthew and Electra. They were definitely having a lover's spat. He hoped it wouldn't end up in the kind of misunderstanding that he had so frequently experienced with his lovers, and especially not like the one he had with Molly.

"Well, you really ought to consider that he might be taking advantage of a circumstance," Matthew said with sharpness to his tone.

"And you're not?" Electra said accusingly.

"What are you saying?"

"This story you are writing about the band. Hasn't that all worked out in your favor?

"Yes, but that is different. I came for the opportunity, but as we got to know each other we hit it off."

"And what if I don't go along with the band and what if Jimmy decides you cannot write the story. What then? Would you choose me?"

Jimmy was relieved that the limo had arrived at the airport, breaking up the conversation. Soon they were all boarded in the small aircraft heading for Sligo and Jimmy's mum. As they settled down in the plane, Jimmy said, "Now don't be surprised if my Mum is a bit abrupt. Also, she won't be having the two of you sleep in the same bed."

"Fine by me," Electra said, still upset with Matthew.

"The two of you need to put your argument aside for the moment. We're here to see my Mum, do a little work and get some rest. And Matthew, don't forget that you are here to cover a story for the band. You're not here on holiday, and as much as I have been okay with your romance, you are not family. Please be respectful."

Matthew was a bit taken aback by Jimmy's speech to him and he was still chewing on the news about Electra's surprising reaction to want to help B.J.. However, as they descended into Sligo, everyone stopped thinking about their troubles and stared in awe at the beauty of what they saw below. There were large lakes which provided a striking contrast to the county's rugged uplands and the dramatic coastline. And the land was so green. Electra understood why Sligo provided inspiration for W.B. Yeats.

As they arrived at Mrs. O'Conner's cottage, the older woman came barreling out of the house to greet them. She had a silver bun of hair that had been braided and wrapped into a neat knot. She was wearing a white blouse and simple skirt that was presently covered in a green apron. She wore wide shoes with a thick heal and, though she walked fast, she was a bit bow-legged. Her blue eyes sparkled as she spoke.

"Jimmy O'Connor, give your Mum a big hug and kiss." Her thick Irish accent completed the image. Jimmy embraced his mother and then stepped back to introduce Electra and Matthew.

"Who are your young friends?" Mrs. O'Connor asked.

"This is Electra and Matthew," Jimmy said. "Let's go in for some tea."

"Of course, where are my manners?" Mrs. O'Connor said, opening the door and then wiping her hands on her apron. "I've baked some oatmeal raisin cookies." She winked and then added, "Jimmy's favorite." Matthew made a note in his notebook.

They all settled down with their tea and cookies. Jimmy decided he should have Matthew leave the room.

"If you don't mind Matthew, I need to speak to just family for a moment," Jimmy said.   Matthew politely excused himself and said he would go for a walk. Mrs. O'Connor kept her eyes on Electra, thinking the only thing possible. Jimmy had brought this young girl home to marry.

"Now Jimmy. I'm thrilled about this kind of news," the older woman said. She stopped and looked Electra up and down a few times. "And she is about the prettiest thing I have ever seen. But lad, she's half your age!"

Jimmy, catching on to what his Mum was thinking, quickly said, "Oh, no. It's not what you think. I'm not asking Electra to marry me. What I came to tell you is..." and he paused as his mother sat on the edge of her chair. "Mum. This is my daughter." There was a brief and awkward silence before the older woman spoke.

"What are you talking about?" she said finally. "This is a grown-woman. What are you, 20 years old?"

"Twenty-two," Electra clarified.

"I don't understand." Mrs. O'Conner said. Jimmy stood up and started to walk around the small sitting room.

"Back when I first moved to Boston, when I was first starting out in the music business, I met a girl named Molly," Jimmy began. "She was Irish herself. We were very much in love and Molly got pregnant."

"You mean to tell me you've been married for twenty two years and you're just telling your poor Mum right now?"

"No, I've never been married, Mum. What I am trying to say is that Molly had a baby, but we didn't stay together. I have only just met Electra myself. I didn't know until recently that I even had a daughter."

"You're telling me your woman left you when she was pregnant?"

"No, Mum. I left her. I didn't know she was going to have the baby."

"What did she tell you she was going to do with the child? Have an abortion?" Mrs. O'Conner said, crossing herself.

"No. Mum. She wanted to have the baby and I didn't. She stopped talking to me so I thought she must have made a mistake or had a miscarriage. Anyway, it's a long story, but I never knew the child was born."

Mrs. O'Connor could not believe what she was hearing. She stared at Electra until Electra, who was feeling quite uncomfortable, suggested that she might need some fresh air. She excused herself and stood up to go.

"Wait, don't go," Jimmy begged, suddenly regretting that he had sent Matthew away.

"I think you two have a bit to discuss," Electra said.

"Now listen up Jimmy," Mrs. O'Connor said. "I don't know what is going on, but before you leave you are going with me to see Father Patrick. Lord knows Jimmy you will need to do some confessing." Mrs. O'Connor said very sternly. There was a silence while Mrs. O'Conner stared at Electra. "Who could believe I have a granddaughter," she paused and then asked, "Where is the young man you brought along?" She headed toward the front porch, and as she held the door open she asked Jimmy with a sarcastic tone, "You're not planning on telling me that this boy is your son as well, are you?"

"No, Matthew is a friend who is working on a story on my band."

"Oh, ok then," Mrs. O'Conner said thinking it odd that Jimmy would bring someone like that home when he was doing something as important as introducing Electra. She didn't really understand what her son did with his rock band, but it paid her bills so it was one thing she was willing to keep silent about.

Electra walked out ahead of Jimmy and reached her hand out to Matthew, "Why don't we go explore the town a bit. Let those two catch up." Matthew took her hand and Electra helped to pull him up. She turned back to Mrs. O'Conner and Jimmy and asked,

"Is there any shopping that you need done while we're in town?"

"As a matter of fact, there is. I wasn't expecting three of you. Maybe you could buy some extra meat and vegetables for our dinner," Mrs. O'Connor said.

"I tell you what," said Jimmy, not wanting to be left alone with his mother and thinking he was about ready for a Guinness, "It's near about supper time now. Let's go round the pub and have a nice dinner there—my treat."

The four of them went into town and entered a small stone pub. They sat down at a table in the corner. Electra's chair wobbled slightly as it was caught in between a crack on the cobbled floor. She sat next to Mrs. O'Connor. While they were drinking their Guinness and eating their dinner, Mrs. O'Connor asked when she would be meeting Molly. Electra explained that she herself had not yet met her.

As the night wore on, Jimmy and Matthew talked about music and Electra and Mrs. O'Connor talked woman to woman. Mrs. O'Connor kept putting her hand to her mouth and saying, "Oh you poor child." Electra had told her about her adopted parents and she also told her about Molly. When Mrs. O'Connor learned from Electra that Molly had never married, she pulled her son by the ear and told him that he best be finding the woman and making things right for Electra by marrying her. Jimmy tried to object that he couldn't just ask Molly to marry him after twenty-two years. Mrs. O'Connor, however, would hear nothing of it.

After everyone had gone to bed that night, Matthew, who was still a little drunk from the whiskey nightcap he and Jimmy had, snuck over to Electra's room and tried to slip into her single bed. Electra was already worried about how Mrs. O'Connor felt about them showing up with Matthew. She quickly pushed him out.

"We can be together when we get to Munich. Be patient," said Electra. Matthew was still worrying about B.J. and wanted to make sure that Electra was still his. Instead of retreating, he put his arm around Electra and started kissing her. Electra pushed him away.

"I mean it Matthew. Please, not here." When Matthew approached her again, she could smell the whiskey on his breath.

"Did you have something after the Guinness?" She asked.

"Jimmy and I had a little whiskey."

"You know Jimmy is not supposed to be hitting the hard stuff so soon after the heart attack. What were you thinking?"

"He had a rough day. You've got to admit, we all had a rough day."

"That doesn't mean you have to make it worse by putting his health in danger. Honestly, are you thinking of anyone beside yourself?"

"Wow, you're a real bummer. What happened to you? You were so much fun in Dublin. Is this about B.J.? You're thinking about him again, aren't you?"

"You need to go back to your room," Electra said, not wanting to get into an argument with Matthew. "Please don't get us in trouble. I'm thinking about Mrs. O'Connor. This is her house and she wouldn't want you here."

"That's just an excuse," Matthew complained.

"Please, just go," Electra said one last time. With that, Matthew slipped back out of her bed and skulked back to his own room. He flopped onto his own bed without getting into the covers and lay staring at the ceiling. Everything was going so well with him and Electra before. He was not going to let some businessman screw things up. Electra was an artist. She wouldn't want to be with someone like B.J.. She needed to be with him. In Dublin, Electra had told him that he made her feel things that she hadn't felt in a long time and that he had seen something in her that she didn't even know existed. He would take her on a walk down one of the roads they had passed on the way to Mrs. O'Connor's, and they could cut across one of the expansive green fields. He would remind her about all those things she said in Dublin. He would kiss her like he did then. He smiled at this thought. Then he closed his eyes and was asleep within minutes.

The next morning, Electra went down to breakfast and found Jimmy sipping coffee at the kitchen table. She could smell bacon and, although his plate was empty, there were yellow streaks across it.

"Did you have bacon and eggs?" Electra asked.

"Yes. Why?"

"You shouldn't be eating like that. And the whiskey last night!" she said scolding him. "You can't be doing that."

"What's this? You meet my Mum and now you're going to be nagging me too?" Jimmy said with a grin.

"No. I'm just concerned. Don't forget, it was only a week ago I was visiting you in the hospital."

"Don't worry. I only had one little shot last night and just one egg today. That's improvement really. Anyway, what's life if you can't enjoy it a little?"

"Just be careful, okay?"

"Where's your man, Matthew?"

"I think he had a little more than just one shot of whiskey," Electra said.

"That boy knows a lot about music," Jimmy said. "You know, he's only giving you a hard time about B.J. because he cares. Give the boy a break, okay?"

"That reminds me—I need to give him a call."

"Who?" Jimmy asked.

"B.J.."

"Why would you do that?"

"You heard the story. It sounds like he needs my help."

"I suppose it's none of my business, but I think it bothers your man Matthew a bit. Anyway, it's the middle of the night back in the States."

"Oh, you've got a point." Electra said, "Maybe, I'll just text message him and let him know that I am here for him. As for Matthew, let's hope that he can be a big enough man to understand that B.J. has been my friend my whole life."

"You know yourself," Jimmy said, repeating the old phrase. "My Mum has run 'round to the store to shop for dinner tonight. Would you like me to fix you some coffee?"

"Sure," Electra answered as she started her text message.

Electra was surprised when she received a call instead of a text message back.

"Hello, Electra?" It's B.J.

"Wow, isn't it late?" Electra asked.

"Yes, but I've been pulling some pretty long hours lately."

"How are you doing?" Electra asked with concern. I got a call yesterday and I need to talk to you."

"What is it?" B.J. asked, not yet realizing that she was calling about business.

"Larry Johnson, who has been running Richards Investment Bankers since Dad died, called to ask me to vote to dissolve the partnership between Richards and the Geld Group. Did you know anything about this vote?"

"Yes," B.J. answered honestly. Electra felt a pang in her chest.

"So, what you told me yesterday—it was about business then? You want me to vote against it, don't you?" Electra said.

"If you're talking about me telling you I love you, I said that before I heard the news. I do love you and I always will love you."

"Oh," Electra said, realizing that the pain had quickly washed away upon hearing that he loved her. She hadn't expected to have such strong emotions about B.J.. It was slightly confusing to her, especially with her new found feelings for Matthew that had so suddenly gripped her while she was in Dublin.

"Did you know that the Geld Group was losing your Dad's company so much money?"

"To be honest, I haven't been paying too much attention," Electra admitted. "I always tell Mr. Johnson to just go ahead with whatever decision he thinks needs to be made. My father trusted him. But what he is asking now is something I cannot do lightly. When my father inherited the company from his father, there was a clause that he should not dissolve the partnership between the Richards and the Gelds. In turn, I received the same request."

"I guess it's hard for other people to understand the loyalty our grandparents had for one another."

"Well, you know—business is business."

"Yes, but I doubt if our grandparents would be too proud to see us give up on each other so easily."

At first, Electra thought he was talking about the two of them. Then she realized that he was truly concerned about a promise that had been made between their grandfathers.

"My father is a complete wreck," B.J. told Electra.

"Really?" Electra asked surprised adding, "Your Dad is always cool as a cucumber. What happened?"

B.J. wanted to tell her what his father had asked of him the day before. Then he thought better of it in case Electra would see it as a manipulation.

"He is at his wit's end," he said. "The business was on autopilot for so long. Then, with things being so good in the late 90's with his tech stocks, I think he just doesn't know how to build something from scratch. I hate to say this about my Dad, but he is not capable. It's really up to me to get thing back on track. I hope that you can give me a little more time, but I will respect whatever decision you make."

"How much time do you need?" Electra asked.

"I have a new customer who has a client that could really make a big difference. It's actually an actor that I am sure you are familiar with. I'm not allowed to disclose his name, but trust me you'd be impressed. Anyway, he has a lot of money to invest, and he told my client that the only funds he can select must be 100% Green, as in that they must provide a positive environmental impact. I'm trying to get such a fund set up in time to get this guy's business. I also want to make it a niche for the Geld group, but it will take some time."

"Wow, that is interesting," Electra said, truly impressed. "It's good to hear. Celebrities have so much visibility and attention; I like hearing that they are such advocates of recharging the Green movement." Electra thought about it a moment and then added, "I am sure you could make a success out of that."

"Yes. I'm counting on it."

"Do you remember the last year of business school when you told me how you were nervous about going to your Dad's firm? You were afraid that your new ideas might not be the right fit for his company?"

"Yeah, I'm sorry about all those late night calls. I thought I probably bored you to death. I also didn't think you were actually listening."

"You're my friend. Of course I was listening. I think your ideas will be great. I love the concept of a green fund. That would be a business concept that would interest me!" Electra said looking out the kitchen window at the green hills. "You can't believe how beautiful it is here in Ireland."

"I'm sure it is. I wish I were there with you." B.J. said.

"Well, I want you to know that I'm not going to sign anything about dissolving a partnership, and I'll make sure that you get a chance to present your new green fund to the Richards group."

"Thank you for texting me," B.J. said. "I wish I could go to Munich to see you."

"I wish you could come too, but it sounds like you've got a lot on your plate. Tell your Dad everything is going to be fine." Electra could hear Matthew coming down the stairs. "I've got to go. I just wanted to let you know that I'll support you however I can."

B.J. had hoped to talk to Electra longer. He wished that he could fly over and surprise her at the concert in Munich, but he knew that he was under a tight deadline to launch his new fund.

CHAPTER TEN – The Song

Pictures of Jimmy's father were scattered about Mrs. O'Conner's small cottage. Electra was looking at a picture of Jimmy with his father that was on a baby grand piano in the room off the kitchen that served as both a dining and living room. Electra noticed that they did not look very comfortable together, and that the baby grand seemed a little out of place in the small cottage.

"Jimmy bought that piano for his father. He barely got a chance to play it before he passed on," Mrs. O'Conner said crossing herself. Electra wasn't sure if she should comment on the piano or the grandfather. She decided on the former.

"It's a beautiful piano."

"Do you play?"

"Yes. It's quite a passion, actually," Electra said. She sat down on the piano bench and ran her hands across the ivories.

"My husband," Mrs. O'Conner started to say, and then continued after a pause, "Your grandfather would have been so proud." Mrs. O'Conner noticed that Electra sat very upright on the piano bench as had her late husband.

"Let's hear you play," Mrs. O'Conner said to Electra.

Electra hadn't even realized that she had so quickly taken her place at the piano. Mrs. O'Conner stood with her hands clasped and Electra knew she had no option but to grant her grandmother's request. Not knowing what to start with, Electra played a few scales to warm up. Then she looked over at Mrs. O'Conner. It seemed to Electra that the old woman was actually holding her breath. Electra smiled at her eager audience and then switched her attention back to the piano.

Jimmy was in the kitchen talking to Matthew about the upcoming show in Munich when they heard Electra start to play. Jimmy and Matthew both looked at each other thinking the same thing about Electra's talent.

"Have you thought about Electra playing keyboard?" Matthew asked.

"No, George wouldn't go for that. As it is, I'm surprised by how accepting the band has been about her just showing up," Jimmy told Matthew.

"Of course, I'm biased," Matthew said. "But I think she is a brilliant addition to the band."

"And you know yourself—I'm biased as well, but it's true. She is the perfect addition to the band. Our agent told us that the show in Munich sold out in an hour. I guess the story leaked out about me introducing a mystery daughter on vocals." Jimmy got a couple of beers from the refrigerator, opened them and handed one to Matthew. "This whole 'father- daughter reunion' campaign has gotten a bit out of hand. But the good news is that we will be making more money." Jimmy downed a few swigs of his beer, chuckled a little and then added, "I'm guessing the up in pay is one reason the band members aren't complaining too loudly."

Matthew was a little disappointed that Jimmy hadn't given him some of the credit for getting Electra to sing with the band. He also couldn't admit it, but he had been responsible for the story leaking out, and therefore, the increase in revenue for the show.

"I'm glad it's working out for everyone," he said. "Don't forget that it was my idea that she try to sing for you in the first place." Matthew paused and pointed toward the living room where Electra was still playing. "I'm not saying you should get rid of George, I'm just saying you should have Electra play piano on some of your songs." Jimmy didn't answer, but listened intently to Electra, who had started a new song.

When Electra finished her piece, she looked up and saw her grandmother standing in front of the piano with her eyes lit up—as though she were a child looking at a Christmas tree. Electra knew that even though she had left music school before finishing, playing the piano was something she would always pursue. She loved to see the pleasure that it brought to another human being. Electra smiled at her grandmother, who still seemed mesmerized by her last piece. She decided to play a song she had been writing, but had never played for anyone. Electra paused, her hands over the keyboard and, then slowly began to play. It was a song she had worked on the first year after her adopted father was listed as missing in the rubble of the World Trade Center. Electra had never been shy about performing, and through the course of her studies, she had performed at some fairly large venues. When she left music school after the tragedy, it was not to run away from school or for fear of becoming a performer, as some had thought. For Electra, it was a time when she simply needed to be alone. Electra knew that being alone with her music was the only way she would ever be able to work through the loss of her adopted father or the profound sadness she felt towards humanity after the tragedy. Living alone in Maine was a necessary time of mourning and in no way any kind of defeat. Electra had perfected the song in the last year and played it nearly every evening, almost like a prayer.

As she began, Electra nearly whispered the first verse. Then the song gained in speed and volume before it receded again. To her knowledge, she had never played this song or sang it for anyone else (she did not know about her late night lawn audience). The lyrics were a poem written in French. It spoke nothing of the tragedy of 911 and was actually about a small sailboat getting caught in a sudden squall. The song ended with the small vessel being moored safely in the harbor. Electra was saddened at times by the cruelty of humanity, but she had a profound faith that those with a good heart would always survive and find light in the harbor of love.

Jimmy and Matthew entered the living room as that song ended. Electra sat in silence for a few moments after she had finished the piece. The power of it had even surprised her. Finally, Electra pushed the stool away from the piano. Standing up, she asked, "Well, what did you think?"

"I don't even know what to say," Jimmy said, thinking to himself that it was probably one of the most complex and satisfying pieces of music he had ever heard. Jimmy, who didn't normally comment on other people's music, felt he had to say something more to his daughter. He added, "I don't know if I have ever said this about anyone's work before, but that song is perfect. I have only dreamed of writing something so powerful."

"Wow," Matthew said, still wanting more credit for getting Electra to sing for Jimmy's band. "Do I know how to spot talent or what?"

"You get this from your grandfather," Mrs. O'Conner said, with a bit of sadness in her voice. Mrs. O'Conner wished that her late husband could have known he had a granddaughter who carried on his musical talent.

Electra hadn't thought about when she would ever play that song for others and was still surprised that she had chosen to play it then. She felt as though she had opened the pages of her diary to people she hardly knew, but she was relieved that it had been so well received. It left her feeling very emotional and she suddenly felt that she needed to leave the confines of the small cottage. She wanted to go for a walk out along the green hills to the ocean.

"Thank you for the generous compliments. I've been working on that one for quite some time." Electra walked over to Matthew and took his hand. "Let's go for a walk, shall we?"

Matthew and Electra walked out of the cottage and down the main road toward the ocean. They didn't speak. Electra felt as though they were walking through a magical tunnel as they passed through a section of the road where the trees on either side of the road had arched over, creating a canopy of green. Once on the other side, she felt as though they were the only two people who had ever passed through that piece of the Irish countryside. Electra walked more quickly, anxious to get closer to the sea. She felt an urgent need to get to the beach and spill her emotions like water across the sand. Once they climbed down a path that led to the water, Electra pulled Matthew down into the sand. They sat on the sand and kissed with a passion all their own. Matthew soaked up all that Electra offered him. He reached for her kisses and pulled her closer to him each time, claiming her as his. Electra felt as though she had finally been freed from some kind of chain that had held her back from loving another person. She closed her eyes as Matthew pulled her closer and wrapped his arm around her waist with a satisfied tug of possession. Electra opened her eyes to gaze into his—and was horrified. Electra could not mistake his look of satisfaction, but could also not recognize any glint of love. She realized suddenly that she was about to make a terrible mistake. Matthew noticed Electra open her eyes and he felt her slowly pulling away from him, he asked, "What's the mattter? You got me all excited. I thought you wanted to do it right here down on the beach."

Now that's romantic Electra thought. She wanted desperately to change the mood as she realized that the emotions she had been feeling had nothing to do with Matthew. Electra gave Matthew a gentle kiss on the lips and said, "I wanted to thank you for being the one to suggest I sing with Jimmy's band."

Matthew was elated that finally someone was giving him credit. "Well you can thank me for that anytime," Matthew said. "In fact, how would you like to finish up with the appreciation and give me some more of those hot steamy kisses?"

Electra wanted to roll her eyes, but she managed to look away from Matthew out toward the ocean and wistfully tell him, "Maybe later. How about if we head back up to the house and you see if Jimmy wants to go to the pub and have a pint with you. You know just you boys. You could talk about the upcoming show in Munich." Electra hoped to appeal to Matthew's obvious idolization of Jimmy and the band in order to give herself some time away from him. Matthew was disappointed by what he thought had been a real tease, but he was happy about the suggestion that he should go have beers with Jimmy so he conceded.

While Electra and Matthew were down on the beach, Jimmy and his mother sat in the kitchen having tea. It was the first time Jimmy had been alone with his mother for a few years.

"I'm sorry for everything, Mum," Jimmy began, adding lots of milk to his tea like he did when he was a boy.

"I can't say that it's all right, but I'm glad that you have come home. I'm glad that you have told me everything. Didn't you say that Molly never married?"

"I don't think she ever did. Why?"

"It's not too late then. You can still make things right."

"I don't know about that Mum."

"This has happened for a reason. Can't you see that? I have been praying for you everyday."

"But you didn't know about Molly or Electra. So how could you pray for this?"

"I've been praying that whatever the devil's been keeping you away would stop keeping you away," Mrs. O'Conner said quickly.

"I know I haven't come home often enough, but I have visited," Jimmy objected.

"Yes, but you've never really visited me. Not like this visit. You're really here this time."

"What do you mean?"

"I mean you're here as the real Jimmy, my son. I'm proud of you for bringing Electra here too." Mrs. O'Conner looked Jimmy straight in the eye.

"Can you bring Electra's mother here to meet me? Will you do that? Can we all have Christmas together?" she asked. Jimmy shifted in his chair. He had no idea if he would be able to visit her at Christmas, let alone bring Molly and Electra.

"Mum, I don't know— they have their own lives. Maybe you can come visit me for Christmas."

"Why would I want to go anywhere? This is my home. Anyway, I'm too old to be traveling all over the place." Mrs. O'Conner poured herself some more tea and said, "I wish your father could have met Electra. Oh, I wish he could have seen her play."

"He had always wanted me to play like that," Jimmy said, going to the refrigerator to get a beer. He opened it and pushed his teacup to the side.

"I didn't mean that you were a disappointment," Mrs. O'Conner said.

"Ah—but I was mother. It's okay. Pop and I just had different expectations for each other."

"He only wanted what was best for you. Sometimes I think he died from heartache of you going away."

"Don't say that Mum."

"He never asked about you, but I know that he thought about you every day. I know that I did."

"I am sorry. I promise to come home more often."

"I think that Electra is just the angel I've been praying for," Mrs. O'Connor said.

Jimmy was uncomfortable with the conversation about him bringing Molly to meet his mother, but he was at least relieved that she had accepted Electra.

"Electra has turned out to be the silver lining of my life," Jimmy said. "I'm glad you are happy to meet her."

"Why would you ever think otherwise?" Mrs. O'Conner asked incredulously.

"The fact that she was born out of wedlock."

"Don't get me wrong. Of course I am not happy about that. But it's hardly her fault. And anyways, there is time to correct all that." Mrs. O'Conner took a final sip of her tea and set the cup back in the saucer with finality.

Jimmy was not prepared to continue the Christmas conversation with his mother. When Electra and Matthew returned, he was more than happy to accept Jimmy's proposal that they go off to the pub for a pint. Jimmy and Matthew headed out the door forgetting to even say goodbye to Electra and Mrs. O'Conner.

"I've already had my tea, but I'd be happy to fix a pot for you if you would like," Mrs. O'Conner said to Electra.

"That would be nice," Electra answered.

"I talked to Jimmy while you two young ones were out on your walk," Mrs. O'Connor started to say as she set out a new tea cup and put the kettle back on. "We talked about you and your mother coming out here for Christmas. Don't you think that would be nice?"

Electra was surprised. "Well, I suppose that would be good, but it's a bit early to talk about Christmas, isn't it?"

"I'm used to my Jimmy being busy so I thought I'd pick a good date out in the future. Christmas is family time so I thought it would be appropriate."

Electra knew that Molly still hadn't made the decision to even meet Jimmy, but she didn't want to give her grandmother the wrong impression about her. She decided it was best not to say anything, and Christmas was still quite some time in the future. Electra put her hand up to refuse the milk for her tea.

"Well, how about that. You even take your tea like your old grandpa – straight up, nothing in it." Mrs. O'Conner noted as Electra drank her without milk.

Electra asked Mrs. Conner to tell her some stories about Jimmy as a young boy. "Let me show you some pictures," Mrs. O'Conner had said excitedly as she ran to the living room to pull out her photo album. Electra listened carefully to every detail of each story she was told. It was hard for her to imagine that less than a year ago she hadn't even decided to look for her biological parents and there she was in Ireland learning about her birth father.

The two women had long since put away the photo album and had finished preparing supper. "I can give Matthew a call," Electra suggested as she noticed Mrs. O'Conner pull back the curtain to look down the street for the men.

"They won't be answering the phone down at the pub this time of evening. Not with the music playing," Mrs. O'Conner answered with slight despair.

"Oh, I meant I can call him on his cell phone," Electra offered again.

"Can you do that?" Mrs. O'Conner asked.

"As long as he can get a signal in there," Electra answered not realizing that Mrs. O'Conner, who had never seen or used a cell phone before, would not know what she meant by signal.

"Oh no need dear," she said her voice a lot more chipper. "I can see them now coming down the road."

"Sorry we're late Mum," Jimmy said entering the door as though he were still a young boy.

"Yeah, sorry about that," Matthew added.

"You're lucky we didn't start without you," Mrs. O'Conner said sternly.

"Thank you for waiting," Jimmy said bending down to give his mother a kiss as he pulled out a kitchen chair and sat down.

After dinner was finished, Mrs. O'Conner asked Electra to play another song for them in the living room. Jimmy pulled up a chair and sat next to Electra and Matthew took a seat in one of the armchairs. Electra played several pieces and stopped when she realized that Matthew was snoring.

"Well, I think I will head up and read for a bit myself," Mrs. O'Conner said and then added, "I am so happy that piano is getting some use."

"Maybe you'd like to go upstairs and lie down for a bit," Electra said to Matthew after shaking on his shoulder a bit.

"Oh, wow, did I fall asleep?" Matthew answered with a groggy voice. "Maybe I will go lie down for a bit," Matthew said getting up from his chair.

When Electra and Jimmy were alone, Electra asked, "What did you say to your mother about meeting Molly?" Electra closed the top of the piano lid and then added, "She seems to think Molly is going to be visiting here for Christmas."

"Oh that," Jimmy answered sheepishly remembering his mother's Christmas wish.

"You shouldn't raise her hopes like that. We don't even know if Molly is going to agree to see you," Electra reminded Jimmy.

"True enough," Jimmy said, "but we still have some time. "I just don't want to disappoint my Mum."

"I don't either," Electra agreed thinking she would do her best to help get Molly to meet her grandmother. The two of them thought about the enormity of the promise they had made to Mrs. O'Conner and then Electra asked Jimmy, "I have a favor to ask you."

"Of course. What do you need?" Jimmy asked.

"Well, I'm in a bit of a sticky situation with Matthew. I think I have led him on a bit more than I meant to. Could you maybe set some house rules that we need to stick to work until the concert? I need to keep focused."

Jimmy thought it over. He was not happy about being in the middle, but he did approve of the idea of them all sticking to work until the Munich show. He hadn't realized how much the press was going to gobble up the father-daughter story. Jimmy wanted Electra's debut to be perfect.

"I should tell you to talk to him yourself, but I understand about focus. This is going to be a big show. I will do it, but only because of the show." Jimmy gave a conspiratory smile and added. "And I'll do it for you if you do something for me?"

"Sure. What do you need?" Electra asked.

"You see if you can use your charms to get Molly to meet my Mum. Like you said before we have until Christmas to get her here."

Electra was surprised and didn't think the deal was particularly fair, *but*, she thought, *Christmas was a long way away and anything could happen in that time*. "Ok. I don't know how I'm going to do that, but I will try. Deal." And she shook Jimmy's hand.

The next day when Jimmy talked to Matthew, he appealed to Matthew as Jimmy the lead singer of the Quarter Moons and not Jimmy, Electra's father.

"I hate to ask this of you lad, but I need your assistance." Jimmy said to Matthew as the two of them sat out on the front porch steps having their morning coffee. "I noticed that you've been getting closer with Electra."

"Nothing happened down on the beach," Matthew said in quick defense.

Jimmy paused and looked at Matthew wondering what he meant by that statement, but then continued to speak. "Oh, that's not it. Or not exactly anyway. What I wanted to ask you is to hold off on the romance right now. You two will have plenty of time for that back in the States. Now that you have made this great suggestion that Electra sing with the band, I need you to make sure she focuses on her music until then. I also like your idea about her playing piano and doing a song on her own." Jimmy put his coffee cup down and put his hand on Matthew's shoulder. "You see I don't think she realizes quite how big this show is. Especially, now that the press is leaking out the story about her."

"I didn't leak it," Matthew said very quickly and very defensively. He had in fact called a couple of his contacts back in the States and let them know the subject of his story. Matthew tried to avoid Jimmy's eyes. He was worried that Jimmy had found out. Matthew had made the call when he was pretty drunk at the pub the night before. He thought that Jimmy was in the restroom and worried that maybe he had heard some of the conversation or that maybe someone else had overheard and let him know about it.

"Don't worry I'm glad the story was leaked. The show is now sold out because of it. Just do me the favor and help Electra stay focused."

"Hey, so you know I think you're very hot," Matthew told Electra after Jimmy's request to him.

Electra looked at Matthew with a raised eyebrow.

"I was just thinking that this is going to be a pretty big deal for you. You know the show in Munich." Matthew continued stumbling on his words. "I just think that maybe you should focus on what you and Jimmy will play together, and I'll stay out of your way and work on the story." Matthew grabbed Electra by her butt and pulled her in next to him. "We'll pick up where we left off back in the States."

Electra tried to feign surprise and said, "Oh, OK. Probably that is a good idea. I guess things were moving a bit fast, huh?"

Matthew gave Electra a kiss and said, "No, it's just because of the show." He was actually thinking that in his mind things had been going too slow.

"How are you two kids doing?" Jimmy asked as the screen door slammed behind him.

Matthew pulled away from Electra and said, "We were just discussing how we should probably all focus a bit on the show coming up."

Electra flashed a smile at Jimmy.

"Oh, that's very responsible of you two." Jimmy said with fatherly approval. "Electra how about you and I work out a schedule for the next couple of weeks?"

"Yeah, sure," Electra said trying to sound as though it was not her idea.

During the next two weeks in Sligo, Jimmy and Electra spent six to eight hours at the baby grand piano working on different songs, deciding which song would be best for the big show. Matthew worked on the father -daughter story and also frequently excused himself and went down to the pub.

Jimmy didn't sleep well at night. He never had slept well at home. When he was a kid, he always knew that he wanted to leave Ireland. Looking at the same walls and ceiling that he did as a child, when his only dream was to go to the States, made him feel restless. He also spent a lot of time thinking about what it would be like to see Molly again. He remembered when they were dating, how much Molly had talked about wanting to return to Ireland. He thought he'd have Electra remind her of that when she asked her to go to Ireland for Christmas.

Electra settled in to the music practice routine very easily and slept soundly despite a couple more drunken attempts by Matthew to sneak in and sleep with her. On those evenings Matthew cursed himself for ever suggesting that Electra join the band in Munich, but then reminded himself of how much better it made the story he was working on. He spent a lot of time day dreaming about his story being published in Spin Magazine.

At the end of the two weeks, Mrs. O'Conner had tears in her eyes as the group waved goodbye to her. The time went by quickly for everyone, and they were soon back on the plane flying over the green hills heading for Dublin to catch a direct flight to Munich.

CHAPTER ELEVEN – The Munich Concert

hen they arrived at the Olympic Stadium in Munich, Electra told Matthew that they were going to be about an hour warming up and doing their sound checks and that he should meet the band later for dinner. The concert venue had catered a meal backstage that would be set up after their warm-up. Electra said that she was nervous and needed some time to get herself together but the truth was, she needed time away from Matthew. Their time apart in Sligo had completely cooled their romance. It occurred to Electra that maybe the whole experience with him had been designed as a lesson to get her to see that she was really a performer—and to get her to open up to love again. She had learned her lesson with him, and she was certain she would always be grateful. It felt right for her to share her music with the world and she felt as if the few years she was alone in Maine was simply practice time for this one night.

The truth was she was not nervous at all. She was eager and ready to take on the crowd. She felt powerful. She felt as though she had really found what she was looking for in life. As she looked over at Jimmy, she thought that he and Molly had not only given her birth, but allowed for this sudden rebirth that was happening.

Matthew was a little irritated at first because he knew that Electra had basically told him to take a hike. He really didn't understand women. She had been so attentive before he had gotten her involved in the band. He was also a little surprised by how quickly she had relented to his suggestion that they cool it off. Matthew also wondered if she had been talking more to the guy she knew back in Maine. *Well, good luck to him if he likes bossy women who don't know how to have fun,* Matthew thought, as he set out to find a beer garden.

Matthew spoke a little bit of German from his college days and, after hopping in a taxi outside the stadium, gave instructions to be delivered to the nearest beer garden. He was a bit surprised when he was dropped off in front of a place with many tables, but not one garden. It was very crowded and the only place he found free was at the end of a table with a guy and two women in their twenties. He asked in German if they would mind if he joined them. They all answered back to him in English that they would not.

"You speak English?" Matthew asked.

"I'm from Australia," one of the girls answered with a thick Aussie accent. Matthew thought the accent was adorable and took an instant liking to her.

"My name is Helen and these are my friends," the Australian girl said, introducing the young German couple. "This is Gunther and his girlfriend Andrea. They're German but speak very good English." Helen thought that Matthew, with his tossled preppy look, was very cute and she wanted to be sure he knew straight away that she was the one who was single.

"How do you do," Matthew stretched his hand out first to Helen and then to Andrea. "I'm Matthew."

"Nice to meet you," Andrea answered. She had very short and slightly spiked hair that was shockingly red. She was sitting with her back to the sun. It looked to Matthew as though she had tiny little candles alit on her head.

Helen added, "I met Gunther and Andrea when they were traveling in Australia last year. This year, they invited me to visit them."

Gunther shook Matthew's hand. "You have found the best beer in all of Munich," he said, waving over a waitress.

"What is it?" Matthew asked.

"It is Tegernseer Hell. They serve it here at the Hirsch Garten."

Gunther ordered a round for the table. Matthew counted out a handful of Euros that Gunther waved away.

"You'll get the next round," Gunther said.

"Why do they call this a beer garden if there are no flowers?" Matthew asked.

"I wondered that myself," Helen said, smiling at Matthew.

Gunther and Andrea laughed simultaneously at what they thought to be a most ridiculous question.

"We're the flowers and we need to be watered," Gunther said, chugging down a long swill of his beer. Everyone started to laugh. Matthew, who was not long out of college, took this to be a challenge and tipped his beer back. Spilling only a little down his chin, he slammed the stein down on the table, and waved over the waitress to order the next round in German.

"So you've been to Germany before?" Helen asked.

"No, this is my first time. I've been to Austria skiing though." Helen loved to ski. She took note that Matthew was also a skier.

"Your German is good," Andrea said politely. Matthew knew that it was not, but said thank you all the same.

They chatted for a while longer, and when Helen asked what Matthew was doing while on his visit to Munich. He realized that he had not been paying attention to the time.

"I'm actually here with a band."

"You play in a band?" Helen asked with great interest.

"No, I'm a journalist. I'm writing about the show and also a special feature on the lead singer."

"Which band?"

"The Quarter Moons."

"No way," Helen said, shaking her perky hair from side to side.

"Who are the Quarter Moons?" Gunther asked.

"They're a band from the States. They're great. Wow, I can't believe it! Are you doing the story about the daughter? Oh, my God. Have you met the daughter?" she squealed.

Soaking in his touch with fame, Matthew answered, "Yeah, the Quarter Moons. I could take you back stage if you like."

"That's amazing—all of us?" Helen said, suddenly worried that she would have to leave her hosts behind.

Matthew was feeling a bit cavalier with the steins of beer under his belt. He didn't give any thought about what Electra or Jimmy would think. "Sure all of you," he replied. Matthew continued to brag by telling them all about his trip to see Jimmy's birthplace, and how it was his idea for Electra to join the band. Helen listened with awe. After some time Matthew thought to look at his watch. "We better get going," he said with a bit of panic. "They've already started dinner."

They caught the first cab they could and Matthew, who had a backstage pass, ushered his new friends forward. They each took a plate and filled them up with the complimentary food. Then they took a seat.

"Oh my God! I bet you that is Electra!" Helen squealed again as Electra approached Matthew.

"Where have you been?" Electra asked Matthew in a very stern tone as she got closer to the table.

"I went out while you were warming up, like you suggested." Matthew said reminding her it was her idea that he leave earlier.
Electra turned her gaze to the three people seated next to Matthew. Matthew quickly introduced them. "Electra, this is Helen, Andrea and Gunther." The three quickly stood and held out their hands.

"Nice to meet you," Electra said politely and quickly turned to Matthew with a look of disapproval.

"I met them at the beer garden," Matthew said in explanation. Then he added, "They're big fans. I hope you don't mind."

"No, that's fine," Electra lied and then asked for Matthew to step outside a minute.

"We just need to take care of a little last minute business," Matthew said, excusing himself from the table.

"What do you think you're doing showing up with a bunch of strangers you just met at the beer garden?" Electra asked Matthew as soon as they got out of ear's reach.

"I didn't think you'd mind," Matthew said, giving her a quick kiss.

"Well, I do mind. You're responsible for them. You're here to write a story. Jimmy will not be too happy if he sees you treating this like a party."

"Oh, come on. Don't be so uptight. Jimmy won't mind."

Electra's cell phone rang before she could say anything else. She recognized the number as B.J.'s. "Go back and make sure you all stay out of trouble," Electra said, wanting to get rid of Matthew so that she could take the call from B.J. in private.

Matthew, who was anxious to get away from Electra's scolding, turned and quickly rejoined his new friends. He sat down next to Helen.

"Just a little pre-show jitters," Matthew said. Helen asked if Electra was his girlfriend. Matthew pretended that he didn't hear the question. "She's just nervous that we might get too loud so we need to be sure to keep it down."

Electra answered her cell phone and went down the hall to her dressing room to talk.

"Hi Electra. It's me, B.J. I hope it's not too close to the show. I had a business lunch I couldn't end soon enough."

"No, you're fine. I have a little more time. It's good to hear from you. How is business?"

"Actually, it's going quite well. I pitched the green fund to some of the other portfolio managers and it turns out that they also have some clients who would be interested. Anyway, I didn't call to talk about my fund. I just wanted to wish you the best. How are you doing? Are you nervous?"

"It's funny, but I'm not nervous at all."

"Wow, I couldn't even get you to come to a party with 20 people and now you're going to be singing in front of thousands."

"Pretty crazy, huh? I'm not shy. I just needed some time alone. But anyway, I'm glad you called now. I wanted to tell you that I've been thinking about what you told me."

"It's okay. I know you're with Matthew. I should have said something sooner."

"Well, sometimes sooner is too soon. I might not have been ready then." Electra thought of how only a couple weeks in earlier in Dublin she had thought that there was something special between her and Matthew.

"Really?" B.J. asked, very interested in what she was about to say. He was on his way back to the office and had stepped into a coffee shop to find a spot a little more quiet to continue the call.

Electra hadn't intended to be so blunt. Maybe it was seeing Matthew behave so childishly by showing up with a bunch of drunken friends, she didn't know.

"What I'm trying to say is that I'm going to break it off with Matthew," Electra said quickly. "I love you and I always have loved you."

There was a brief silence as B.J. soaked in what he was hearing.

"Wow! This day is going better than I thought," B.J. said. He wanted to ask more, but suddenly Electra seemed to be interrupted.

"I'm sorry," Electra said as the band's manager knocked on her door. B.J. could hear him asking, "Are you ready to go on soon?"

"I thought I would have more time to talk, but it looks like I'm going to need to go. I'm glad you called. I wish you were here."

"Do you say break a leg to rock stars?" B.J. asked.

"Just tell me that you still love me."

"I love you, Electra," B.J. said with a solid tone. "Now go sing and hurry home."

"I love you too," Electra said, hanging up the phone.

Jimmy walked in as Electra was putting her phone into her purse.

"Who are those people that Matthew is with?"

"I don't know. Maybe they're guests from the warm up band," Electra lied. Electra took a look at herself in the mirror. An Italian designer had given her a dress to wear during the show as a promotion. Electra appreciated fashion and she was fairly pleased with the ensemble. Her cream colored silk dress was strapless, beaded at the top with citrone crystals and it tied up the back from her waist with a yellow ribbon. Electra turned slightly in the mirror to admire the back.

"You look stunning," Jimmy said as she stepped out of her dressing room.

"Check out the back," Electra said turning so that he could see. While Jimmy was admiring the back of her dress, Electra smoothed out the bottom. The skirt was ankle length although it had several slits of varying sizes that slightly exposed her legs when she took a step. Having finished straightening herself out, Electra took a look at Jimmy. He was wearing his usual light cotton button up shirt, slightly open with dark pants and stylish shoes. She nodded her approval and then reached for Jimmy's hand.

"You're not even the least bit nervous?" Jimmy asked as they headed out toward the cheering audience. "I mean, this isn't just a small gig. This is a stadium." Jimmy was worried that she would be surprised once she went out on stage.

"I played in Carnegie Hall when I was eighteen. I was nervous then. People were there to judge me. Out there tonight, that is a crowd of people wanting to be a part of something. I'm not nervous. I just hope that some of them leave feeling like they were a part of something beautiful."

"Well, let's go do it," Jimmy said. The crowd started to cheer as they saw the two emerge from backstage. Jimmy surveyed the audience from the front of the stage, and then he took a step back. Electra stood, microphone in hand. A silence came over the crowd as they waited intently for Electra to speak. Electra looked back at Jimmy who nodded his head and smiled at her.

"Hello," Electra said into the microphone. She continued, "My name is Electra." Before she could say another word the crowd started to whistle and shout. Electra looked back again at Jimmy as if to say 'help' and he stepped forward again. Silencing the crowd he started to speak.

"It's great to be here. As you all know, I have someone special here with me tonight all the way from New York (Jimmy couldn't quite bring himself to say Maine since he suspected half the audience wouldn't know where it was.) Let me introduce my daughter, Electra." Jimmy put his microphone back in its stand and started to clap. The audience joined in.

"Thank you very much," Electra said to the cheering crowd. "Thank you." The crowd, anxious to hear what she had to say, calmed back down. "I am from New York, but I have spent a lot of time up North in Maine on the coast in a little place called Misty Cove." Electra paused thinking about the piano in her living room back in Maine that looked out onto the ocean, and she continued, "I have a song that I wrote while I was there." Electra turned from the crowd and started to walk to the piano. She sat down and arranged the microphone and resumed speaking, "It's a song about needing a safe harbor when times are hard." As she had done in the cottage back in Sligo, Electra began playing very softly. The crowd raised their arms and started to sway ever so slightly. When Electra reached the stormy point in the song, the audience slowly started dropping their arms back down. When it was over, they began energetically clapping their hands and raising their lit lighters.

While the crowd was still cheering, Jimmy stepped back up front and began the saxophone solo that usually came in the middle of their hit song "Full Moon and High Tides." The crowds' arms were immediately up in the air again. George was back on keyboards and Electra was dancing in the background and singing backup chorus. Jimmy could see that the crowd was completely on fire. He put the saxophone down and started to dance in a sliding motion back toward Electra, cuing for the band to stop playing when they got to the chorus. Next he motioned for the audience to chime in. As the audience sang, Jimmy danced with Electra letting the audience continue to sing the chorus several times over. Jimmy twirled Electra around and then cued the band again to start back up from the top and he started the song from the beginning. The energy in the stadium was at its peak when the band finished their last song. The audience started clapping and stomping their feet for an encore. One by one the band-members walked backstage. Electra followed Jimmy as the last one off.

Electra's heart was pumping. She had never felt so exhilarated. She turned to look for Jimmy when she saw Matthew making out with Helen who he had invited backstage. Matthew saw Electra as she turned away from him, and Jimmy who was also looking for Electra was witness to the scene.

"You wait here." Jimmy said to Matthew in a terse tone. Jimmy reached his hand out for Electra and they headed back out to the thunderous crowd to do their encore.

"Guess he doesn't like public displays of affection," Helen teased Matthew giving him another kiss.

Matthew used the pretense of wanting to hear the encore to pull away from Helen. He knew he had been busted. He hoped that Jimmy would forgive him and understand it was a guy thing. "You should go find Andrea and Gunther." Mathew told Helen after the first encore, "I have some stuff to finish up with the band." Matthew handed Helen his card and added, "My cell phone is on there. Give me a call later on" he said to her and then disappeared to sneak out the back.

Helen thought he would be inviting them to an after hours party with the band and she happily ran off to find her friends who had been placed on the other side backstage. Matthew escaping out the back with his press pass decided that he would greet the crowd as they exited the stadium to get some candid quotes to complete his article. He had a bad feeling that it might be his last review, but at least it was being picked up by Spin Magazine so he knew it was still his big chance. As he thought about Electra, he shook his head and rationalized that it was better not to get involved with a rock star anyway.

The crowd was not satisfied with just one encore. Jimmy who loved his audience more than anything prompted the band to do one more. When they had finally finished their last encore, Jimmy took Electra's hand and they bowed together. With the roar of the applause all around her and her father's hand in hers, Electra was certain she would never forget that moment for the rest of her life.

CHAPTER TWELVE – The Return

olly had just showered after her morning swim when Nathan knocked at her door. She put on one of the Gelds' bathrobes that she had snuck down from the big house, wrapped her hair in a towel and went to let him in.

"Hi. I'm sorry to bug you so early," Nathan said thinking to himself how he'd love to see her more often that early in the morning all wrapped up fresh in a robe. He was tempted to grab her and ravish her, but he had more pressing matters at hand. "I have Electra on the phone. She called this morning desperate to speak to you."

"Is everything ok?" Molly asked concerned and holding her hand out for the phone.

"Yes, everything is fine," Nathan replied handing her the phone, "but she needs to talk to you."

"Hello Electra. It's Molly. Is everything ok?"

"Yes, everything is great. I just need to talk to you."

Molly was nervous about what she might say and so she sat down in the overstuffed chair as Nathan looked on with a concerned look. Electra had already told him that she wanted to talk to Molly about Jimmy.

"How was your show?" Molly asked.

"It was great. It was better than great. The crowd loved us and it felt really fantastic." Electra sighed remembering the afterglow of the show.

"The crowd always loved Jimmy," Molly said with a little more harshness in her voice than she had intended, she still felt jealous of his success.

Electra however, did not notice, "Yeah, the crowd definitely loves Jimmy. Actually Jimmy is why I called. You told me you would think about whether you would want to meet Jimmy, and well we're going to be flying back to the States tonight so I wanted to check with you on your decision.

Molly still did not want to see Jimmy, but she felt that telling Electra that would only make her seem that much weaker to Electra. Molly also thought having dated someone who was a rock star might at least be some kind of accomplishment. Molly had been thinking over the past couple weeks about what a big deal everyone had been making over Electra having a rock star father that maybe she could get a little credit and recognition as having been the 'girlfriend'.

"I always believed in him." Molly lied to Electra. "I'm so glad that he has become a success. I would consider it an honor to get a chance to see him."

Electra put her hand over the receiver of her phone and mouthed the word 'Yes!'

"I'm so happy to hear that." Electra said getting back on the phone. "We will be arriving in Maine tomorrow. I can't wait to see you."

"Me too," Molly said trying to put some enthusiasm into her voice as Electra said her goodbyes.

Nathan had been listening very intently to the conversation. "Did you just tell Electra you would be honored to see Jimmy?"

Molly got up from her seat and handed Nathan his cell phone back. "Yeah, I think I just did that."

"Do you really feel that way?" Nathan asked trying to mask the jealously from his voice and expression.

"No. I'm terrified to see him. But I can't let her think that. It would only look bad for me. I need to show her I can be strong."

"So you are doing it for Electra?"

"I'm certainly not doing it for Jimmy," Molly said noticing the concern on Nathan's face she added. "Really I don't have feelings for Jimmy,"

"Then why are you afraid of seeing him?" Nathan asked.

"It's just uncomfortable." Molly said, not wanting Nathan to know how poorly she had behaved those many years ago. She knew she hadn't given an exactly accurate account of the relationship with Jimmy.

"I can understand that," Nathan said hoping to sound more supportive.

"Plus, he is such a success and... well I'm not."

"Well, I think you are perfect." Nathan said sliding up toward her and slipping his hands in her robe and around her waist. Molly was more than happy for the affection and the diversion from the topic of Jimmy.

Molly and Nathan each released their own fears about her decision to see Jimmy in the bedroom.

As they lay together, Nathan started to think again about Jimmy. He was still worried that there was only one more day before Jimmy would arrive. He was amazed by the progress of his relationship with Molly, but he still felt that he needed some more intimate time together. "Can you come by my house tonight?" Nathan asked kissing Molly on her bare shoulders.

"I'd like that," Molly said feeling that she also wanted more time alone with Nathan.

"If I can get some help from the guys over at the boatyard, we may be able to get my boat in the water." Nathan told Molly.

"Really? That's amazing. When did you have time to finish the boat? I was just over at your place last week. I thought you had a long way to go."

"I can work fast." Nathan said with a self satisfied grin. What do you say I pull out the good stuff and we christen her?"

"That sounds like fun," Molly said rolling over and looking at the time on her alarm clock, "Oh, Shoot," she said grabbing her robe and rushing for the bathroom. I'm late. Mrs. Geld will be done with her yoga soon." Molly rushed back to the bed and leaned over to kiss Nathan. "I'll be over tonight though."

Nathan stretched out across her bed. He hoped he would be able to get his boat in the water. He knew it would be the perfect distraction and had also hoped it would endear himself to Molly that much more before she saw her ex-boyfriend, the rock star. Nathan had hoped that Molly could see herself spending her future days with him.

On her way out to Nathan's, Molly heard Gina call to her. Gina was walking out to the back driveway with a dishtowel and a full Tupperware container. Molly had feared that she was going to be needed to help that night, even though it was one of her nights off—the one night she really needed off. She was relieved to discover that Gina just wanted to give her some leftovers to bring down to Nathan's.

Molly told Gina about the news of Nathan's boat and her plans to help him christen it.

"I'll bet you will," Gina teased her.

"No, seriously Gina," Molly said, "He just wants to celebrate the boat being done."

"Yeah, but that's not all. Don't do anything I wouldn't do?" Gina said with a wink.

"And that would be what?"

"Oh go on get out of here," Gina said swishing Molly with a kitchen towel still in her hand. "Tell Nathan I said hi."

"Ok, thank you for the food. I'm sure Nathan will appreciate it," Molly said putting the Tupperware on the passenger seat as she jumped into her truck.

Nathan had been anxiously awaiting Molly all day, and so when she arrived he quickly commanded her "Can you take that bag?" He spoke excitedly telling her, "Go on down to the dock. I'll be right behind you."

Molly was impressed when she saw Nathan's boat. It was even more attractive than she had imagined it would look once in the water. "It looks beautiful," Molly said, admiring the deep blue boat that was on its new mooring to the left of Nathan's dock. Nathan caught up to Molly and jumped into the dingy tied to his dock. "Come on in and be careful with the bag. There's some good champagne in there."

"Okay," Molly answered, carefully placing the bag in the dingy. She untied the cleat, and joined him. The small dingy tipped from side to side with each placement of her foot. Nathan rowed toward the stern of his sailboat, and Molly quickly saw the name painted on the back. She gasped.

"You didn't tell me you named the boat already," she said.

"Well, how can I christen her without a name? I wanted to name her Molly but I thought that might be a bit too forward."

"So you named her Irish Eyes instead?"

"Yeah, you know—a lucky way of seeing things," Nathan answered with a wink. He tied the dingy to the mooring and said, "Well, let's get the champagne out."

"Wouldn't it be nicer to have the champagne on the new boat?" Molly asked.

"And we will—but first we must christen the boat." Nathan popped the cork and poured the champagne so that it ran over the letters Irish Eyes. Then he jumped on board and poured it all around as he hopped from stern to the bow.

"I should have done this before I floated her in the water," he said. 'But I didn't want you to miss the moment."

"That was a very expensive bottle of champagne," Molly said, surprised.

"Ey, and Irish Eyes is now christened!"

"I guess it just seems a bit extravagant dumping the whole bottle of champagne over the boat," Molly said.

"And a thirty foot custom designed boat is not extravagant? There are some things you only do once. So stop talking and hop on in here. We're going on the maiden journey."

Nathan had the sails up and the boat on tack so quickly, Molly thought she should have used a stopwatch to time him.

"Okay then. Let's get some of that extravagant champagne opened for the skipper and first mate. Take the tiller for a moment," Nathan said as he reached in one of the bags for the second bottle of champagne and a couple of glasses. He opened the champagne, poured two glasses, returned to the captain's seat and traded the tiller for Molly's champagne.

"Cheers," Molly said, reaching her glass out to his. "And Congratulations!"

"Cheers to you and my Irish Eyes," Nathan said.

"What were you going to name her?" Molly asked. "I mean, originally."

"What do you mean originally?" Nathan asked.

"I mean, before you met me?"

"You think I named this boat Irish Eyes because of you?"

"Well, I don't know," Molly said suddenly embarrassed that she had made the wrong assumption."

"I'm just kidding you. Of course I did. You were the inspiration. I never thought about what she'd be named before. I guess I always knew that the day I finished her, I'd know her name."

"Well, thank you." Molly said, unsure what else to say. No one had ever named anything after her before.

"You're welcome. Now let's toast to Irish Eyes and then we need to come about." Nathan took Molly's glass and placed it in a special glass holder he had designed. "This will only work when it's calm like this. Do you remember how to do it?"

"Ey ey, Captain. Ready about...," Molly said to Nathan. He smiled as Molly efficiently let out the jib, changed sides of the boat, and quickly pulled the lines back in. There was hardly any wind so the boat moved very slowly at first. Before long, however, the sails were luffing in the wind. Neither Nathan nor Molly paid too much attention as they sat thoughtfully sipping their champagne.

"This is so beautiful, Nathan. Thank you so much for bringing me out here."

"You're most welcome. I am so happy right now. I feel like I always knew that you would come and that somehow I knew I was building this boat for you."

Molly was slightly tipsy on the champagne, started to cry.

"What's the matter?" Nathan asked.

"Nothing, that's just the sweetest thing anyone has ever said to me."

"What about Jimmy? Did he write songs for you?"

"Jimmy?" Molly asked, surprised that Nathan would bring his name up. "I never listened to the lyrics of his songs, but I doubt there are any songs about me."

"What do you mean, you were his first love. Of course there are songs about you."

"Let's not spoil this moment," Molly said, putting her hand on Nathan's thigh.

"You're right. I'm sorry for bringing it up." Nathan said taking the empty champagne glasses and tucking them back away in the duffel bag. He used his knee to hold the tiller and gave Molly a big hug. "Everything will be okay. It's going to be a very big weekend all around. Did I tell you that this weekend is the Round the Island race that the Gelds have won every year since I have been on their boat as crew?"

"Yes, you did mention it," Molly said.

"This year, a couple new boats are entering the race. They're fiberglass and I have no idea what that will mean for us." Nathan let the sail out a little, trying to catch some wind. "I do know, however, that if there isn't more wind than we have this evening, we'll have a hard time getting back in time for Electra's dinner party."

"You better be back. Swim if you have to. I'm not going to be meeting Electra and Jimmy by myself."

"I'll be there for you. Don't you worry." Nathan said. "I know that it will be a very big day for you. What do you say we take Irish Eyes back in and test out the cabin?

CHAPTER THIRTEEN- The Party

he band flew back from Munich to Boston without Matthew. Electra took advantage of seeing him kiss Helen during their big concert, as an excuse to break up. Matthew was guilty and a bit too drunk to argue. However, he seemed to adjust fairly quickly. Matthew had stayed behind in Munich with Helen and then traveled with her for the rest of her holiday, which was a backpacking trip through Europe.

The story Matthew had written about Jimmy and Electra turned out to be poignant after all. Jimmy and Electra were both impressed. Electra was glad that she hadn't let things go too far with Matthew, but she didn't regret Matthew going on the overseas trip since she knew she never would have found her place in the band without him. When Electra said goodbye to Matthew, she had told him that she hoped they could be friends and work together again in the future.

With the show over in Munich, Electra was anxious to get back and see B.J. and to finally meet Molly. Electra felt bad that Molly had been stuck working for the Geld's all summer. She thought it would probably be a relief for Molly to be able to tell the Geld's who she was and then stay on with her until she went home to Seattle. It had bothered Electra that she had kept Molly a secret from Mrs. Geld, but she knew the woman all too well and she didn't want to make things difficult for Molly. She would be the one to tell Mrs. Geld and not put Molly through that.

B.J. was waiting for Electra and Jimmy at the small municipal airport in the Geld's island-designated Jeep. He had parked just shy of where the paved runway stopped.

It seemed like a long time before the small plane came into sight and slowly descended onto the single strip of pavement. The runway was surrounded by a field of wildflowers, mostly lupines and daisies and there was a barn that was being used as a hanger; otherwise there were no other buildings or public waiting areas. Aside from a small sign off the dirt road that led to the field, there was no way of knowing it was an airport.

B.J. had taken small planes up there himself. A couple of times, he had bumped into some celebrities who had homes on the island and always traveled there by air. He had never really expected Electra to be one of those celebrities, yet he was more excited about seeing her than any celebrity he had ever admired. Once the small plane had come to a stop, B.J. approached it with a huge grin on his face. Electra jumped out of the plane first and ran up to B.J.. She gave him a big hug. B.J. lifted her off the ground and twirled her around. Once she landed on her feet, Jimmy walked toward B.J. with his hand outstretched.

"Nice to meet you lad. I have heard a lot about you."

"Good to meet you as well. Or should I say 'an honor'?"

"I want you to be thinking of me as Electra's dad, not as Jimmy from the Quarter Moons."

B.J., reading a little more into the statement than Jimmy meant, quickly responded, "Yes, sir. May I have permission to date your daughter?"

They all laughed at this question and Jimmy said, "I don't know. You'll have to ask her." The pilot placed their bags in the Jeep and they headed down island to Electra's house.

"It's going to be a bit dusty," Electra apologized as they wheeled their luggage toward the front door of her house.

"No, it will be fine. Mother arranged for it to be dusted, remember?" B.J. said.

"Oh, yeah," Electra said, remembering the awkward fact that Molly had been assigned to clean her house. "Why don't you check with your mother what the schedule looks like for today? I'd like to meet Molly before the party. Just the three of us—me, Jimmy and

Molly." Electra knew she should probably first meet Molly alone, but she was also nervous and wanted Jimmy with her.

"No problem. I'll send my mother off for lunch at the yacht club."

B.J. knocked on Molly's cottage door and told her that Electra was home and waiting for her to go over for lunch. Molly was surprised. She had thought she would go over later in the evening and had been counting on Nathan going with her for moral support.

"I'll be right over," Molly answered trying to sound upbeat. She was terrified. After pacing around the cottage and checking herself in the mirror a few times, she headed across the lawn to Electra's house. She found herself once again in front of the lion's head door knocker. She hesitated a bit, but this time she knocked. Then she stepped back as Electra opened the door.

"Come on in," Electra said, as she greeted her.

Molly paused at the door. Electra was even more beautiful than she had remembered. She had spent so many days thinking about what it would be like to be in front of Electra. She had thought it would be scary, but somehow at that moment, it wasn't scary. It felt too unreal to be scary. It felt to Molly like she was in a play and Electra was just pretending to be her daughter. She was almost waiting for someone to say 'cut!'

When Molly didn't move, Electra advanced with her arms outstretched and gave Molly a hug. Jimmy stepped up behind Electra and when Electra let Molly go, he stepped in and gave her a hug as well.

Molly instantly remembered how natural it had always felt to be in Jimmy's arms. For a moment, she forgot time and just let him hold her. Electra cleared her throat and Jimmy let go of Molly. As she stepped back, Electra said, "Welcome Molly. I must admit, when I sent letters to both of you last spring, I hardly dreamed that we'd all be standing here at my house together. This is truly amazing. Please come in. Would you like something to drink?"

"I already thought of that," Jimmy said. "I have champagne chilling in the fridge."

"I don't need champagne," Molly objected, already feeling off-guard by letting Jimmy hold her as long as he had. She didn't want to give him the wrong impression. Molly knew that Jimmy would be at Electra's party, but somehow hadn't expected to be meeting him at the same time as Electra. She didn't know if she would be able to handle sitting alone with the two of them. They both seemed so relaxed whereas she felt as though she might break down into one of her sobbing fits.

"Nonsense. Of course we will all have champagne," Jimmy said with a smile that showed he still had the boyish dimple. Jimmy led the way to the porch as though it were his house. He handed Molly and Electra a glass of champagne.

"I'm going to let the two of you say your hellos," Jimmy said recognizing that Molly was feeling uncomfortable. He stepped back into the house.

"So how have you been?" Molly asked Electra as Electra motioned for her to sit out on her sun-porch.

"I am great. It's so good to finally meet you. I wanted to tell you again that I am so sorry about making you wait so long."

"No, it's ok. I told you things have been working out quite well next door."

Electra folded one leg over the other and then said, "That is so serendipitous that you met Nathan and could help out next door." Electra had been under the impression that Molly had taken the job next door as some kind of favor. It hadn't really occurred to her that Molly might have needed a job. She realized there were a lot of questions she had yet to ask. Electra looked thoughtfully at Molly and then said, "When we talked on the phone, I meant to ask you what you do back home in Seattle. I was thinking you must be a school teacher to have the summer off. I was hoping that you would be able to stay with me and not leave too soon."

Molly fidgeted uncomfortably in her chair. "Actually, I've promised the Geld's that I would stay on for the rest of the summer."

"I'm sure they could find someone else. Mrs. Geld is brilliant at finding help. She is always so generous. I've never known her to have trouble getting help."

Molly wasn't sure how to respond. She told her, "It's true she is generous. Well, to be honest I was hoping to collect on a bonus she offered if I finish out the summer season." There was a moment of silence and Molly regretted what she had said.

"What is it? I can cover it. I should have offered to help with your expenses in the first place." Electra was starting to realize that maybe Molly had stayed on for the money and not just as a favor until her return.

Molly felt very uncomfortable and was not sure how to respond. Again there was silence.

"I'm sorry. I didn't mean to insult you. It's just that I know it was probably not cheap for you to travel." Electra felt bad that she hadn't given more thought to Molly's circumstances.

"No, you didn't insult me," Molly lied. "I just want to honor my commitment."

"Well, at least you will be close by," Electra said smiling at Molly. "When do you have to be back in Seattle?" Electra asked as Jimmy rejoined them on the sun-porch.

Jimmy noticed that they both looked a little stressed. "How are you two doing?" he asked.

"Why don't you join us?" Molly quickly offered, not wanting to answer any more of Electra's questions.

"Actually," Electra said getting up. "I'm going to go check on lunch. Why don't I give you two a chance to catch up as well?"

Molly realized that things were not going to get any better. She would eventually need to answer everyone's questions. She felt her new life slowly slipping away from her.

"Congratulations on all your success," Molly said doing her best to sound upbeat and genuine.

"Thank you. You know yourself; I'm a bit surprised to be seeing you after all these years." Jimmy brushed his hair back with his hand and took a seat across from Molly. Jimmy was nervous and the tension that lingered in the air didn't make it any easier. He took a few sips of his champagne and said, "You're looking very well."

"You too," Molly said. She was actually fairly shocked by how little he had changed. "What's it been, twenty years?"

"Twenty two years, hard to believe, eh?" Jimmy said. "I tried to visit you a couple times after I moved to New York. The last time I stopped in your uncle told me that you had moved to Seattle. So do you like it out there?"

"Yes. It's a good city."

"You still doing your art work."

"Yes. Never became famous like you though," Molly said.

Jimmy brushed the comment aside with his hand and then focusing on Molly asked, "So why did you never tell me you had a baby?" He didn't seem angry, but Molly could tell he wanted an answer.

"You know I told you." Molly answered defensively.

"You told me you were pregnant. You never told me you had the baby. I came by the pub a number of times before I left for New York. I asked for you, but you never came out. Then later I gave your uncle my phone number in New York, but I never heard from you."

"He never gave it to me," Molly said matter-of-fact.

"Well, I guess it's all in the past now." Jimmy said. He didn't want to ruin a chance for friendship *or maybe something more,* he thought to himself thinking about how it felt to hold Molly again. "I should have tried harder to see you.   Electra is such a lovely girl. It's amazing that she has found us. Don't you think?"

Molly was still thinking about Jimmy's comment that she had never told him she had a baby. She felt indignant, and upset that she had actually told Electra that she would be honored to see Jimmy again. She wasn't honored. She was mortified. Molly wasn't sure how much longer she could sit there. She had not looked forward to seeing Jimmy again, but never had she imagined that she would feel as low as she did.

"I really want to thank both of you for responding to my letter. I cannot tell you how much it meant to me." Electra said reentering the sun-porch and sitting in-between Molly and Jimmy. "And I really can't believe you're both here. "I just have one wish left," Electra said. "Or rather, I have been asked for just one more thing."

Jimmy and Molly took a sip of their champagne and at the exact same moment asked, "What is it?"

"Well, I've promised Grandmother O'Conner that we will all three go visit her in Ireland."

Molly put her glass down. "What?" she said.

"I don't mean right now of course—in the winter, maybe around Christmas time."

"I can't do that. I don't have the same kind of money you all have. I don't just decide to go to Ireland and then just go." Molly added. "It was hard enough getting here."

"Of course I will pay for the tickets," Electra said.

"That's very kind of you, but I really don't think it is appropriate."

"I know it is a lot to ask, but I promised Grandmother O'Connor. She is not young, and I just know that you will be as happy as I was to have met her. It would really make everything complete. It's really the right thing to do."

Molly was certain she would never do such a thing. Still in a bit of shock from the request, Molly thought to herself about all the times when she was pregnant with Electra, how she had fantasized that Jimmy would tell her that he changed his mind about the baby and that he wanted to marry her and take her back to his family in Ireland.

Jimmy looked at Molly, who was absorbed in her memory. He was shocked that Electra would blurt out that request so suddenly. Wanting to clarify things he said, "My Mum sees this as a way to make things right."

"Make things right for whom?" Molly asked. Meeting Electra was one thing, seeing Jimmy another, but going to Ireland and meeting Jimmy's mother was a bit further than she was prepared to venture. There was an awkward silence. Then Electra blurted out, "I'll forgive you for giving me up for adoption if you do this one thing for me."

Molly could not believe what she just heard nor could she believe that Electra would force her into such a corner. She was feeling completely ganged up on. She wanted to get up and run away and never look back. They both stared at her, and though she could not imagine being able to go through with it, Molly said, "I will think about it, if it is that important to you." It was the only way Molly could think to end the conversation.

Electra put her glass down and went over to give Molly a big hug.

"You will love her. And you will love Sligo. It's so beautiful. Jimmy told me that you often talked about going back to Ireland. This would be a perfect chance," Electra said triumphantly.

Jimmy winked at Electra and followed suit. As he got up to give Molly a hug as well, Molly froze and turned her shoulder away from him. He sat back down.

"The Gelds are having a cocktail party before your dinner tonight. I will come over just as soon as I can get away," Molly said, getting up to leave.

"You're leaving already? We haven't even had lunch." Electra asked, disappointed.

"I'm sorry. B.J. told me that you wanted to meet ahead of your party tonight and, of course, that is what I wanted as well." Molly twisted her hair nervously and added. "I really appreciate the offer for lunch. And we will have lunch soon. I hope you can understand that I have a lot of work to do before tonight. I'm sure you know that B.J. invited a lot of friends to stay."

"Speaking of B.J., where is your man now?" Jimmy interjected.

"He is taking his mother to the yacht club and then getting ready for the big race," Electra explained feeling a bit concerned by how abruptly Molly was taking her leave. "It's called the Round the Island Race. The Gelds have won the race for the last fifteen years in a row. Hopefully, it will go well. I want everyone in a good mood tonight." Electra wanted to be sure Molly knew what a special night it was.

After Molly left, Jimmy said to Electra, "I don't think that went too well. I don't think Molly was too happy to see me."

"It's my fault. I shouldn't have told her about meeting your mum so soon. I'll say something to her later. I'm sure it will all be fine. Did you see how long she held you at the door? I needed to break it up."

"Well, you've got a point there," Jimmy said. "I was glad that you're the one to ask Molly about going to Ireland. But you might have let her settle in a bit first."

"I'm sorry," Electra said, furrowing her eyebrows as she recalled how carelessly she had blurted out her request. "That was so stupid of me. I also cannot believe I told her that I would forgive her for giving me up for adoption."

"That surprised me as well," Jimmy said.

"It was just stupid. Now she is going to think I am resentful of what she did," Electra put her hand to her forehead and thoughtfully added, "I could never be resentful. I have had a good life, and lately it has gotten even better. I'll talk to her tonight at the party. I'm sure she is just busy like she said. You know I may have not mentioned that we were planning on lunch today. I was just so excited to finally meet Molly. I guess I didn't think about what else she might have needed to do today."

"Yeah, I'll talk to her as well. That doesn't really make sense for her to keep working as a housekeeper. I know you have plenty of money, but maybe it's most appropriate for me to be the one to give her some money. You know, kind of like delayed child support or something." Jimmy took a sip of his champagne and told Electra, "You know I would have helped her with you back then if I really knew. My Mum is right, it's not too late to make things right."

"Don't worry everything is going to work out. We have all found each other and that is the only thing that matters to me."

Jimmy smiled at Electra and said, "Yes, and we have you to thank for that."

Molly crossed Electra's lawn back over to her cottage. There was no way she could have stayed with Electra and Jimmy for lunch. She had never been so uncomfortable in her whole life. Molly also could not stop thinking about Electra's comment that she would forgive her for the adoption if she visited Mrs. O'Connor in Ireland. She had dreaded the thought that Electra would resent her for giving her away. Molly realized that her daughter did have poor thoughts of her. Electra's comment just reminded her how temporary happiness was.

Molly noticed that the Geld's circular driveway was completely full with new cars, but she was glad for the distraction. Her thoughts turned to her duties at the Geld's. She guessed that the cars belonged to B.J.'s friends who were up from the city for the party and the private appearance of the Quarter Moons. Molly liked just being the 'help' and having everyone buzzing around her. She didn't like suddenly having such an active role in the unfolding events. Thinking about her immediate job as housekeeper helped make her feel removed from her situation with Electra.

She was uncertain of what to do with the extra time before her duties started. She tried to take a short nap. Although she was tired, she was too excited to sleep. Instead she made herself some coffee and sat in her favorite overstuffed chair. She thought about Jimmy and how at ease he had been with Electra. It seemed as though they had known each other for years. It should have made her happy that they had gotten along so well, but somehow she felt irritated. She was also surprised by how unaffected Jimmy seemed, despite the fact that he had become so rich and famous. She didn't know what she had expected, but she did expect him to be different. She hadn't expected him to treat her exactly as he had when they were just kids. He was the same positive, confident, tall and slender man she knew decades ago. Molly was very surprised by how gracious Jimmy had been to her. His magnanimity made her feel even smaller.

Molly's thoughts were broken by the continual shutting of screen doors up at the big house. She could hear voices on the porch and, though the start of the cocktail hour was still an hour away, she decided she better get her uniform on and get up to the party. Again, she wanted to take her mind off of Electra and Jimmy. She would be seeing them again soon enough.

"Thank God you're early," Gina said to Molly as she entered the house through the kitchen. "B.J.'s friends caught the earlier ferry and they're all in a partying mood. Can you get out to the bar? Mrs. Geld should be here soon and she'll want to see everyone settled in with a drink."

"No problem," Molly answered. Then she asked, "How many guests do we have this weekend?"

"It's a full house. I'm not sure how many are couples. It could be near twenty people."

"Oh," Molly replied. "I hadn't realized it would be so many. B.J. sure does have a lot of friends."

"That isn't all. He has a crowd staying over at Electra's as well. In fact, they're all invited here first for cocktails, so you should be prepared for a busy hour." Gina pulled a large bowl of something from the refrigerator. As she placed it on the counter, she asked, "Is the bar well stocked?"

Molly panicked slightly. She was angry at herself for not thinking to restock the bar. Gina was always so efficient and prepared. Molly was feeling pathetic that Gina had to remind her how to do her job. Molly didn't want to disappoint Mrs. Geld so she went to the bar to check exactly what they had. She also needed to serve the small crowd that had already gathered. When Molly got to the bar, she saw a big box beside it with a note on top:

Hey, Molly. I took a quick run to the mainland this morning. One of B.J.'s friends who is going to help crew needed to be picked up. He was a bit late so I took the opportunity to pick up some more booze. You'll find B.J.'s friends are pretty big partiers. Cheers, Nathan.

Molly smiled and let out a sigh of relief. *What would she have done this past summer without Gina and Nathan helping her out?* Molly reminded herself that they had both worked for the Gelds for a while and that she was still new. She pulled herself together, determined to do a good job that evening despite her personal problems.

Two young women approached the bar as Molly was putting the last of the new bottles into place. She looked up and before she could ask what she could get them, one of the girls demanded, "Can we get two Cosmos?" without looking away from her friend or acknowledging Molly. She was wearing a very slinky dress with an open back and cleavage so low that Molly wondered if her nipples would pop out if she turned too quickly.

"Excuse me," the woman said, clearing her throat toward Molly, "Did you get that?"

Having worked in bars before, Molly was used to rudeness.

"Coming up," Molly answered, mustering her best bartender enthusiasm and smile. The other girl, who was wearing a simple powder blue cocktail dress with a pearl necklace, smiled and said thank you while the first girl turned back to her friend and resumed talking.

"I'm not sure if this is the best or the worse news, B.J. getting hooked up" the girl said excitedly, "James tells me he is completely whooped. It's hard to believe. I mean, I came on to him at several parties—and nothing. He didn't respond at all, and I gave him my best so I assumed he must be gay." The woman nearly finished her drink before Molly was even done pouring the second one for the friend.

"I think it's great," her friend responded. Then, as she got her drink, she held it up and said "Cheers! Here's to a great weekend."

"Here's to B.J. not being gay," said the first one with a wink.

"You're terrible," the second girl said and they walked away.

Molly had heard such talk at bars before, but this time she was offended since it was her Electra whose boyfriend this girl wanted to steal. She wasn't too worried, though, because while it perplexed Molly that B.J. called some of these people his friends, she knew he would never go for a girl like the one in the slinky dress.

The requests for gin and tonics, Cosmos and Mojitos kept flowing in and the chatter on the porch had become so loud, she could barely even hear the drink orders. Then there was a short lull in the noise level and Molly looked up to see B.J., Mr. Geld, Nathan and B.J.'s friend enter the porch with B.J. all smiles and leading the way.

"You are looking at the crew of the winning boat," B.J. shouted out proudly.

Everyone cheered and Molly mouthed 'congratulations' when she caught Nathan's eye.

Gina brought out the sailing race themed appetizers and Molly started to pass them around. As each person took Gina's bite-sized creations, this time in the shapes of sailboats and markers, Molly wondered what they would think later at Electra's dinner party when she took off her apron and became a guest.

Before long, B.J. clinked his glass and requested everyone's attention, announcing that dinner would soon be served and to adjourn next door. There was a quick rush of excitement. Molly heard Jimmy's name mentioned a number of times and soon the porch was empty except for Mrs. Geld who said, "You did a great job. I never saw anyone in need of a drink." Mrs. Geld gave Molly a quick look and a tense smile as she walked toward the door back into the house.

"Thank you," Molly answered. "I guess I will see you at Electra's soon then."

Mrs. Geld stopped walking toward the door and looked at Molly with a slight bit of confusion on her face. "I thought Electra was having caterers take care of the whole event. I didn't realize she needed help. What a long day for you."

"Oh, no," Molly quickly corrected, "I've been invited as a guest."

"Oh, a fan of that rock band then I suppose," Mrs. Geld said awkwardly. "Just make sure you're up early in the morning. As you can see, we have a full house."

"Yes, of course," Molly answered. She wanted to tell Mrs. Geld about Electra. She knew it would be a big shock and that Mrs. Geld would no doubt feel slightly betrayed, but it was Electra's message to deliver. Nathan had made her promise she would wait.

He had convinced Molly that it would help with her relationship with Electra to keep that confidence.

After Mrs. Geld left the porch, Nathan, who had gone off to change for the dinner party, reappeared to help Molly clear the glasses and food. "How about you and me sit right down, put our feet up and have a drink before we go over?"

"To be honest, I'd like to just sit here alone with you all night and never go over. This is going to be so awkward," Molly said with a certain amount of despair. "I thought it was going to be a small party, just family and a few friends. I mean, the thought of springing this on Mr. and Mrs. Geld was bad enough, but now I have to face a bunch of debutants."

"Come over here," Nathan said, patting a spot on a loveseat next to him. "I'll make you a drink. What would you like?"

"I made so many drinks tonight, I don't think I want anything," she said.

"How about a beer then? Let's have a couple beers. I'm sure you're thirsty after all that work. I know I could use one. Besides B.J., the rest of the crew was more in the way then anything else." Nathan got up and retrieved a couple beers. Then he quickly sat back down next to Molly, putting an arm around her.

"You'll be okay," he said reassuringly.

"I've met Electra and Jimmy," Molly told Nathan.

"Really? When?" Nathan asked.

"She invited me over for lunch," Electra answered. "It was awful."

"What did you have?"

"Nothing. The lunch wasn't awful. The experience was awful. I left before lunch was served."

"That bad?" Nathan asked concerned.

"Yes, it was that bad. They really made me feel small."

"You shouldn't feel that way," Nathan said rubbing her shoulder.

"But I do. They both get along so well. You'd think they'd known each other forever. And wait until you hear this. They

207

actually suggested that I go to Ireland and meet Jimmy's mother to 'make things right'."

"What do they mean by that?" Nathan asked concerned.

"I guess Jimmy's mother wants to meet me and they both think it's a good idea. Electra even went so far as to say she'd forgive me for the adoption, if I did that one thing."

"Wow. That doesn't sound like Electra," Nathan said.

"Well, she did. I don't know what they're expecting from me. I am glad to meet her, but I have a new life now." Molly looked up at Nathan. She wondered why it was that he made her feel so safe and accepted and Jimmy, though he clearly still had feelings for her, made her feel so inadequate. "Oh, and the other thing," Molly added, "Electra also seemed to be under the impression that I would just leave the Geld's now that she is back. She is expecting me to stay on as her houseguest before I go back home to Seattle. I don't think Electra could appreciate how hard it is to get a job like this." Molly took a sip of the beer Nathan had given her and added, "I was also hoping to come back next year, but now the whole situation seems to be so awkward."

Nathan wanted to talk to Molly about moving in with him for the winter so he was elated to hear that she was even considering returning the following summer. He had never asked anyone to live with him before so he wasn't sure when or how he would ask her, but it seemed to him that he needed to do it soon before Electra and Jimmy scared her away.

They sat sipping beer each absorbed in their own thoughts until Nathan started to worry that dinner would start without them. Nathan looked at Molly realizing that she was still in her uniform and asked her, "Why don't you run down to your cottage and get changed for dinner?"

Molly thought of all the women she had served and the many beautiful cocktail dresses they wore. Suddenly, she gasped, "Oh, no."

"Oh no, what? I'm telling you, you'll be fine. I will be there for you."

"No, it's not that. It is that I haven't got anything to wear."

"Oh, you women, you always say that. You'll look great no matter what you wear."

"The only dresses I have are my uniforms. I don't even have a skirt. This is Electra's big day. I can't show up in jeans. What will she think? She'll have to introduce me. 'Oh, here's my mother. Not quite the success as my father. You might recognize her. She is the one who was serving you drinks. Don't forget to tip.'"

"Oh, come on now. Don't be ridiculous. Electra's not like that, and I doubt it matters to her what you're wearing."

"What won't matter?" Gina asked as she entered the room.

"Molly doesn't have a dress to wear tonight." Nathan offered.

"Seriously? Geez, Molly, if I were you, I'd have been thinking of what to wear tonight for days."

"Thanks Gina. That really helps." Molly said, irritated.

"I'm sorry. I'm just surprised you'd forget something like that."

"Well, I've had a lot to think about," Molly said defensively.

"Don't worry, sweetie. I have the perfect dress for you. It's green and will match your eyes. You two have another beer. I'll call Stew up and ask him to bring it on down. He'll be excited for the excuse to come over. Maybe we'll sneak over to Electra's after the music starts."

"That's too nice of you." Molly said, though she had every intention of accepting the offer.

"Don't worry about it."

Molly and Nathan entered Electra's through the back kitchen. There was quite a crowd and Nathan suggested it might be a better way to mingle in slowly. Tables had been set up both in the dinning room and on the back porch. Nathan's nametag was on a table on the porch and Molly's at the main table seated with B.J., Electra and Jimmy. It was hard for Molly to think of herself as a guest of honor in Electra's house.

At Nathan's table, the conversation was mostly about sailing. Either someone had a great story of their own successful race or they were trying to get sailing tips from Nathan. On the other hand, at

Molly's table not much was said. Electra, Jimmy and Molly were all absorbed in their own thoughts about what the evening meant to them.

It had been announced that the music would start after dinner so it seemed like most people at all the other tables, who might normally linger through dinner with bottles of wine and conversation hurried through the main course and desert. Within the hour, folks were already up and walking around the living room with expectations of music.

Electra nervously clinked on her wine glass. It wasn't quite loud enough, so at first no one besides B.J. noticed. B.J. clinked his own glass and shouted out, "Can we have everyone's attention?"

"Thank you B.J.," Electra said, slightly blushing. "Today is a big day for announcements. First of all, a toast to our neighbors the Gelds for once again coming in first place in the *Round the Island* race." Electra smiled at B.J. and applauds swept through the room before she continued. "But I'm sure you all know, since I haven't thrown a party in many years, I have a much bigger reason than sailing to have gathered everyone this evening." Electra paused and took a deep breath. "As some of you know, after my father died a couple years back, I went through some pretty hard times," again Electra paused. She looked into her champagne glass and watched the bubbles rise up as the crowd waited to hear what she would say next. "One of the things I had to struggle with after his death was learning that I was adopted. You can imagine that this came as a great shock to me. I spent a lot of time being upset about learning this news the way that I did." Electra looked around the room and caught the eye of Mrs. Geld, whose mouth hung open. She turned her gaze to Jimmy and then got the courage to finish with her speech. "I did a tremendous amount of thinking about it," Electra said, fixing her gaze on Molly. "Then I made the decision to look up my biological parents. I was fortunate to have located both my biological mother and father this past year. And tonight, I am pleased to introduce them. Can you both stand up—Molly, Jimmy?"

Mrs. Geld, who was the most in shock of everyone so far, let out an audible gasp when she saw Molly stand up. "This is too incredible. Why didn't Electra tell me who she was?" she whispered not so silently to B.J.

"You heard her mother. She didn't know until just recently herself."

"I knew there was something different about Electra. She was so unlike any of the Richards I ever met," Mrs. Geld said with her jaw tense.

"Shh," B.J. said, slightly elbowing his mother. "Don't be ridiculous. You're going to have to start liking Electra. Someday, I hope you'll be crossing the lawn to come see your grandchildren."

Mrs. Geld raised her eyebrows and turned her head to look at her son directly in the eyes. "Now look who is being ridiculous. Are you going to stay home and mind the children while she is off touring with that band?"

"I said someday, Mother. We're both young. Anyway, let's listen."

Jimmy kissed Electra on the cheek and then turned to speak to everyone.

"Electra has turned out to be the silver lining of my life, and now the band's as well," Jimmy, always the performer, stopped to cheer the members of the band and the crowd joined in. When the room finally settled back down, Jimmy continued. "We had an amazing tour in Munich with Electra joining us." Jimmy gave Electra a big pat on the back. "It turns out that she is a natural performer. I wish that Molly, her mother, could have been there to see her." Jimmy said, turning and flashing his dimples at Molly and then he motioned for her to speak next. Everyone's eyes turned to Molly.

Molly cleared her throat and scanned the room desperately looking for Nathan. "Hello, everyone." Molly said with a weak and nervous voice, "You probably recognize me from next door. I was the one serving drinks. And yes, it's true I am Electra's birth mother." Molly stopped and looked this time for Mrs. Geld as Nathan suddenly appeared by her side. "I know I haven't exactly been honest about why I am here. And I want to apologize to you Mrs. Geld. I know this must come as somewhat of a shock to you. I really appreciate everything you have done for me, and I have every intention of staying on as your housekeeper this summer."

One of B.J.'s guests turned to B.J. and said, "Your girlfriend's mother is the housekeeper?" Electra heard her statement and gave the girl an icy stare." Electra looked over at Molly and was shocked to see that she was holding hands with Nathan. Electra gave Nathan a disapproving look which Nathan immediately saw. Electra was not pleased with how things were turning out in the least. She realized that she should have given a lot more thought to the circumstances before bringing everyone together. Wanting a moment alone, Electra headed towards the kitchen. On her way, Nathan who had left Molly's side, caught up with her,

"Electra, I'm sorry. We should have told you."

"Told me what?" Electra asked her voice cold.

"That Molly and I are dating. I need you to know that I love her."

"It hardly seems appropriate. I mean you work together and anyway she is just visiting."

Electra's words about Molly just visiting stung Nathan. He was painfully aware that the summer was coming towards an end. Nathan knew that he would be faced with the likely possibility that Molly would be leaving, but he had not been able to face that fact yet. "Well, thank you for the party. I'm glad that you and Molly have met. I need to get going. I'm sure the guests will want to go out on boats tomorrow." Nathan said abruptly.

"I'm sorry Nathan. I didn't mean to snap at you. I'm just a little disappointed that this introduction has turned out to be so shocking to everyone instead of being a nice time with family and friends like I had envisioned while I was away. Everything else has just been so fairy book lately."

"Don't worry about the people who don't see this as a happy evening – they are not your friends, and family is family. It was a lovely dinner." Nathan said. Nathan excused himself and walked ahead of Electra and out through the kitchen to the back door where he took his leave. Nathan quickly crossed the lawn and went down to the Geld's dock to take his boat home. He had hoped he would be bringing Molly with him that night, but he was feeling overwhelmed. He couldn't recall any other time when his heart felt so afraid. He had always felt safe. It was uncharted waters for him that evening.

Just after Nathan left her, Mrs. Geld grabbed Electra's arm "What are you doing? Who are these people?" She demanded, "You can't mean to tell me that the Richards were not your parents, but I guess it makes sense doesn't it?" Mrs. Geld's face was all wrinkled up and her voice high pitched.

Electra tried to pull away from her, but Mrs. Geld gripped her arm tighter. "You may have gotten all this by luck, but don't think for one minute that you'll be getting anything from us or marrying our boy." She continued.

Mr. Geld who was holding on to Mrs. Geld's other arm blurted out, "I don't care if you were adopted." He leaned over and slurring heavily continued to say, "It's your responsibility to do the right thing with our companies."

"Darling, you're making a fool of yourself," Mrs. Geld let go of Electra and turned to face her husband.

"You don't understand dear. We're in deep trouble and Electra can help us." Mr. Geld pleaded, "You can help us can't you Electra?"

Electra gave a horrified look at Mr. Geld. B.J. had been right. The man was completely undone. Out of Mrs. Geld's grasp, Electra continued with her escape to the kitchen. B.J. saw her and followed.

"How are you doing?" B.J. whispered to Electra as the swinging pantry door moved back and forth behind him.

"I don't know. This is beyond awkward. It's not how I pictured it to turn out."

B.J. stroked Electra's cheek. He felt bad that he had not done more to help make the introductions go more smoothly.

"And what is Molly doing holding hands with Nathan?" Electra blurted out.

"I guess they're a couple now," B.J. said.

"You knew this?" Electra asked upset.

"Well, yeah, it's not such a big deal. I think they make a nice couple."

"Everyone has gone crazy!" Electra said throwing her arms dramatically up in the air. "Can't you see how this would be the least bit upsetting?"

"Why are you so upset about Molly holding Nathan's hand?" B.J. asked confused. "You told her that you didn't mind her taking the housekeeping job. So what if she hit it off with the Captain?"

"So what?" Electra repeated incredulously. "I thought she came here to see me. And now suddenly she is living next door and dating an islander? Didn't you hear how shocked the guests were when she talked about being the housekeeper?"

"Electra you need to calm down. It's not such a big deal. She did come here to see you and remember you've been gone for weeks. She waited for you. The other thing is Jimmy is here for you and a whole room full of people expecting to hear you sing."

Electra knew that B.J. was right. She was the hostess and should not run out on the party, but she was still irritated with the scenario. "I know," Electra said. "but I just really hoped it would have been a little smoother and that Molly hadn't found it so important to tell the whole crowd that not only had she taken up a job housekeeping next door, but that she would be staying on in that capacity. I just don't see why it was necessary to make that announcement in front of everyone." In truth Electra could care less if her mother was a housekeeper, but with her budding romance with B.J., she wanted desperately to gain Mrs. Geld's approval, and it was obvious that this latest announcement, done at a dinner party no less, would not get her any closer. Mrs. Geld had made it very clear that she disapproved of her. To make matters worse, it almost seemed to Electra that Molly didn't really like her very much.

Electra grabbed a paper-towel and blowing her nose said, "Okay. I better get back out there. I think Jimmy promised everyone I was going to sing my song." *At least I know that Jimmy approves of me,* Electra thought as she pulled herself together.

"That's more like it," B.J. said, taking her arms and holding her hands out in front of her, he kissed them. "I know I would love to hear you sing."

Electra gracefully walked across the room and took her seat at the piano. When Jimmy, who had the crowd going, saw Electra, he quickly finished up his song and then announced, "And didn't I tell you, my friends, we'd be warming up for the star of this evening? I might proudly add, my daughter, Electra."

Once Electra started playing, B.J. went to sit by his parents who were on a sofa off to the side. With her son back by her side, Mrs. Geld whispered, "This is just a bit too much. I hope Electra's not planning on having rock bands playing over here all the time."

"Shh Mother," B.J. said, annoyed. "Why don't you take father home?"

Mr. Geld, who was sauced on Bourbon, said "B.J. needs to marry that girl. She's beautiful don't you think. And you know she could save our business. I think we'll all be sunk without her."

"Come on dear, you're just drunk."

"No, really." Mr. Geld protested with a slur, "Doesn't she sing like an angel?"

"More like a siren," Mrs. Geld said under her breath and then pulled up her husband, hoping no one noticed him staggering behind her. Mr. Geld left willingly, but turned once to B.J. before he left.

"Don't forget what I told you about Electra."

Molly tried to look at Electra with the pride of a mother, but somehow she still remained a total stranger. Molly couldn't even think of Electra as someone in her everyday life. She was ashamed to admit it, but she was jealous of her own daughter. *Hadn't she also been an orphan? Why wasn't she in a beautiful house being admired and getting along fabulously with her newly found father?*

Molly hated that she couldn't stop feeling so inferior to Jimmy and Electra. She hated that they had not only become great friends, but were now both famous. She hadn't been surprised when she discovered that Jimmy had made it big. She thought about how determined he was back in Boston and how so many of the girls at his shows liked him because they thought he'd be famous someday. Molly thought about how his being a musician was never the reason why she pursued him. She wasn't a groupie. It was in that split second of thinking, that she realized she didn't know why she was so set on him other than the fact that she had always wanted to marry an Irishman. She thought that there must have been a stronger reason, a reason why she was so in love with him. She kept looking at him, trying to remember what it was. He felt her gaze upon him and smiled back. She saw the same smile that he used to give her so many years ago. She remembered how he had made her feel loved. He had loved her for a time, she knew that. She knew that he had sacrificed all his free time with her when he wasn't working his carpentry job or doing his gigs. She was pleased seeing him happy, but she realized it was mostly because she thought that meant that would lead to marriage. She never stopped to just enjoy what they had. She never thought about what they were to each other, only what he meant to her. She was always thinking about where it was leading—and always wanting more. It hadn't been good enough that he loved her. To her, that was only a start. She knew that she had tricked him into being with her. She remembered that fateful night twenty some years earlier and she blushed at her own naiveté. She was so busy building her own dream of getting married and having a family of her own, and with him the further fantasy of having that family in Ireland, she realized with self-loathing, that she had been very selfish. She never stopped to think about what he wanted. After their fight, she had made it impossible for him to talk to her. It was true; she hid from him when he came to the pub. She had wanted to wait until she was showing before she would let him see her. She wanted him to feel bad, and she had to admit, she had wanted him to feel obligated. As it turned out, after three months, he had moved out of town and the opportunity never presented itself. When she did start to show, Molly had to explain herself to her uncle. She had stretched the truth when she told him that Jimmy moved away intentionally abandoning her and the baby. She told her uncle that Jimmy had used her. It's what she wanted to believe because she could never admit to herself that indeed she had some responsibility. Molly looked on again at Jimmy and at Electra and felt disgusted with herself. Molly had not expected that after all these years of feeling betrayed, she would be sitting in the same room as Jimmy and the child she had given up, and not be feeling mad at Jimmy or sad for giving up the child, but instead angry with herself for not seeing her own blame. The only thing she felt good about was giving up Electra because she knew she could never have given her the kind of love she needed, not while she had no idea what it really meant to love someone. That was her problem. She had always thought of Jimmy and the child she gave up as a lost opportunity for her. It had always been about her. She had never felt sorry that the child might want to know her mother, and she had never really wondered what happened to the child. And finally, she had ended up being jealous of that child and denying the father the right to know she ever existed.

Molly felt that she owed both Jimmy and Electra a better effort. Electra had invited her into her home and into her life. She had cracked the door open, and it was up to Molly to step in and let them both know that she did care. She needed to shed her own ego and test the waters of love. Molly weaved her way over to Electra as soon as she finished playing and asked her to go out on the porch so they could talk. She wasn't sure what she would say, but she knew if she didn't try then, that she would probably leave and never get the chance again. It would be the biggest and most tragic defeat of her life. She didn't think she could live with that kind of failure.

After they settled into their chairs facing each other, Molly said, "That was a lovely song."

"Thank you."

"I like your dress. It's very pretty. It matches your eyes."

"Thank you," Molly answered.

Each had so much to say, but no idea where to start. Finally, it was Electra who spoke.

"Thank you for coming here. I know it wasn't easy for you," she said tentatively.

"No, it wasn't easy. I was worried that you would be disappointed in me. Well, to be honest, when I got your letter I was just disappointed in myself. I think that coming here and meeting you has probably turned out to be just as important to me as it is to you. It's hard to explain, but I think me being a disappointment to myself started with the mistakes I made back when I had you."

"Do you think I was a mistake?" Electra asked in a quiet voice. Electra worried that her fear that Molly did not like her was true.

"No, no, of course not. I mean other kinds of mistakes—the things I told other people, like your father and my uncle. It's hard to explain, but I learned a lot about myself. I suppose over time I might be able to explain it to you. I am so happy, though, that you decided to find me. It may sound a bit corny, but in your reaching out to find me, I think I found myself."

"I'm sure it was meant to be. It doesn't always work out this way. I have talked to some other people, others who had tried to find their parents. Sometimes the parents just deny they are who they are. I think that would have been very hard for me. I was a little scared to test it, but after my adopted father died, I had a lot of time to think. You know, I had not even known I was adopted until just a few years ago after his death."

"Yes, that must have been very strange to be left behind and then to find out you were never the same flesh and blood."

"You cannot imagine. My whole life, everyone always told me I took after my Dad. He was such an amazing person. It really hurt when I found out that I couldn't have taken after him."

"Well, maybe not through his genes, but he raised you. So I'm sure there are many ways you take after him." Molly said. She wasn't used to being the one to comfort someone. It felt nice.

"I guess I didn't think about it that way. I just felt so alone. Maybe you felt that way after your parents died."

"I am sad to say it, but I don't remember them at all. I have little glimpses of things in Ireland, but not much." Molly thought to herself that maybe those tiny glimpses of her parents in Ireland were what fueled her fantasy to be married to Jimmy and live in Ireland with him.

"I wonder which is worse, remembering or not remembering," questioned Electra. "It seems to me like you'd avoid a lot of pain by not remembering."

"I think not remembering is much worse. The fact that you felt so alone was because you had been so connected. I had never really been that connected to my parents." *Nor to anyone else,* thought Molly.

Electra sighed, thinking of her adopted father.

"Yes, we had a very special bond. I think it was probably fate that he adopted me. He needed me. When his wife, Evelena, left him we took care of each other. She was a selfish woman. He only saw what he wanted to see of her. Physically, she was stunning. I remember when I was a little girl, having people always say to me, 'Oh, I bet you will grow up to be as beautiful as your mother,' and I always cringed. I didn't want to be anything like her. That was another reason why I loved people telling me I took after my father later in life. Anyway, after he died and I spent time by myself, I thought of so many things. One of the things that I kept wondering about was who it was who had brought me into this world and given me a chance to spend the time I had with him. That was when I decided to look you both up. And of course, a part of me was just curious. I guess most of all; I wanted to have a chance to thank you. Thank you for bringing me into this world." Electra was glad that Molly had asked to talk to her. Their conversation was more in line with what she had been expecting. Her motivation for meeting Molly was in fact to thank her. She was glad that she was finally saying what she had meant to say in the first place.

Molly didn't know what to say in return and so repeated Electra's earlier comment.

"I guess it was meant to be."

"I'd like to get to know you," Electra said, feeling the awkwardness in Molly's voice.

"I'd like that as well," Molly replied. Although she still felt so inadequate, she knew that getting to know Electra would be the first step in having a chance to be someone more than who she was when she first started her journey to Maine.

"I know I pushed you hard this afternoon about Ireland. I guess I hadn't really thought about what it would be like for you. I just wanted you to meet Mrs. O'Conner. I also didn't know about Nathan. Probably, he wouldn't like it too much. If it's too much to ask right now, I understand."

Molly had also thought it had been a lot to ask. But she also realized that it was the only thing besides just acknowledgment that Electra had asked of her. She didn't want to do it, but maybe Electra and Jimmy were right in thinking that it was the best way to heal things for everyone. Nathan probably wouldn't like it, but she knew he would support her if she were doing it for Electra. Hadn't he told her to take care of Electra first? He was a man who knew a thing or two about being a friend.

"I think if it is something that you would like for me to do, than I will be happy to do it," Molly told Electra. She didn't want to burden Electra with how hard it would be for her and so she added, "I think it will be an adventure. I haven't been back to Ireland since I was a child. Maybe I could show you where my side of the family comes from. It's actually not too far from Sligo."

Electra gave Molly a hug. While they were both trying to think of more to say, B.J. came through the door clearly looking for Electra.

"Well, I think the music has been a big success," he said, squishing in next to Electra on the loveseat she was sitting on. "I'm sorry to break up your cozy chat, but I need you to come in and stand by my side a while. That Deborah is shamelessly hitting on me."

"Is she wearing a very slinky dress?" Molly asked.

"I don't know what she is wearing. I just know I need some help getting rid of her."

Molly found it hard to believe that any man wouldn't have noticed her dress, but she suspected it was probably the girl she overheard earlier. She said, "There was a girl with a slinky dress talking about you back at the Geld's during the cocktail hour. You should go in with B.J. and set her straight. I enjoyed talking to you. I need to get back next door. It's going to be a big day for me tomorrow." Molly got up from her chair and then awkwardly bent down and gave Electra a quick kiss on the cheek. "Thank you for the talk, and for everything," she said. "We'll talk again tomorrow about going to Ireland. Say goodnight to Jimmy for me."

B.J. hopped up from his seat and gave Molly a hug, "You did great tonight," he said. After Molly left, he pulled Electra closer to him and said, "How was your talk?"

"It was nice. I felt like we might have connected a little bit. I have to admit though that I still feel a bit weird about her going over to your house and taking Benilde's place."

"Well, Molly said she will talk to you about going to Ireland so that is something to celebrate, B.J. pulled Electra up. "Let's go find Jimmy."

B.J. was becoming more and more fond of Jimmy and a new fan of his music.

Electra was happy that she had such a good conversation with Molly, but disappointed that Molly had retreated next door instead of making a further presence at the party she was throwing in her honor. She had also hoped that Jimmy would have more time with Molly. She felt that given some time Molly would be comfortable with Jimmy again. She knew that Jimmy still cared about her and thought that he and Molly could be friends again.

On the way back to her cottage, Molly stumbled across Stew who was sitting on the lawn not far from where Molly had sat with Nathan listening to Electra play piano.

"What are you doing out here?" Molly asked a little surprised.

"I just needed to get out for a moment," Stew answered his voice slightly cracked and shaky.

"Are you ok?" Molly had never seen Stew upset before. When he didn't answer her she said, "By the way, I wanted to thank you for bringing Gina's dress down for me to borrow. I really appreciate it."

Stew looked up at Molly at the mention of Gina's name and he blurted out, "She broke up with me."

"What happened?" Molly asked. She wanted to sit down next to him, but she was afraid of getting grass stains on Gina's dress.

"After I brought the dress for you, she said that we were also invited to Electra's for the music after dinner. I don't really know anything about the Quarter Moon's, but you know I love a good party so I agreed to go." Stew started to pull at the grass while he tossed the pieces to the side of him. "I thought everything was going so well. We were having champagne and then she asked me to go out on the sun-porch to talk." Molly was thinking that the sun-porch certainly was a location for serious talks that day.

"Just like that she broke up with you?" Molly asked knowing that Gina could be very direct, but surprised that she would break up with Stew so quickly.

"Well, she told me that she has put an offer in on some property in Hopeville and that she plans to live there in September while she renovates it to be a restaurant. She told me about the place she was looking at, but I didn't know she was going to move that quickly."

"Well, that doesn't mean she broke up with you." Molly stated.

"She may as well have. She knows that I leave for the Keys in September. I have commitments down there."

"They have regular flights to Florida. It doesn't mean you have to break up." Molly pointed out.

"Remember when we first met? Remember Gina talking about us settling down once we figured out where?" Stew asked excitedly.

Molly remembered the conversation well. She also remembered how Stew tried to avoid the whole topic. "Yeah, I remember." Molly answered.

"I never said I didn't want to settle down or that I didn't want to have kids," Stew added defensively.

Molly thought the obvious which was that he also never said he did, but she didn't want to get in the middle of their relationship.

"I'm sorry this has upset you so much. I can understand." She said instead.

"What should I do?" Stew asked desperately.

"Well did she tell you that she wanted to break up?"

"No, but it seems like she is moving on without me."

Molly thought that it seemed premature of Stew to be upset. She thought that Gina probably would have said something to her if she was planning on breaking up with Stew.

"I think you're jumping to conclusions. She hasn't said a word about a breakup to me. I think you need to talk to her about logistics of you working in Florida and her staying up here."

Stew who had partially been fishing for information from Molly was relieved to hear that Gina hadn't said anything to Molly about leaving him. "I guess you're right," he said his voice already more cheerful. "It's just been so convenient having her go down to Florida with me every year. I thought she was trying to punish me or something."

"You know what I think?" Molly offered. "I think she found a place that was too good to turn down and it's just been too hectic around here to have a chance to talk to you about the timing of the whole thing. You said she told you she was looking at places, right?"

"Well, yeah. She asked me to go take a look with her earlier this week, but I had too many lessons scheduled."

"OK then. No more talk of breaking up. You knew you were going to have to broach the subject of her starting a restaurant in New England at some point didn't you?"

Stew was starting to get annoyed with Molly for driving home her point and so he changed the subject and asked Molly.

"How did it go for you meeting Electra and Jimmy?" Stew asked spreading his jacket out and offering for Molly to sit on it.

"Well, Electra was disappointed in me working at the Geld's. I'm sure it's uncomfortable for her." Molly sat down carefully on the jacket. "I'm doing my best to try to connect with her though. I think it's just hard for her to imagine anyone with a lifestyle like mine. Oh, and she has an obsession that I should go meet Jimmy's mother."

"Why that?" Stew asked.

"I don't know. I guess she really bonded with her and feels it's her obligation to make the old woman happy." Molly paused for a moment. "That's just the thing she has bonded with Jimmy and his mother, but we just seem so distant."

"What about Jimmy? What was it like seeing him?" Stew was worried for his friend Nathan that things might go too well with that reunion.

"He really hasn't changed very much. He wants to be friends." Molly looked up at the stars and thought about how he had held her when they first greeted and how he had smiled at her all evening. She felt as though he still loved her. It made her feel good, but uncomfortable. She was still angry at him for the past, and was not ready to let him back into her life any more than she must for the sake of Electra.

"How did you feel?" Stew asked interested. "Are you still in love with him after all these years?"

Molly wanted to divert the question. "You know I really just focused on meeting Electra," she answered.

"That's probably the best thing." Stew replied. "So are you going to go to Ireland and meet Electra's grandmother?" He added with curiosity.

"I think I will. I'm thinking it might be one way for me to get closer to Electra."

Stew noticed that she hadn't answered the question about Jimmy. "So how is it going with you and Nathan?" he asked.

"He is so wonderful," Molly exclaimed and added "I don't know how I could have gotten through all this without him."

Stew was glad to hear Molly speak well of Nathan. "He's a good man for sure. I hope it works out for you both." Stew said sincerely.

"Me too," Molly replied and then added, "You should go back inside and find Gina." Molly got up and shaking out Stew's jacket she handed it back to him and added, "I'm sure you two will work something out."

Stew took the jacket and pondered her last statement. He knew that she was right. He stood up and gave Molly a hug.

"Thanks for the chat. I'm glad that you finally got to meet Electra. Do you think you'll work for the Geld's for another summer season?"

"You know I would love to do this job again. I'm just worried about whether or not Electra would like that."

"She'll come around. Gina always thought she was a snob, but I think she is just shy. And as for Mrs. Geld she'll probably be happy to rub it in B.J.'s face that she is employing Electra's mother. I heard her talking earlier today, telling one of her friends that she would like to find a way to get B.J. to understand Electra isn't the right girl for him. "

"Well, I certainly don't want to come between that relationship." Molly said with a bit of concern. "Mrs. Geld told me that she was worried that Electra didn't know what she wanted."

"She is mistaken on that point. Electra is the most focused person I ever met," Stew paused and then corrected himself, "Well except for Gina of course."

"Well, if it harms Electra in any way, I will find another job. I'm just hoping that Mrs. Geld can start to see what everyone else has observed which is that Electra and B.J. make a pretty darned good couple."

"It's ironic how mothers sometimes say all they want is their child's happiness, but then get all upset when the kid does something that makes them happy, but that goes against their own will." Stew thought about his own mother's reaction when he told her he would be spending his winters in Florida. He told Molly, "My mother will love Gina because she hated me moving down south. She will be voting for me to stay up here with Gina."

"Well, at the end of the day we all have to do what is best for ourselves. The big trick is figuring out what that is. I know for myself making this trip is the closest I've come to doing what is right for me."

Stew gave Molly a hug and said, "I'm going to take your advice and go find my sweetie. "

Molly returned the hug and said her goodbyes.

When Molly got back to her cottage, she saw an envelope tucked into her door and she quickly scanned the backside and saw Nathan's familiar signature. She took it and walked over to her favorite overstuffed chair. Sitting cross-legged, she opened it up.

Dear Molly,

First let me start by telling you that I love you. I loved you the moment I saw you. What I want to say is that I fear that maybe I have been distracting you more than I should be. I know you had come here for a reason, and it wasn't to meet me..."

Molly put the letter down in her lap. She was afraid to read further. It seemed as though something about it all being a mistake was going to come next. She thought about his words, how *she had come for a reason and it wasn't to meet him*, but he had been such a big part of her being able to do what she came there for. She couldn't help but think there was a reason why she met Nathan. She had thought recently that it was because they were meant to be together, but maybe that wasn't it. She thought more about the events of the evening and all that had led her to where she was at the edge of the water, and then finally picked the letter back up.

"I know that you came here to meet Electra. I know how much it meant to both of you, and I am so happy that you both did meet today. I'm sorry that I left the party. I was just a little overwhelmed. In any case, I really hope that you both get to know each other. You're both two very special women. I have been so absorbed in my feelings for you, that it has been hard for me to remember why you are here and scary for me to think you might not stay. I am a little embarrassed to say it at my age, but I think you are the first person who I have really been in love with. I do love you so much. The summer is near about over. I would love for you to stay on with me. But I need you to think about what kind of a choice that would be for you, because as you have heard me tell Gina, I don't ever plan a life other than an island life. It's what suits me. The winters here are long, there is not that much to do and not

even really any work. You might be able to teach the kids some art or do your own art in my barn if I can figure out a way to keep it warm enough. What I'm trying to say is that a life with me would be very simple. I know that you have some feelings for me. They weren't immediate like mine were for you, but I know you do care. So please think carefully about this. I just want you to be happy. I know I should have said all this in person, and I will if you give me a chance.

Love, Nathan

Molly put the letter back in her lap. At first she felt a wave of love for him, but then she also felt something else. She wasn't sure what it was. Molly realized that what she felt was sadness. Nathan was right. The summer would be over soon as would her comfortable routine. It would be time to make choices that she felt ill prepared to make. Molly envied Nathan being so sure of where home was for him. And of Jimmy for always knowing what he wanted to do with his life. Molly realized that before she could find a home or know what she wanted to do, she needed to understand what it truly meant to love another person.

As Nathan drove back to his house in the Geld's motor-boat, he couldn't stop thinking about how strange the evening had turned out. When he rounded the corner towards his house and saw *Irish Eyes,* his new sailboat, he decided he would go out, take a seat and treat himself to his private stash of rum, his most treasured comfort. It was hard for him to believe that just the day before he had been so sure of his relationship with Molly. It deeply disturbed him when Electra looked at him with disapproval while he held Molly's hand. It had never occurred to him that anyone would disapprove of that relationship. He didn't want to interfere with Molly's connection with Electra and he certainly didn't want to upset their employers, the Gelds.

After tying up the motor-boat, Nathan stepped into his dingy. Even though the water was still that evening, the boat tipped back and forth with his weight. He settled himself as much as he could in the center of the seat and put the oars into position. Each time he pulled, Nathan watched as he stirred up phosphorescent in the small waves of water. The moon was full and lit up a path that seemed to lead right to *Irish Eyes. She is beautiful*, he thought.

Once on the boat, Nathan went below deck to his Captain's bar. A friend of B.J.'s had smuggled an Havana Club Anejo 7 year old rum into the U.S. and B.J. had given it to Nathan as a birthday present. Looking at the bottle, Nathan smiled at the thought that B.J. had finally gotten together with Electra. *Some things are turning out the way they ought to* be, he thought to himself.

He poured some rum and slowly sipped on it while he thought about his own relationship and the letter he had left for Molly. He was feeling uneasy about what he had said and started to regret leaving the note. Watching the flag on the front of his boat slowly wave back and forth in the wind, he contemplated whether or not he should try and retrieve the letter. Nathan worried that he had been presumptuous writing about a future life with him. He wouldn't normally mention things like that to someone he had known for so short a time, but he had become very worried about how things might change after Molly saw Jimmy again. Nathan couldn't help but compare himself to Jimmy, and he hated that he felt jealous. He had never been jealous of anyone before and it felt very unsettling. He could see by the way Jimmy looked at Molly, that the man still had feelings for her. He wondered if Molly would be tempted by the kind of lifestyle that Jimmy could offer. He had put a lot of effort into getting *Irish Eyes* ready in time to take Molly out for a sail, hoping that it would be the kind of experience that she would want to repeat. It had been a special night, but Nathan felt that he still needed more time to win her over completely. *Why did I have to push it*? Nathan questioned himself. Checking his watch, he saw that it was still before midnight. He chugged the last bit of rum in his glass and climbed back into the dingy. Rowing much faster this time, he quickly switched from the dingy to the motor-boat and headed back to the Geld's.

Nathan's heart skipped a little as he stepped off the Geld's dock and saw the light on in Molly's cottage. *She has already seen the note*, he thought nervously as he walked up to her door. After knocking lightly, Nathan let himself in and smiled when he saw Molly sitting on the sofa holding a cup of tea.

"Chamomile," Molly said when she caught his eye. Putting her mug down on the coffee table, Molly stood up and gave Nathan a welcoming hug. "I got your note," she said and held him a little tighter. "Thank you."

"I'm sorry that I left the party without saying goodbye."

"Don't worry about it," Molly said disengaging from Nathan's arms and leading him to sit back down on the sofa with her. "I'm glad you came back."

"I came back because I was worried that I was a bit too serious in my note," Nathan said stroking Molly's cheek with endearment. "And because I wanted to see you."

"I'm glad you did. And I think we should start thinking about what we're going to do after the summer ends."

"I want you to know that you are more than welcome to stay with me for however long you want."

"That means a lot that you would offer that to me," Molly said. Taking Nathan's hand in hers she added, "I don't feel like I have much to give back to you though."

"You are too hard on yourself."

"You just don't know enough about me,"

"I want to know everything about you," Nathan said rubbing her hand with his.

"Are you really sure?" Molly asked. "I'm just realizing stuff about me that I don't like much."

"We all do that." Nathan said and then confided "I didn't like learning that I am jealous of Jimmy."

"That is normal." Molly paused for a moment and then added, "I mean it doesn't make you a bad person. I haven't been completely honest with everyone about what really happened all those years ago."

"What do you mean?" Nathan asked.

"Well, after Jimmy walked out on our fight about the baby, I avoided him intentionally."

"Well of course you did. It was pretty cold of him to tell you to get rid of the baby and just walk out."

"Well, that is just the thing. He did walk out that night because he was upset, but he tried to come see me, but I wouldn't talk to him." Looking straight into Nathan's eyes, Molly added what she thought was her deepest confession. "What you need to know is that I hid from him intentionally. I wanted to wait until I was showing with the baby. I thought maybe if he saw me with the baby showing that he would feel guilty and change his mind."

"Molly," Nathan said keeping her stare, "You were eighteen years old. Maybe you think what you did was not the right thing, but you can't beat yourself up over it. He had told you to get rid of your baby. It seems to me like you were very brave. "

"Well, when I think back on it now, it seems so deceitful," Molly said her voice choking up and tears welling up.

"Shh." Nathan said tenderly. "No one faults you. The most important thing is that Electra has had a chance to meet you. What if you had talked to Jimmy after the fight. What if he had convinced you to have an abortion? With the way everyone feels about Electra that would have been something to be sorry about. I really don't think that Jimmy or Electra have a single thought on their mind about you being deceitful. " Nathan took Molly's hand and tenderly kissed it as he reminded her, "Electra contacted you to thank you for what you did all those years ago."

"You always know how to say just the right thing," Molly said smiling at him. "I was very touched by your note. I've never gotten one like that before."

"And I've never written a note like that before," Nathan said smiling.

"Actually, when you showed up tonight I was thinking about what I am going to do when I am finished here. I would like to stay in Maine at least until I take the trip to Ireland. Gina had mentioned if she found a place she would love to have me help her fix it up. Also a while back when we were chatting, Gina told me that I could display my paintings throughout her restaurant." Molly looked over at her latest painting that was resting on an easel in the corner of the room. She was picturing it hanging above the fireplace of Gina's new restaurant. "Stew told me tonight that Gina put an offer in on a place."

Nathan was ecstatic that Molly was thinking about staying in Maine, "That's fantastic news about Gina. She told me about the place she was looking at the other day. It sounded perfect. I'm sure she'll make a quick success. Her cooking is the best I've ever tasted."

"I was planning on asking her about it tomorrow."

"I'm so happy to hear that you will be around a little longer. You mean more to me than anyone I have ever known," Nathan told Molly as he bent over and kissed her on the lips. He looked deeply into her eyes and held her gaze, speaking to her heart.

Molly felt the same way she had when Nathan had first approached her at the edge of the water, enveloped in warmth. "Do you want to go lie down with me?" She asked him.

There was nothing more that Nathan wanted at that moment than to hold Molly in his arms. "I would love that."

As they walked slowly into Molly's bedroom they lay down on the bed still clothed. Facing each other, they fell asleep. Both their fears were at rest. When they awoke in the morning their eyes met, followed by a smile.